The
SERPENT'S
VEIL

The SERPENT'S VEIL

~

Maggi Feehan

Maggi Feehan

thistledown press

Thistledown Press Ltd.
633 Main Street, Saskatoon, SK   S7H 0J8
www.thistledownpress.com

Library and Archives Canada Cataloguing in Publication

Feehan, Margaret, 1962–

The serpent's veil / Maggi Feehan.

ISBN 978-1-897235-56-0

I. Title.

PS8611.E398 S47 2009   C813'.6   C2009-900755-X

Cover photograph by Julia Margaret Cameron, courtesy of the George Eastman House International Museum of Photography and Film

Cover and book design by Jackie Forrie
Printed and bound in Canada

10 9 8 7 6 5 4 3 2 1

Canada Council   Conseil des Arts
for the Arts   du Canada

SASKATCHEWAN
ARTS BOARD

Canadian   Patrimoine
Heritage   canadien

Thistledown Press gratefully acknowledges the financial assistance of the Canada Council for the Arts, the Saskatchewan Arts Board, and the Government of Canada through the Book Publishing Industry Development Program for its publishing program.

For you, Dad.
For understanding the slant of dreams.

"Invisible before birth are all beings and after death invisible again. They are seen between two unseens. Why in this truth find sorrow?"
— The Bhagavad Gita 2:28

This game, his affection

THERE THEY ARE, THROUGH THE BUBBLES, *those three long strands of hair on Father's big toe. The right foot because his left is over a little, out of sight, leaving sparkles in the sand, cracks too.*

Any second now, he's going to let me up, I just know it.

This game, his affection. His hand on my head a kiss. But my heart is beating too loudly. It's all I can hear beneath the water. Thug, thug, pause, thug. Moving from this shoreline out into the Arabian Sea, filling every bluish inch of it with the sound of coursing blood. Mine.

I'm a song for whales. The beating of my heart is music for fish.

His hand squarely on the crown of my head, he still has not let up. His palm like a cap on a sealed jar of cherries. My eyelids puffing up from the salt, nostrils flaring. I need oxygen. I need air.

I want to come up now. I need to come up now. I'm butting my head into his hand, desperate to signal to him that the game is over, that his turn is up. But his fingers dig deeper, grasping my head all round.

Like cricket. Grown men grasping the ball, squeezing it hard and then throwing it away with a blur of their arm. That's going to be me, I just know it, whipped out to sea in this manner. Arms and legs snapping off from the pressure. I would float, wouldn't I, float for a second before the sinking begins? Sinking slowly and soundlessly into the darkened arms of the ocean floor. First, a curiosity for fish. Then, the smell of my blood a bidding for sharks who would move into me, pointed teeth gaping, each vying to take the first bite.

It is too long, now. Father, let me up.

All of me inflating now, swelling up like a balloon.

His foot blurs, appears to be floating away. Everything is a wash of aqua. My lungs want to explode, want to gush out into the water, stain the green liquid with a burst bubble of blood.

The little stars on the sand are the only things I can see.

Let me up, now! Please, please, let me up! Oh dear God, he's keeping me down here too long. Oh, dear Jesus, he's trying to kill me. Father's trying to kill me.

Air slaps me in the face.

He is laughing, laughing. Everyone on the beach is laughing, too. There is a huge crowd of people in long swimming costumes and mid-calf shorts. They point at me and shake their heads. Their jowls heaving from the rich wave of belly laughter washing between them.

Even Mother has a smile on her face. Mother, who is dead. Mother, whom I have never even met. She laughs at me.

One

~

Constance and Ank
London, England
1899

ANK MAGUIRE STANDS NEXT TO HER hospital bed, his fingers just above the sheets. He longs to touch her, light upon her skin, give a lick of comfort. Constance's eyes are hollowing out the ceiling above her. White-grey paint. A flattened presence, scarred with cracks and crevices that thump with secrets. Like her skin.

Constance can tell by the way his nostrils first flare and then squeeze together that the stench is still around her bed. Here he is, the surgeon's dresser, an Irishman with a thin, attentive body and mismatched black hair and blue eyes. He carries a faded bag filled with cotton bandages and ointments that he wants to smear over the scars on her legs. Legs that tumble out of her pelvis like bloated worms, ready to burst. Young legs that are suddenly ancient. Legs that cannot walk for her; can no longer take her away.

Constance is in the corner bed, where the L-shape of Dorcas ward veers to the right. To her left, the tall window is slightly masked by the striped curtain which, when drawn, surrounds her bed. To the right, a walnut table with a white porcelain washing bowl. And a plant - the pushy leaves of a fern.

All she can smell is the sweat under her arms. The musky scent of unwashed flesh. How long has it been since the last sponge bath? Constance cannot guess; time has slid by her, an unseen serpent.

Ank longs to know what is going on inside her head. Her auburn hair has been mopped off her youthful face. He purses his lips; they long to speak, Constance knows this. His tongue is thick with waiting.

He has been here since the beginning. The corpulent nurse Shoemaker told her this. He comes to the ward and stays for long periods. Most unusual. Nurse Shoemaker has offered this wisdom in a voice that reminds Constance of a turkey just seconds after her father shoots it. A gobbling, an inward suck of air.

The smell of urine stains the air between them. Constance clenches her top teeth into her bottom molars, pushing down the way one would on a trunk crammed too full, careful that nothing spills out the sides. Ank's adam's apple bobs as he swallows, but no other expression breaks through on his face.

"Get the nurse then, shall I?" He is already stepping off the wood onto the fat track of carpet that dissects the ward.

"Please don't."

He returns to her bedside. She finally allows herself to look at him, directly look into his eyes.

"Please don't call her. She's so tightly wound. She's no comfort to me."

A laugh breaks out between her cracked lips. Despite himself, Ank snickers, her darkly comic plea settling itself into his understanding. She, a body just barely held together; a thorn bush tethered by rope. She has no right to comment on another's winding.

When her laughter subsides, she reaches down to touch her pelvis. A broken picture, a smashed human being. She lies back on the bed, gives her weight to the mattress and the pillow beneath her. She closes her eyes.

Inside her body is pain. Ruptured energy, pulsating energy, wanting to escape. She feels a red hue from deep inside begin to foam. Small bubbles rise from her extremities, overcome with larger bubbles that soon burst out through the centre of her body. So red, so hot, she feels herself slipping into the boiling mass, allowing herself to catch fire and steam into the air. She is crimson. She is burning.

She opens her eyes. Mr. Maguire is still there. He has been watching her. Did he feel the heat?

"I'm so hot," she tells him, certain that he already knows this. His eyes narrow.

"I know, girl, I have water." Ank lifts the glass to her mouth.

"I feel as though I am on fire."

Constance flicks her tongue into the glass. Cat licks.

"I had a strange dream," she is babbling now, loose with the fluid connections in her mind, "a peculiar dream." Her mind rambles off a list of dreams she could relate to him. Mixed, blurred images swimming around in the stew of her imagination.

"Dream?" A muscle on the left side of his mouth twitches.

"You were in my dream." She pauses, considering. "In it, we were riding the horse - both of us were on him - the one, you know, Ceylon - and you told me to watch the sky, because the weather was changing. I looked up and it was red. Not blue, red. And you said that it was a sign."

She can tell by the tightness of his face that he doesn't know she is lying. There has been no such dream, but there could have been. He could have been on the horse with her. He could have seen the sky as red.

"A sign of what?"

"I don't know." She wants him to solve the riddle, find the missing piece.

"Constance, you've been badly hurt, see. You may have ideas, thoughts, that other people don't understand."

He says this in a tone which makes her feel that he too is lying. She knows he understands.

The bed is hard again. Her body is warm, no longer hot. The bubbles have cooled. She remembers the breeze on the horse that day - a burst of air that felt more like a window opening than a breeze.

"It's fine. The heat is lifting." And with these words, she closes her eyes again.

Ank pats his thick hair distractedly, pulls at his moustache, his eyes studying Constance, as if she were a painting by some long dead, mysterious artist he's sought to understand.

She has been in this room for many weeks now. His mind wanders back to when she first arrived, the lengthy surgery that took place in the theatre where dozens watched. Ank himself stood to the left of the table, ready with the instruments the surgeon grunted for. Behind him, men surrounded the circle, looking on, whispering to themselves throughout the hours. It was hot in there, too. Housemen propped up on the steel railings, or sitting on the steeply slopped benches that reached to the audience exit. And nurses, four of them, in their white cone-shaped hats and over zealous bows around their chins.

Ank remembers waiting for Constance, as they all did. Days dragging into weeks, waiting for her to awaken. She murmured in her lost sleep, but speech defied her for some time after waking. He wanted to hear her thoughts, her first words. When they came, they meant nothing. Something about the rain.

It was a relief to hear her talk. A young woman's body had been laid out as a meal for vultures. But the vultures did not come.

~

The woman looks overtop her papers, her eyes dissecting Constance with studied intensity. Constance begins to groan, hopes her bodily pleas might send the woman packing. But she is the predator, and Constance is her prey.

"The hospital records say that it wasn't your father who came to the hospital with you, but ah . . . Mr., ah . . . Baron."

"le Baron."

"I suppose he is French?"

"I suppose."

"And he was — a friend or — "

"He worked with my father."

"And your father — he was stationed in India?"

Constance has a flash of a young Indian boy with no arms who skilfully caresses the sleeping body of an older man with his toes. With no arms to aid him, the boy's sensitive foot skims the outline of the man's arched back, searching for money, or food, for anything that might make his world a little more comfortable. Constance remembers the boy's stumped arms swaying, the creased, remorseful look on the man's face, despite his being asleep. All this in a few moments of unprotected sight, before Father snapped her head away and cursed at Ayah, as if it were all her fault.

It is far too complicated to explain, especially to this woman who sits in front of her with peaked lips that look like a badly painted picture of the Swiss Alps. She cannot talk to this woman about India. How could such a woman understand? This woman could never possibly believe that India is a world where the roads themselves have their own voice, their unique rhythm. How even the garbage-streaked streets seem to sing out despite the squalor they are a part of. How can she possibly tell this woman that looking at anything in India is to look into the eyes of a mystic, a gifted elder. The wisdom and memory that shines back at you is dwarfing.

The woman cuts in to Constance's thoughts.

"You spent some time there, have you? In India I mean."

Constance feels a muggy puddle of sweat collect across her chest and down towards her belly. It was unthinkable to her how she could be so hot and swollen in the rain. The monsoon rains, where the sky opens up and shakes itself like a wet bird, water splattering.

"Yes. My father worked for the ICS — The Indian Civil Service. He was an administrator."

"When did he come back?" The woman's voice is edgy.

"He came back when I did."

"You are how old?"

"Seventeen."

"And your Father, he was with you, that day. The day of the accident?"

"Yes."

"But it was Mr. Baron who signed you in?"

"le Baron."

"Yes, yes."

The story clearly makes no sense to the woman.

"And your mother is dead."

She says this with too much conviction, Constance refuses to reply.

"You are an only child, then?"

"Yes."

The woman scribbles something on the page. Constance wonders what she keeps writing. Watching the movement of the pen, Constance has a dance of ideas. *Ask her, don't ask her. Be silent, speak up.*

"Where is my father?" The question comes out starkly; even Constance is surprised by her own bluntness.

The woman licks her upper teeth.

"We don't know."

"He hasn't sent word?"

"No."

"Why?"

The woman does not answer.

"Where is Mr. le Baron?"

"India."

"Then my father is there, also."

"No."

"What do you mean no? Have you checked?"

The woman half closes her eyes, a cat look, a tracking look. "Of course we have." Her voice clipped again.

The woman rubs the side of her nose and scribbles on the page. Then she gets up from her chair, pushes it back over the carpet with a ram of her hand. She says nothing more, does not look at Constance again.

∾

Constance wakes to a red sea. For a moment, she thinks she is back at the accident, she has just been crushed. Fans of blood splatter over her. The crack inside her opening.

But she isn't on the ground, the air is not warm. It is cold. Cold and sticky. She rolls over and the starched cotton of the bedclothes scratches at her face. Her eyes come to focus on the metal rail around the bed. She is still in Guy's hospital.

But what is all this blood? Constance has a gummy feeling all the way down her legs. As if there is something clinging to her, some massive leech that has attached itself to her, glued itself down the length of her thighs, unwilling to be pried off.

She sits up in bed. There is red everywhere. Blood. Constance shouts for help.

The nurses encircle her. They are looking at the sheets, at the blood, but not at Constance. With fingers stiffly bent, Nurse Shoemaker hikes up her bed sheet, peers inside.

"Call the doctor."

One nurse is gone, clipping through the ward and out the door to get help. Constance begins to pant in fear.

"What happened? What is it?" she asks.

Nurse Shoemaker finally makes eye contact.

"Complications."

Doctor Watts is rushing to the bed. A nurse staggers after him, holding a thick cotton pad. He lifts the sheet and she shoves the pad between Constance's thighs, wrapping it like a huge nappy.

"Lie down. Breathe calmly." The doctor's voice has a measured beat to it, a practised rhythm.

Constance focuses on the water stain on the ceiling above her. She can tell the doctor and nurse are looking at each other, exchanging meaningful glances that she is not privy to while lying on her back.

The doctor clears his throat. He moves over the edge of the bed, coming in range of her eyes. He seems to focus exclusively on her pupils, without taking in any other part of her.

"You've lost a lot of blood. How do you feel?"

"Dizzy. Light headed."

"Yes," is his only reply.

Again, the word complications is uttered. Nurse Shoemaker is clicking her teeth, quite softly, but to Constance, it sounds shrill, a screeching in her head. Constance lifts her head up with an intention to stop the noise.

"Lie down!" commands Nurse Shoemaker.

Constance reluctantly obeys. At least the Nurse's command has interrupted her clicking. Constance stares at the ceiling, sees how the black hanging light sways whenever someone makes an abrupt movement. She still feels sticky, and very thirsty now.

"May I have some water?" She speaks to the ceiling.

"You'll have to wait. We need to see that things are — " Shoemaker is cut off.

"Under control," finishes the doctor.

Nurse Shoemaker pats Constance's knees, which arc the bed sheet up, away from the cotton that is propped between her legs. There is silence coming from the foot of the bed, though Constance knows that some kind of communication is going on.

That's when it enters her right ear. Not the high-pitched squeal she heard during the accident, but a base note, a deeper tone. It sounds as if it may be spiralling, twisting through her eardrum.

The sound clings to the back of her throat, sticking there for a moment, then breaks in a wave against the root of her tongue. Curdles into a muttered voice. Says something she cannot understand. She is listening for the words, but is delivered an image instead: a picture of herself seated in a chair, her face wrinkled, her fingers crippled, and no one to help her, no one else in sight.

Then an image of Doctor Watts, his hand on his chin. But she cannot see him, he is at the foot of her bed. Words mouthed, words whispered, words thought but not spoken. Constance lifts her head again, despite knowing that a quick reprimand is to follow.

"Did someone say something to me?"

Everyone shakes their head. Constance slumps back onto the pillow a second before Nurse Shoemaker commands her to.

The murmuring continues inside her, rambling away. Constance wishes her head didn't hurt so much, she wants to hear words. She decides to silence her breath, hold it in somehow, stifle her body so she can understand.

A moment passes. The message is no clearer. Constance exhales heavily. Doctor Watts probes her abdomen with his fingers. She wonders what he is searching for.

Her head an open window, contents jutting out. She imagines an even crack down the centre of her skull, a clean incision. Then the piercing in her right ear again and words coming through a tube. 'Let the nurses tell her.'

Finally words in her head, gloriously clear. Constance is sure of it. Five words strung together in a gift. Constance looks up again at the congregation at the foot of her bed. "Tell me what?"

There is silence.

"I beg your pardon?" Nurse Shoemaker sounds indignant.

"Someone said, 'let the nurses tell her'." Constance turns to the Doctor, "That must have been you."

The Doctor looks at her as if she is mad.

"No, Miss Stubbington, I didn't say that. In fact, I didn't say anything. Furthermore, I haven't decided anything. We need to watch this situation. It will be some days before we know anything for certain."

"But I heard you."

Nurse Shoemaker edges her back down to the bed.

"But I heard you say you'd get the Nurses to tell me."

There is silence from above. Then she hears Doctor Watts stride away.

Nurse Shoemaker leans over her face. She is smiling, a feigned, holy kind of smile. A smile that seems to say 'we'll pray for you, child'. It makes Constance burn with anger.

"I'm going to give you something to help you sleep. We need to watch and make sure no more blood is lost."

It is later, in the middle of the night that Constance awakens to find the ward in darkness. She glares at the ceiling once again, and puts all her concentration into the area of her right ear.

It is humming. It is alive.

~

Father smiles crookedly. Good lord, what should I do now?

He holds a perfectly hideous hat, wide brimmed with pink lace tied around it. Baiting me. He's always had appalling taste. Does he really think this is going to work?

His eyes sparkle the way they do. The way they do before he scolds me. Searing those cold grey eyes into me, telling me that I look hopelessly slothful or something equally vile. He's seen a sloth — many of them. He'll describe them in detail if I ever give him the chance.

But there's something unusual today. No scolding, no piercing silence. Just icy grey and a baiting. I think he may even be happy, although he'd never use such a word. Happy. A woman's word, he'd say. An emotional word. But whatever he might call it, it's unnerving me. Gives me the willies.

"Come, get the hat. It's only proper that a young lady should wear a hat when she goes riding."

"Riding, Father?"

"Yes, long lineage from chivalry, courage, carriages. You've heard of these, have you not?"

No Father, I've never heard of them. You've never once talked about such things. Not during the dreary dinners you condescend to eat with me, not during the long embroidery lessons you insist I take, never.

"Whose horse is it?"

"Roger le Baron's. You'll recall him from India, I'm sure. But of course, when you weren't in the rain, you were sick in bed. I don't suppose you remember much. Nevertheless, he is a remarkable horseman. He requests the honour. Come."

∽

Ank lies on his bed in the dormitory, book open in a tent on his chest, words unread. The writing on the page not filling him, leave him wanting more. More.

The top surgeon's dresser. Ank feels pleased with this, proud that an Irish orphan like himself has a proper job in an important hospital. But the bandages and cotton and encouraging words of Dr. Watts are not enough. He awakes each morning, scurries through words, diagrams, examples. He needs to study, to learn as much as he can from the books, impress Doctor Watts, look good to the surgeons, to all the English doctors. The pressure to read, to learn, to memorize. But still, the dream will not leave.

A wide-open sea, a boat full of women coming to the shore. The whole lot of them, weeping, calling out, "We're starving!"

Need to feed them, feed the women, as soon as they are on shore. A soup kitchen, free government food, because of the hunger.

Women off the ship, the soup in stout copper kettles. Constance disembarks, with so many others. Need to feed her. Feed them all.

⁓

Constance's voice rebounds off the white tile walls and echoes through the swimming baths. The sun leaks through the window in the ceiling, creating splashes of light that swirl into tiny whirlpools in the water. It is her first time here. She has finally made it into the arched cavern where, at last, she can submerge her entire body in the warm liquid.

"Does this mean I've had the last of the sponge baths?"

Nurse Shoemaker looks at her carefully and shakes her head. "Let's not get ahead of ourselves, shall we, Miss Stubbington."

Nurses Shoemaker and Woost are on either side of her, and on some inaudible cue, they bend over and hoist her out of the wheelchair. Constance swings her arms around their shoulders. Supporting her weight carefully, the Nurses free her from her seated prison. Her legs float out from her, as if they could be easily carried away in a tide.

Nurse Robbins is in the pool, already wet, wearing a hospital issue bathing costume identical to the one Constance wears. The material clings to Robbins's skin, and blushing, she tries to hold herself beneath the surface of the water so that the peaked, anxious bulbs of her breasts will not be revealed. She lifts herself up only at the last minute, when it is necessary to ease Constance into the water from the front.

As soon as she is in the baths, Constance laughs noisily. She wants to hear herself, wants the sound of her own voice to hit the low ceiling above and come crashing down with emphasis.

It has been so long since she has been fully wet, she desires to inhale every inch of the experience.

A wave of water caused by Nurse Robbins laps up and sprays Constance's face. It feels like a loving stroke against her skin. She wants to fling her arms, kick her feet if she could, splash with delight in the water's warm embrace.

Constance cannot remember being so happy. She thinks of the word delicious and decides that this is how she feels. Robbins and Woost smile to see her so excited. It is a veritable party for her, a watery homecoming.

"The last time I was in water like this was the day before the accident. I had a brilliant bath that day. I remember when the water hit my head, I thought I could hear music coming from my hair. The way the water soaked it through, it sounded like each hair was singing to me. But my Father — "

Here Constance pauses and looks at the Nurses, their faces turning an instant shade of grey.

"But Father yelled at me through the door. There I was singing, enjoying the water so, and I heard him order me to get out. Doesn't anyone know where he is?"

The sudden shift to such a pointed question rattles the nurses. They both look to Miss Shoemaker, who in such a moment of awkwardness, receives reverential authority. She merely shakes her head.

Constance grows quiet again. She dangles her fingers in the pool and then clears her throat to make an announcement. "I wish to get out now."

The nurses exchange a conspiratorial glance. Miss Shoemaker is silently elected to speak. "You're to have a good washing. Doctor's orders."

Constance knows immediately what they mean. A sting of shame runs through her, and the sight of all that blood on the sheets comes into sharp focus. But the question of her Father lingers. She looks at the nurses for clues. Surely they know something they aren't telling her. Surely he has made some kind of contact with the hospital. Surely he's yet to arrive.

The questions shape Constance's face but the nurses, deaf to her expression, continue to scrub her down. She allows her body to go limp, inviting easier access to her depths and curves. The Nurses wash around the outline of her swimming costume, following the seams with the diligence of tailors. No one dares to lift up her suit, wash beneath it. Constance watches the concentrated effort of their task and smiles at them, feeling some awkward need to reassure them.

"You're awfully good to me. Thank you."

For some reason, she wants to apologize to them, make amends for mentioning her Father. But the nurses would blush, shake their heads no. So, Constance laughs instead, and launches into more talk. She knows she can win them over with her tongue, and she decides, in a moment of defiance, that she can speak about Father if she wants.

"I'll let you in on a secret, shall I? Father was one of those gentlemen who had his cup of tea brought in at precisely two o'clock each afternoon. In India, however, sometimes his duties forbade such a siesta time, but he was loathe to give up his ritual. I have seen him, pinkie lifted, be served chai on the back of an elephant no less! Can you imagine?"

She pauses for a second and eagles in on Miss Shoemaker, determined to crack the mask of her face. A buried face. Forgotten features.

"The Natives would get the tea tray ready, and command the elephant to fold up its knees and bow, literally bow before him. Then, my father would snatch the elephant's tail between his hands and hobble up its back to sit behind the guide. Have you ever been on an elephant before? I guess not, not in England. But there he would sit, posed like an ancient warring prince of some lost kingdom, handed his china and a linen napkin with his initials embroidered on."

Robbins relinquishes a small smile. Shoemaker tightens. "Open your toes. Clean between her toes please." Shoemaker flashes her hand at Robbins in attempt to pretend she isn't listening.

"Do you know what it is like to ride an elephant?"

Despite themselves, all three nurses are listening to Constance, alternately washing and hanging onto the words.

"You would think that it might be a lurching ride, wouldn't you? As if the elephant might positively lumber along? But not so, quite the opposite. That beast is graceful, it almost floats along in a seamless stream. Whoosh! The right legs glide forward. Whoosh, the left legs purr. Pure rhythm, like a well tuned melody."

There is a moment of silence. Against their better thoughts, the nurses find themselves envisioning themselves atop an elephant's back.

The patter has had the desired effect on the Nurses. They have stopped scrubbing her roughly and now softly dab. Constance, having lulled them, gives herself time with her own thoughts.

They'll not speak a word of Father. That much is clear. I'll ask Mr. Maguire, she decides. He'll tell me.

～

Ank is waiting for her when she is wheeled back to bed. He rises, his book falling off his lap onto the floor.

Shoemaker has gone, and Miss Woost and Miss Robbins are on either side of Constance, ready to lift her.

"Mind then, I'll help." Ank offers.

Ank reaches out to take Constance's arm, but in the grasping space of two nurses and a wheelchair, his hand lights upon her neck instead. Three cupped fingers, an unintentional caress, and when he moves them away, Constance feels a tingling that dwells there for minutes afterward.

She is back in bed and the nurses gone before she dares lift her hand to her throat, examine the quivering skin. As she does, his eyes follow her fingers and linger for a moment on the spot, before he squirrels about, foraging for his book.

"Thought I'd beguile you with the written word. " Ank says, shifting the book from one hand to the other.

"What have you there?"

"'Tis Irish, and that's a warning."

"Like you?"

"Indeed."

Constance folds herself into the covers, closes her eyes.

"Who's it by?"

"A man named Yeats."

"Never heard of him."

"He's new, mind. Listen up then, will you?"

Ank clears his throat and begins.

"Where dips the rocky highland
Of Sleuth Wood in the lake,
There lies a leafy island
Where flapping herons wake
The drowsy water-rats;
There we've hid our faery vats,
Full of berries
And of reddest stolen cherries.
Come away, O human child!
To the waters and the wild

With a faery, hand in hand,
For the world's more full of weeping than you can understand'."

Ank has read only the first stanza when he notices that Constance's breath has changed. Water washed, clean fatigued, she is asleep.

~

Sitting in her steel chair, Constance inhales the fresh air of morning outside the hospital walls. A tomb has opened and life breathes through her once again. She feels like a mummy finally unwrapped from a sticky sarcophagus.

She waits at the main entrance of the hospital. Nurse Shoemaker has wheeled her up to the statue of Mr. Guy, and unceremoniously deposited her there. Below Mr. Guy, the statue gives way to four plaques facing in each direction. On the first plaque, Constance reads: *Thomas Guy Sole Founder of This Hospital In His Lifetime AD. MDCCXXI*

Constance wheels herself to the second side. There is no writing here, just an engraving of a woman, with three small children lolling across the front of her body. One of the children is suckling at the woman's left breast, and her gown, looking more like an Indian sari than a dress, has slunk down to expose her nurturing nipple. The other child sucks fruitlessly at her right breast, which the material of her gown covers. Then the third child, his body facing away from the mother, appears to be sliding down from her lap, uncared for and unloved. Constance cannot understand this. Why does the mother not reach out for him, save him from falling?

Constance swivels around to the third side of the statue. The engraving here shows three men with long hair and beards, but even the immutable stone exposes a malevolent gleam in their eyes. The watery lustre is one she has seen before, in India, when she and her father encountered the snake wallahs. Father snapped at them in anger, commanded them to stand. Three men, hair in matted locks wavering down to their shoulders, runny eyes that didn't know how frightened they should be. Father leaned over the basket, chose from among two cobras and a python. Grabbed the python by the tail, swung him. Even in her terror Constance could see the Indian merchants shaking their heads. *No, sahib, not like that. Not like that at all.* But they spoke another language. One of the hundreds he was deaf to.

She knew Father was coming for her. Standing in a long beige frock, gloves on her hands. Not flaunting her navel, as he complained those Indian women did with their saris, but dressed like a proper English girl, terrified.

She ran to the embrace of a Neem tree, while Father, cherry blushed by her retreat, marched over to grab her. Her spine hardened with his approach, the muscles in her body sucked in towards a shirking centre. His hands hot, his face cold. He clutched at her hair, shook it away from the back of her head, so she could feel the snake on her neck.

The wallahs were saying *no, no, snakes only made to dance,* but father shouted at them to be quiet as the cool muscle of serpent slid across the back of her neck.

Constance pleads for help with her eyes. The older wallah clasps his hands together in front of his chest in prayer position, bows his head, says, '*Snake no hurt you, Miss. No bite.*'

That's when she heard the python's voice. It said, '*I know. You know I know*'.

So she stepped into her mind, imagined eating marmalade on toast; drinking cocoa from a blue, chipped cup; having her hair combed by Ayah. She greedily sucked in images, anything to take her away from the moment, to prove to her father she wouldn't show fear.

Constance grimaces at the memory while she wheels herself away from the sensation, to the last plaque. And then she laughs. Here he is, waiting for her. An engraving of a horse, its front legs lifted up in the air, eyes spooked. Ceylon, of course.

But before Constance has the chance to speak to him as she desires, Nurse Shoemaker is behind her, hands on the chair, wrenching Constance away from the statue.

"You don't need to fill your head with any more of that."

This is ridiculous to Constance. Shoemaker brought her here and now scolds her for looking. The logic of Father.

"What's the trouble?" she asks, her voice in simulated innocence.

"You know very well. The horse. We don't want to upset you now, do we?"

Constance snickers to think how carefully people here try to distract her from any reference to horses. As if the mere mention of them will bring Constance to madness. She knows Nurse Shoemaker once tore out a picture of one from a book, where it gathered dust on the bottom of the trash bin rather than meet Constance's eyes.

The nurse wheels her further into the Quadrangle. Constance looks hopefully towards the entrance, where two muted stone pillars guard the lattice gate. She longs to be on the other side, have the option to pass through the entrance and leave this place.

A bandaged man is wheeled up beside her. His face is a canvas of splattered colours, running down the edges to his chin. With quivering hands, he lights a cigarette. He inhales the smoke in a short, gasping pull.

"Hello there." She says.

He gives her a painful nod of his head.

"I'm Constance."

"So I've 'eard."

Constance doesn't like the way that sounds, pulls back into herself.

"The horse rider, that it?"

She twists her mouth deciding how to answer him.

"What happened to you?" She asks.

"Mine accident. Up north. Those bastards knew they were sending us to our death. Curse the dogs, they didn't care."

Constance watches as his deflated chest pulls tightly, attempting to find room for the smoke in his pancake lungs.

"What were you mining?"

At that, the man begins to laugh. Despite his crumpled presence, it is a thick laugh.

"You ever 'eard of coal?" He snorts.

Constance is insulted by the tone of his voice.

"No." Her voice has an innocence to it that takes him unaware.

"You did have a rough fall. Just like they said."

"It was rough indeed. And you look like the sort of bloke — to understand."

The man pulls his head in, turtle-like, looking indecisively at Constance. She, on the other hand, has the compunction to laugh. She has never called anyone a bloke before. She has heard the term many times, of course, especially here among the patients, but at home, she was forbidden to speak with such commonness. Now, having said it, she is dying to say it again. Let it blot out of her mouth, in defiance of Father.

"In fact, I have you figured as just the right sort of bloke to hear this story. It isn't for all ears, you know, but having gone through such an experience as you have, well, you'll understand.

But don't you dare breathe this to another living soul. Are you ready?"

The man doesn't change the blank expression on his face.

"The horse — when he stomped on me, something powerful happened. He did more than touch me in the physical sense. You see, I sucked his spirit into my body."

He looks at her with a snarl.

"You don't expect me to believe that, do you now?"

"I can feel him inside. His name is Ceylon. You know what it's like to hear like a horse? It's terrifying. Every little sound is like a trumpet blasting. And my sense of smell, it's so very acute — I can smell people's fear."

The man looks confused. There is a struggle on his face - is she mad or is she having one over on him?

"You're queer, you are."

"Ask around. There was a man in this very hospital, only a few years back, who was bitten by a rabid dog. He was so violent after that, he used to fight with everyone who came in sight of him. They had to give him the electrical shocks to calm him down. But he was never the same again."

The man is clearly ill at ease now. "You wouldn't be making fun of me now, 'ould ya?"

"It's like killing a man. You take his life, and forever you walk around with his angry spirit inside your own body. Have you ever met a man who killed? You can see the ghosts of his victims in his eyes."

"The other patients. The staff. I 'eard them talking. Saying you're a wild one. I think I understand now." He flicks his cigarette to the ground.

"That coal — do you feel it in your heart? Is that what you've taken in?"

The man turns his lips into a pouting sneer. "Aye, horse missy, believe what you care to, but you better be careful about who wants to ride ya." He spins out of her way.

When he is gone, Constance allows herself to laugh aloud. Then she looks up and sees Ank Maguire standing there. He has heard every word.

~

It's hot for England, not as hot as India, of course, but too hot for riding. And here I am sandwiched between Father and his watchful, reticent friend, Too-Tall boots le Baron. He just nods at Father, smiles sometimes, but hardly says a word. Lets Father do all the talking. But I don't like being between them. Seeping cucumber between their slices of crust-less bread. Slippery green seeds in the heat.

Still, the horses move onward. Did I really tell Father that I've never ridden a horse in England? I lied. I have, many times. Before he summoned me to India, when Freda was my keeper and she and I went to see the man who kept the stables. That was when I rode, back then. While Freda and the man kissed each other blue.

That's when I learned the horse language. Not words, just thoughts, straight from one brain to another. At first, I thought I had to speak like Father, rough and commanding. But that's not how it works, not at all. You whisper. You tease. You flirt.

Ah, the clink of their shoes. Chink, chink, links of a thick chain. Like the slaves, the ones that came to England from Africa. Captured a long time ago, by the likes of Father. Oh, he would have been one, a slave trader. I know he would have, if he had lived back then. Capturing them in the deep jungle, chains of unwashed human, fear rising up from their pores, putrefying the fragile pockets of oxygen below the deck of a ship being thrashed at sea. Laying, row upon row, matchsticks in a box, head to toe, toe to head, human cargo brought from the brutal sun and flush green of West Africa to clammy, cold, unforgiving England.

Two

❧

Ank
En route to Victoria, BC
1889

YOU SENT ME TO THE NEXT village to gather winter provisions, Ma, not knowing the half of what was to come of it. Two days gone and I'm aching to be home. Long walk on the rocky road that slides by the ocean's shoulder. Singing I am, skipping rocks along the dirt.

'Tis the smoke I smell first, then the knowing deep in my gut that says something's all wrong. Have no idea where the smoke is coming from, but the heart in me is all a' beat, a force that thrusts me on, cuffs me into a run. The egg of a giant bird cracking inside.

Ankles twist ugly on the uneven road, the rucksack digs into the back of me something fierce. But I have to go on. Have to see.

'Til I stop the running, fall at the door. Sugar and flour rain down on me from the rucksack, the bones from the butchers clanks me but good. Can feel the heat. Down on the ground, want to cry, need to cry, but the dinner in me comes up instead. Garish yellow, it is, the smell of rotten eggs.

"Ma!"

You still lying in your bed, a half-burned rafter trapping you. Your arm reaching, thinking, it seems, it would all be grand again if you could just get out from beneath the burning. But you aren't with your thoughts, no, you're watching me. Watching me with open eyes. Eyes that do not blink. Dead eyes, watching me, dead.

And beside you in the cottage is Eoin and Da, their faces red with the insult of smoke. Lying, they are, both of them tucked clean into bed, trapped, too. Roof scattered in angry ashes and broken bits all around them. Chimney blackened. Thatch like darkened dogs speckled all about.

Your mouth sweating, Ma. Hungry you seem for oxygen, famished for another chance at life. And your pupils, your irises, beg me to stay.

Minutes alone with you, not even a blink to send me away.

⁓

The rain yells down and I want to be standing there, so. Feel the wetness soak through and settle into my skin. Get away from the burning inside. Erase the shadow that has settled in my gut.

The pinned down face of Mrs. Cleary, her gaunt fingers on the coins, counting once, twice, again. I want her to stop, stop the small circles on each coin, stop the dusty reading of the face of them, stop it. Silver collected for me, so that I might go to America.

"You're to do the chores now, Ank Maguire."

The chores. The sweeping of the cabin, girl's work, so that the old woman might count the coins again.

I pick up the broom from beside the fire, swipe at the spiders, feel the wee bit of light cut the back of me from where it pries its way through the small window. Thinking of you, Ma.

Oh God, Ma. The back and forth of your broom, hips keeping time and balance between right and left, and you talking, talking about people having the guardian angel at their side to look after them. The first time I heard it, I knew mine was watching, did chores enough for two boys that day, wanting the angel to notice. Look down and feel proud.

But 'tis no angel here. Nor you, Ma. Just Mrs. Cleary, grabbing for the broom.

"Ach, what a waste of black hair and keen eyes. I'll be showing you how to do it. Mind it now."

I watch her, see the way her elbows are up shoulder way, heaving the dirt through the doorway, ridding it. Not the long, clean strokes that Ma made.

"You're to be a sorry lot of fourteen-year old trouble over there if you can't keep yourself helpful."

Over there. The other side of the world.

Which only brings me back to the thinking. When you were a woman who had flesh. And Eoin was a lad with a lisp and Da was a man with wide, milking hands.

Then a sneeze that rumbles my insides, though it comes from her. A tangle of brown hair escaping from her knot, scolding me.

"You're to quit the dreaming, see. Dead and gone and you knows it as good as I. Now get to the sweeping."

Again. Once, twice, the red rash of her fingers boiling up, breaking over the coins. She places a shilling in her mouth, right at the centre of her tongue, and closes up 'round it. Sucking, she is, her lips slack and a bit of spit dripping down, like the dogs when they get hungry. Coins collected door to door by none other than me, now in the hand or mouth of Mrs. Cleary. So that 'the bad luck' may be sent away.

~

The cliff, overlooking the sea. The sea Eoin said he'd drown himself in if ever one was to pull him away from Galway. Water that could have splashed, doused, cut through the fire. Too far away.

Pink in the still dark sky to the west. Warning hues, chiding me as they are. I'm hunched up as Ma would say, knees into sweater, that bird within me still fluttering. Wings whip my heart, clawed feet puncture my lungs. Dreading the break of day and the hard baked loaves of Mrs. Cleary. What's a lad like me to do so far away?

Thinking 'bout that first pint of my life, at the wake, no less, instead of with Da. Drinking my first with the lads out back, half moon slipping in the sky. Splashing down the homemade bitter, lads chanting "Ank! Ank! Ank!" like I was the star of a hurling match, not a boy in the world alone. Them with the yarn, telling me made up stories, trying to pull me out of my own head. Half of me wanting to venture forth, half of me still inside.

Where the smoke is.

Then the men came out, a cuff from Eamon Fahy, his pig lips in my face. "At least come in and drink like a man."

A man. Standing in the centre of the circle, some of the women keening, tea and whiskey wetting their hoarse throats. The men, mugs foaming, saying, "'tis bad now lad, but will make a strong one of ya." But I can see they are lying. Can even feel it in the way they slap my back too hard.

That night was the last of the lads. Pulled ears and smacked heads, away from me, to the cows, the potato beds, into the village. Away from me, the bad luck a fire burned into my too-white skin. Cursed.

Now I just want to die. Like you, like Da, like Eoin.

That's when you come to me, Ma. Your voice, inside me.

The hovering was always with me, it was. Even as a wee one, I saw them. Ghosts, you'd say, the spirit people.

The first one I ever saw was the baby sister, dead of the fever. Da was out, see, selling his tools on the road, and when the doctor realized that Rosa had the fever, he put us up. Meaning, if you will, the quarantine. Me Da couldn't come back, see? No one in, no one out. Those were the rules.

So it was just Mamaí and me and Rosa, who was dying. I held her, cause Mamaí couldn't. Mamaí couldn't stop shaking enough to hold her own baby girl. Rosa was only eight months old at the time, still needing a nipple, see, but Mamaí wasn't up to the job. She just sat in the corner and rocked, her finger all a' rub across her upper lip, back and forth. Like there was some hole there she wanted to fill, tried to fill, but couldn't.

~

Now it's the bleeding ocean beneath me, and isn't she rough. And me, the likes of me, cramped small into a wee egg crate of a bed. How I'd like to be down there, tumbled down there, into the gaping mouth of the Atlantic. Beneath the miles of water, head and feet squeezed by enough water to bring me down, douse the fire in me.

And don't I get my wish.

The first blast cracks a grin in the skylight, the second rips it all the way off, rough and nasty. The men all up, arms arched over their heads, knees folded beneath the weight of water. Curses to the sea, shouts at God and the Devil as if the two of 'em worked this one out together.

But me, Ma, nothing. I lie here, not so much as a peep from me. Just waiting for a big wave to come and take me home to you.

But no such luck.

The ship, she jumps and heaves while the water carves out rivers on the floorboard, soaks the mattresses through and through. Then the men, a good half of them with the vomit, bites of beef and bread they hoarded down. Give it all back they do, all of them give it back with a stench so foul not even the smell of wet wool or the musky sea can hide it.

The lot of them, filled with disbelief. Cursing fate, the new life that waits for them in the West. Murmuring to fathers, brothers, the wives they left behind.

"God help it, I'll see you alive again my beloved."

"Father, send me the prayers, send them now Father, now."

And on it goes, the war of waves. I fear we can take it no more when don't that sea calm. That's when I make for the outer decks, where the living is. Golden belt between endless sky and endless water. Ah Ma, how I love it, your voice in my head yet again.

And I held Rosa, wet my fingers and let her suck on them until she'd howl with the impatience of it all, while Mamaí went on rocking and rubbing, the skin beneath her nose chapped and red.

Then one day, Rosa stopped sucking at my finger. She stared up at me, knowing I wasn't Mamaí and mad as hell about it. She cranked her little head to the side, looking for that woman who brought her into the world, like she wanted to give her a good cussing out, make her stop rocking. But Mamaí didn't look even then. She didn't look when Rosa growled like a rabid dog and left her body for the ceiling. I swear it happened just like that. A low grrrr and then this hissing sound like a tea kettle singing at full boil and Rosa flicked up to the ceiling and waited there.

I don't know what she was waiting for. I guess Mamaí to notice her. But it was only me who saw her, hovering as I've said. From then on, I seen them all, the children when they die.

But if you can hold onto it, I'll tell you a secret. You're not to tell a soul about it, you promise me then? The children, after they die, they don't stay the same. What I mean is that they don't stay the age they died at, see? Everyone thinks that. That if they died at three, they'll always be three, but it don't work that way. See, they grow here. Dead children, they grow in Spirit.

~

That's what I hold on to, your voice a hum inside me. We've made it to St. Thomas, West Indies, but it isn't the town I pay mind to, it's your voice, like the brushed strings of a fiddle in the minor key, singing just for me.

Then the blast from the ship's gun, and those small rowboats dart out from the shore to swarm the vessel, like they're going to cage us. Me, I'm just dying to get off, same as the men. A whole knot of us, gathered round the side, desperate to feel our feet on solid land.

And aren't we tested by the fury of it all. The quarantine flag hoisted and when the medical officer comes on board, I knew we're in for the long haul.

The officer finds a stripped down ship, course. All signs of the sickness floating out to sea. The water a mile or two out like a huge dust bin, the trash heap of us all. I saw them myself, the torn bedclothes used to bring down the fever, empty bottles of whiskey, buckets of vomit swept up from the decks, even a diseased chicken or two. The whole lot of it thrown overboard, gutting up the water so it turns from blue to grey, just a few miles from the shore.

And that officer, he clips right by us. No walking for the likes of him. He prances, he does, as if he's on a white horse in a muddy pond, wanting to get away before the legs of the beast are soiled. I guess that means we're the mud, dirtied flowers all of us, tongues dry and cracked, waiting for the sting. Him in the boots that reach to his knees, not touching a soul. We're the mud, I kept reminding myself, he doesn't want to get those beautiful horse legs dirty.

Standing in front of me is a big bear of a man. Da would have said bellicose, from his reading. Remember how he was always using the big words, Ma, chiding you when you didn't know them? But you didn't care for the big words. Said they most often got in the way. You knew other things, you did. I'm remembering how you watched. You waited. Could tell us all months ahead whether a woman would have a girl or a boy child, knew by looking who had the evil in his eye, heard the keening long before someone died. The banshee that comes lurking, 'tis a family trait, you said. Handed down. Lets us know when our people are going to die. Like smoke in your heart while coming home from the village with provisions.

"What's he afraid of?" I whisper it, hoping no one but the bellicose man will hear.

"The past," he says, "The famine. 'Twas a real mess here when so many left our Island some thirty years back. They came with the famine disease. Boat loads of dead or dying. Here, other places, too. Don't like us now. Think we're filthy, they do."

I look down at my wool jumper, see the black smudges, the holes that peek out like so many windows.

"We are filthy."

"Not our fault."

That officer is near me now and I can smell him. Soap. Freshness. Clean drawers and all. Not like a man who's done a day's work. But he motions with his hands for me to open my mouth, which I don't remember closing, and now I know that I have to have the quiet mind. Worried that he might read it, know that I think he smells.

He stands far away from me so he doesn't have to feel my breath on him. I can see the lines beneath his eyes, three folds under the right, two under the left. I'm busting to ask him why he's uneven.

Then we're off. Has been a few hours and the whole lot of us move as one huge spider down onto shore. The men, their eyes are on the ladies who fan themselves beneath those queer tall trees.

"God" one says, "Will you look at them. They make me hungry, the women do."

So I look at them, and I like the colours on their dresses, even though they are covered like we are with the boat grime. And of course it makes me think of you, Ma, who was never filled with the grime, boat or otherwise. Even when you were in the chimney, dust on your face. Said the grime was a way of looking at the world you just didn't have. So I look and try to see which of the women don't have the grime way of looking at the world. See their white noses and long eyelashes. See them tilt their heads to the side when I smile at them. They make me hungry, they do. Hungry for a hip beneath my head and a kiss on my cheek.

A whole day to pass in St. Thomas. Me, I squat, watching. See for the first time in my life the dark skinned men and women. Can't stop the staring at all that deepness in their skin. Looks full and heavy, it does, like the touch of peat after a long rain. My own skin, it doesn't have this feeling. It's slight. The feel of once risen bread before it is folded in half, kneaded again. By you, Ma. Folded and kneaded by you.

~

Back on the ship, cockroaches all a' skitter through the night. Crusty black jackets flick over my skin like so many bad dreams. Tease me, they do, like licks of a flame I don't see.

"Can't sleep lad?"

A voice from the darkness.

"No, sir, cannot."

"What pains ya?"

"Cockroaches, sir."

"I mean inside, boy."

Inside. Don't want to tell no stranger about the feelings inside.

"Have you been to America, sir?"

"I'm sure if I had I wouldn't be going back. But I've been, dare say, on worse vessels than the one that lay beneath us."

'Tis the bellicose man.

"Where's that then?"

"Feckin' India."

Now there's a word Da wouldn't say.

"Was it beautiful?"

"India's a feckin' whore."

That word. Whore. The word the men use after they've been to the pub. Before drink it is Missus. After, whore. And worse.

"'Twas near your age. On the way back. Made it four days out when the Captain came down. Some grimy tropical fever or another. First mate was going to take us onward, but he got sick too. Was a bleedin' casket by the time they turned us round."

I am sure there is something I am supposed to say, but I don't know what.

"Even the pigs died. Four of 'em. In the pigsty. Had a grand infection, the whole lot of 'em. But you know what happened, don't ya? That cook fed 'em to us still. Bastard pigs, stinking of the chloride of lime they did, from what they swabbed the decks with."

"'Twasn't right."

"No, boy, 'twasn't."

I lose him in the shadow for a moment and then he is back, something shiny in his hand.

"For you," He says.

'Tis a bottle, half full of golden coloured drink, and all I can think of is the word whore.

"Never mind. Don't need it."

"But you do."

"No, don't."

"Go on, be the man you are. Scoff the lot."

He lifts the bottle to my mouth. No force with him, but a clean raising to my lip. He's like the men back home, Ma, good men like Eamon Fahy who look out for a lad. And I so want to be a man, want to keep the roaches away. And don't I open up.

"There you be. For the pain. Inside." He says it like he knows what he's saying.

Down I lie and let the drink take me. I can barely feel a thing when a cockroach flashes across my chest. I feel better and worse at the same time. The cockroaches, my rumbling stomach, the fire under my skin.

Then there is nothing else but my mouth, hot with the drink. Not at all like the pint at the wake, but a bee sting that arches through me and boils up. I don't like the feel, I don't, my tongue scalded, like I've drunk too hot tea just off the fire. And the smell, the smell of the drink, 'tis a curse for the roaches, so don't they just leave me well enough alone.

Bellicose gone now, lying down some out of sight. Just me in the bed with the drink inside and a ship that feels even more like a tilting. But still, the burning inside. I want your voice in me, Ma.

But I can't hear you.

So I squeeze my ears near pain and search for the pictures in my head. I feel the drink well up, feel the legs on me dead. And I'm near desperate for you to speak to me.

Are you here? Put my fingers in my ears, rub wildly.

But it doesn't help none. Your voice just a hum, like a fly buzzing far away, trapped beneath an overturned saucer.

Ma? You here Ma?

But you're gone. Nothing. Your voice all gone.

~

Panama, a town called Aspinwall, 'tis worse. Worse than the boat, even. Garbage strewn 'round miserable huts, buzzards all a' squawk and fluttering about, everywhere a liquor shop. Would rather burn my eyes with hot coals than stay here a night.

Bellicose cups the back of my head with his hand. Like Da did. 'Tis a man thing, I suppose, an open palm on the neck of a boy. Hated it with Da, hate it now. But we're headed for the train and he's decided he's going to get me there.

I can see they're queuing for the bags, and I so hope the Bellicose can pay for mine. Coins nearly gone. Just the shiny ones left, the ones Mrs. Cleary cleaned for me in her own mouth. Got a smack for that, she did, when her husband came home.

Me seeing how mean he was after the drink and knowing how she ached to keep the coins herself and run away.

"Watch for them Natives," Bellicose says.

"Why? What's wrong with the Natives?"

"They'll think nothing of stabbing a knife in your back and robbing ya."

I'm thinking that Bellicose doesn't know what he's saying. He's got to be talking about somewhere else. No one here seems to own a knife. They're too bleeding poor.

"Who says?" I ask.

"I say, boy. And you'd say too if you had a brain in your head."

He's ticked, I can see.

"I think they'll know a poor boy when they see him."

"No one poor in their eyes except them."

Now I've given him the cheek and yet I need him to pay for my bags.

"I'll watch for them. I will."

"Good one. Good lad." He seems calmer with this.

"How 'bout I get us a seat on the train?"

"You do that, lad. Leave your bag with me."

But I have no intention of staying with the Bellicose. When I look at him, I feel the heat in my chest. Burning drink and your voice gone. So I climb on the train, funny thing that it is. Can stand in the centre and see all the way down the entire length of it.

'Tis full, this train. Men squat all the way along its edges, so I dip my head in greeting and keep moving along. Look to sit where there's room only for one. Need to have the silence. Hear you again.

But he's on the train, Bellicose, lumbering the way he does and craning his neck for me a couple carriages back. So I crouch alongside the men, stare out at the dust as the train begins.

The jungle, 'tis purring with life. I see a green reptile, a ridged hump on its back. Sits there deathly quiet it does, not daring to flicker as we go past. I want to be like the reptile with crisp, quiet eyes, but it doesn't last long. I'm up and into a run because Bellicose is clumping towards me. Need to be where he isn't.

So I head for the Natives. The last carriage and here they are, torn clothes and dirt like a sun dog round their mouths. I'm looking for the violence, but don't see none. I'm looking for the rage like the Master with his cane, but there isn't no rage in their eyes. I see them same as I see the dogs in the village back home who don't belong to a soul — ears back, eyes down, nose tucked out of sight.

So I sit with them. Watch as the train takes us through a small village of huts. Past a clearing you would say has been hacked away by angry axes. See the Native men with scarcely the clothes on, arms full of wood. See the Native women, naked almost, blowing into open fires despite the heat of the day. And everywhere, furniture out in the open air — planks here, wine bottles there, rinds of melons and pumpkins that have been dried in the sun. All of it desperate like, too hot to care. But 'tis the boy who gives me the jolt. My age, his right leg tied to a tree, looking like it's to prevent him from wandering away.

Don't want to look at the tied up boy, so I close my eyes, invite the lull in. Let the blur begin. Listen for you. Try to find your voice, Ma. Stretch my mind back home where your voice might still be, home to Galway. Over the waves that can't touch me now, the salt that can't lick at my wounds. I'm almost there, can almost see the smoke again, the cottage burning. Almost

found you. But there's a problem. A smell. 'Tisn't right. 'Tisn't
a smell that lives in the story in my head. Doesn't belong to the
fire or your cooking or even Eoin's hair, smouldering. 'Tis like
something rotten. Flesh, cloth.

I open my eyes and there he stands. Not Bellicose, but a
Native man. I'm looking for the knife but get distracted say, by
the things in his hand. One a yellow-green sliver of moon, the
other a squat green-red oval.

I try to look at him, but he turns away. His arm coming at
me like an altar of saints, his face shy.

"Anana, banana," He says as he places the moon fruit in
my hand.

Then the other. "Mango." And all of him moves away.

Bellicose would say they was poisoned. Can already hear his
daft words in my head. Poisoned and full of the larva that will
rot in your gut. But I'm not scared of the larva or the Natives
or even of Bellicose, so I'm going to eat the fruit anyway. Close
my eyes and count them so I know what to eat first. Which
one comes out seven. Your lucky number. Lucky until it wasn't,
anyway.

The mango wins, 'tis seven. But how to eat it? The outside
skin hard and dry, tastes like dirt on my tongue. But down
deeper, something soft. Something cool like the lips of you on
my cheek after a day working with Da in the fields.

Peel away the skin, finally. Fights me, it does, then it obeys
and I can tear it like leather beaten down by use. Orange flesh
below. Da would have said succulent, you would have laughed.
Said back, "Nothing succulent like the feel of dirt beneath your
nails" and Da would have said you was cracked altogether.

Cracked. Sweetly stinging juice that sops my hands and my
mouth with this rain of orange heaven. The softness of a warm
night riding across my tongue. And doesn't it take me away. To

the place of flowing juices. The yellow haze of a distant sun. Where you are alive and smile your big-mouthed smile, call me the Monkey's Uncle and Eoin His Goodness Me. And Da, book by the fire, teaching me to read in the early hours when there is a warm darkness all around, just broken in tiny flirts from the light of the hearth. Still air, and me knowing what no one else knows — that the earth doesn't move in the early morning. It stands there still, in the glow of that distant sun, and just waits for me to crawl inside and bask in it and dream the day away.

But then it's over and I am on the train travelling into a day that leaves me too fast. There'd be no evening here if you can believe it. The night is like a bad thought that rides out and hits me, a strike of cat's claw. Day just here and gone and it's all over with before you can get used to the idea. No sunsets like in Ireland, when you can see the colour change in the sky. Here, it's a sudden drop of darkness, a blunt end to the sentence that Da would have said wasn't worth his eyes.

And out there — Mary the Mother of us all — what is out there? Those large palmed ferns hiding all sorts of beasts, lurking I'd swear.

So I think I better keep my eyes open.

And aren't I glad I did, or I would have missed the bridge, and a moonlight path cross the sky. We're over a river and I'm leaning far to catch sight of the water below. It's now, when I look at the water with the light from the sky that I know what I've been waiting for. Red winks of light. A twinkle, a flash from under the bridge.

You. Your eyes all the way down here where the world is cut in half. Crocodile eyes flashing. Red eyes, all a' squint. Your eyes, Ma. The moon a candle you hold in your hand.

Acapulco, a numb sea and we're back on the water again. Stone glad we're away from the mosquitoes and the jungle and the stench that seemed to linger over the land like a bad dream.

The Bellicose is on the ship and me pretend pining that he didn't find me on the train. Cutting across Panama isthmus without him, feigning the persecution of it all. And he's raw enough to believe it, think I wanted for him.

But all I want is your voice. So I ask the salt air for it back.

Put my hands over my ears and listen. Squeeze my brain so I see you in my mind and beg you to please give me the words. Imagine, I do, your sturdy legs, your wide face, your thin lips. And there I am, reaching out for your dark hair, black hair like my own, pulled up in a loose knot behind you. Want to untie that hair, let it fall onto your red cheeks, want to smell you.

But I can't. Can't smell. Can't hear you anymore. The smell of your hair and your hands and your breath sinking down into a lost crevice inside me. So I make up the scent, crack it up with the wood fire you cooked over, roll it up with the spray of flour on your hands, let it wash over me like the waves that come across the water same as a song you can't get out of your mind. But I'm lying with the whole lot of it. All I can smell is the scent of burnt flesh and the sweet slap of mango.

You're gone, you are. Dead. Gone.

San Francisco and we're herded ashore again to change vessels. Bellicose by my side.

"Got your bag, lad."

"Thank you for that."

He brings me to the Chinese part of town. I'm thinking this is worse than Aspinwall, but perhaps they're one and the same. Everywhere, a whir of flies and the biting smell of rotten vegetables. Garbage and mud and human waste all round. 'Tis filthy, this new world. Can't understand why a man would leave a clean home to come the likes of it.

We're passing a pub that Bellicose calls a saloon and I can see the men out front, howling as they are. Worse than when the pub in the village lets out, it is. A mess of Chinamen run off in all directions, scampering fast. The whole lot of white men slap at their trousers and bellow each other on. I'm thinking they must be playing a game of the drinking jacks, or the dice, but when we come closer, I see it's not that at all. A circle of white man with one lone Chinaman left inside. Bellicose snatches my arm, tells me I don't need to pry. But it's all I can do not to look, because I hear the pitch of the men's voices and know that all is not well. The Chinaman, he isn't part of the fun. He's the game.

Then a leader of sorts, all stubby arms and long, narrow body, he's got the Chinaman's plait in his fingers. One long dark braid, like the girls have at home. And Bellicose behind me.

"Let's move on, lad."

But I'm not for the going. First I've seen a man with a plait in my life, never set eyes on a Chinese. Bellicose tries to haul me off, but I won't go. Leap away from him, I do, into the group of men.

They chant, "Cut, cut, cut" while the leader holds up a fat blade. Don't know what they're doing, don't know why they're doing it, but the danger feeling is back inside me. And the knife, it goes *schleep* and the stubby armed leader, he slits off the man's plait.

They laugh and those men, don't they stamp on the braid while the Chinaman's eyes go red and he hangs his head. On the ground, the hair unwinds and clots in the mud. The men louder now, louder and laughing like they shouldn't be.

I have a piece of the plait in my hand before I right know what I'm doing, wounded hair piece that it is, and I flick it against my trousers to dislodge the mud. The Chinaman with the rotted tooth just stares at me, doesn't say a thing.

I'm stopped by a hand, sticky wet that smells like old socks over my mouth. Forced to the ground, ankles clicking, an elbow between my shoulder blades. A rusty voice spits in my ear.

"Saviour boy, hmm? Little hero, have we?"

I crane to see, get a knee in my back, a thick block across my head.

The taste of salt in my mouth, along with another thick, full taste I cannot say. The sun hot, a splash of yellow over me, overcome by a red wave.

I hear a dog bark and a bottle crash and that's when I move inside myself. Away from the Chinaman, the braid, the stubby arm holding my hands behind my back.

Just the flailing arms of Bellicose, hitting for me. Swearing for me. Swinging arms and animal grunts.

Everything is pink, then grey, then black.

~

On the bunk, coming back from some far away blackness. 'Tis layers of blackness if anyone cares to know. Sheets of it, long and deep and filled with worms.

Bellicose is by my side, stinking of the whiskey. He whispers something in my ear. But his voice is thick, comes in through the darkness. All a' search for me in here. And me too shocked by the light out there to hear him.

Inside, feel something is wrong inside. Something important missing. Can't think what it might be, but there is a clipped piece, something gone. Some intestine, say, a liver that a fork has seared through. Don't know, but the hole inside is wider than before, letting in more shadows. Deep like the Atlantic.

The mattress is bumpy, fights against me when I try to push up. Bellicose with his arm beneath mine, lifting. And I'm pretending it's your flesh. I open my mouth to catch a taste of you, Ma, but Bellicose is talking, telling me something.

I push up to a sit, then insist to him that I stand. He helps me up, across the cabin and out onto the deck.

I can see what he is saying.

Daybreak. His arm steadies me as the ship rounds into the harbour. Trees about. Land, too. Seems like the coastline opens its arms to welcome me. It's kind, it is, but I'm too sore to give it the greeting back.

All I know is that I'm here. I meet it, Victoria, British Columbia. I meet it with a bruised lip, a longing for you, and a piece inside of me clipped off like a cut plait on a Chinaman's head.

Three

~

Constance
Maharashtra, India
1896

IT'S TOO HOT AND FATHER, AS usual, is angry with me. His rage
an arrow forever marked on me.

But the mali, he's come again, smelling like liquorice. He
slips away from his work in the garden, beckons to me. Ayah is
in the house, too busy to notice. Ayah who should really have
a child to care for, not a fourteen year old like me. But Father
insists. Perhaps I can slip away, sneak before she notices, follow
the mali up the hill.

I walk behind him and only once does he turn his head to
see if I am still here. His brown feet look bleached white on the
bottom, hard on the dirt. Me in these ridiculous sandals that
Father bought, thinking them suitable. He doesn't care how
ugly they are, how clumsy they make me feel.

Above, the sun is fierce hot, my body heavy moist.

The mali brings me to the temple; it's old and cracked, stone
is chipped and missing. He motions to my feet and I remember,
I must slide off my sandals. If Father were here, he'd shake his

head no, remind me of the tape worms that want to slide in between my toes. He said they'll live in me, find my intestines and grow as long as snakes, as tall as trees. But what does he know? Father doesn't go to temples.

The temple is circular, with arched openings all around it, like yawning mouths. As we step down onto the stone lip, down onto the clay-baked floor where small licks of water lie, the mali talks of Shiva and Parvati dancing, dancing together in their God and Goddess bliss. But I only half listen because I am looking for the snakes, afraid they'll crawl from the cool of the rocks, slither across my feet. He laughs when I tell him, says the English only half understand, see only the part of snakes they fear. What about Kundalini, the coiled-up snake in us all?

"Shiva, destroyer of obstacles. Shiva danced on serpent's head to show he had overcome illusion, ignorance." I want to tell him it isn't illusion or ignorance I'm afraid of, it's what the snakes know.

A man with a monkey chained by the neck approaches. The monkey lurches at me, holds up a cupped, pink palm.

"Do not give him the anna," The mali tells me.

"I don't have any to give."

And the mali, he argues with the man, words spew back and forth. The monkey man wields his long stick in the air; the monkey eyes me, lunges near. I am scared of its claws and its teeth and the wild look in its eye but the mali's arms thrash, rough the air, push the monkey man away. The monkey glowers at me, teeth bared.

Now the mali spins me to see a crevice where the rock is old and green moss leaps out from the cracks. I cannot see anything in the crevice, but he bows his head, puts his hands together in front of his chest. *Namaste.* Then he sits me down, crosses his legs lotus style.

"Parvati greatest goddess of all."

He pulls from his dhoti a crumpled painted picture of Parvati and Shiva, their arms intertwined like mating serpents, their blue skin accented with fat bands of gold. Oh, what I would give to trade in my tangled auburn for Parvati's fluid, black hair!

He places his hands on mine, his fingers cold on my wrist despite the heat. "Parvati strong woman. Many good Goddess strong."

I nod my head yes, yes, though Father would burst if he heard this. Good Christians do not take to Goddesses, he has warned me.

"Shiva near when you smell sandalwood. You smell?"

I sniff: dust, rotten banana, sweat. I shake my head no.

But the liquorice smell on him lingers. Then he pushes himself to standing, his whole body now spinning, pink tongue flicking out of his mouth.

"Dance is how Shiva began the world," He says as he dances in a circle around me, but I am thinking of the creation of the world, and I know it was the word, the word, not dance.

"Shiva and Parvati never apart, like fire and heat, cannot be apart."

I am trying to picture how heat and fire might be separated, but he goes on.

"Power in speech, in Muladhara. Power in the rising serpent. In Kundalini."

I am lost, I don't know what he is saying anymore, but he pulls me to standing and begins to dance me about. I want to be Parvati. I want to be Shiva. I want to dance on fire and smell sandalwood, but there are voices coming up the hill. They are English, so he draws me to the back of the temple, where a small cave is cut into a stone outcrop, neem tree swaying. I'm scared of the cobras, pythons, boa constrictors, but his long cool fingers are over my mouth and he makes a *shh* sound into my ear.

Inside, in a cleft, he picks up a candle and lights it with matches that he slides out of a small box. It smells dank in here and beneath my feet, the hard, cold rock floor. He walks deeper in, the light of the candle showing a shadowed way. A labyrinth. Arched alcoves filled with statues along a spiral passageway. He bows, he prays.

I am searching for Shiva, for Parvati, but these statues are not dancing. These statues are not bronze. They are made of stone. I move closer, try to make out the face of one and it is a man's face, open eyed face, the head of a man but the body of a snake. A snake as thick as my arm.

"Shiva?"

"No, Patanjali. In his aspect Adisesa."

I want to get out, away from the snakes, but he stands in front of me, head tilted to one side.

"You not understand. Snakes not bad thing, not bad thing at all."

I cannot listen. I run to the entrance where others are coming in. Two Englishmen with an Indian guide. I turn to see if the mali is behind me, but he is gone.

⁓

Ayah won't say a thing to Father, of this I am sure. She found me sitting at the top of the hill, near the temple, my feet dirty, my cheeks spotted with the rash I sometimes get. And no mali in sight.

I sit in the house and try to concentrate on my studies, but I see only the cave and the statue with the body of a snake and the head of a man. Ayah tells me there is no such thing, but I know she is lying. She is lying so that I won't think of the statue.

I tell her I must get out. I want to walk in the peeling of buildings and burnt-coloured brick. I want to walk in the trees, be in the cool of the shade, away from the heat boredom of the house. Of course, she insists on coming, Father's orders.

In the park, where the hush of trees offers the grace of cool, three women sweep the path. Cotton saris of blue and yellow and mauve, bare feet. Ayah won't look at them, but I want to stop, watch their sweeping dance, long uneven reeds in their hands.

And Ayah, who always lets me get my way, squats off to the side, head angled, eyes scorching.

I hold out my hand, *May I please?* The one with the mauve sari looks to the others, giggles, hands me the broom.

I imitate their broad strokes, their languorous pulls. The surf of leaves, neem, betel juice nudged aside. That's when she touches my hair. Mauve sari woman, stroking my hair like I am a newborn kitten. A chattering in Marathi, then all of them, hands caressing my foreign red hair.

Ayah grunts. I know she disapproves, will tell me later that their saris are worth nothing, made of old cotton, not silk, the only ones they own. But I want to touch their hair, too. Long black braids that sway behind them.

My hands form the request, and the woman in the mauve sari bends forward, motions to me that it is alright, come. Her hair is dense, the fullness of a horse's tail, freshly brushed. The second woman undoes her braid, lets the end unravel from its tie. A soft embrace, a tease of coconut smell, midnight hair tickled by my touch.

But Ayah is up and coming fast to me, the bubble of her stomach leading the way. Her eyes dark now, her mouth a punch. I allow her to take me away. Behind us, the swish of brooms. Dark hair, clean road.

~

On the way home I see the bangles. So many hues that Father won't permit me to wear: purple, gold, greens and reds. A woman in a pink and white sari sits cross-legged on the kerb, her dark eyes pull me to her. Ayah is still pretend-angry with me, and knowing how Father would click his tongue against his teeth, she does it now, but it sounds forced coming from her. I know she thinks this too, because her eyes look away from me, try to escape.

The woman offers me a blood red bangle with little white stones. I extend my wrist, and her hand is on me, warm sweat hand, lapping hand, sliding the bangle on. Her boy, with deer-brown eyes, yoghurt skin, tilts his head from side to side, yes, yes; he wants me to buy it so he can eat. Ayah smelling flowers, yellow flowers with brown eyes. Not daisies, not sunflowers, but what? Her long nose draws up the scent, while I pass the anna to the boy whose face opens when I put it in his clammy palm.

This is the bangle I cannot wear lest Father rip it from me, spin its vanity into the garden. That's why I hide it in my cotton underpants, near the small tufts of my private hair. A shiny, new bangle.

~

When we return, Father and his friend are sitting in the garden, droplets of wet down the sides of their drinks, along their top lips. End of moustaches streamline, pointy.

"Hello Constance. You remember Mr. le Baron? Now, do be a dear and leave us be, will you?"

"Yes, Father."

He waves me away with his hand.

"I am reading about India." I say this to Mr. le Baron with his too-tall boots, thinking that Father won't interrupt me if the comment is not to him. But he and Father sip their beer, continue to talk.

"Do you know the history?" I ask Mr. le Baron.

He looks over at Father, surprise tinted on his face. "What has a girl to do with such knowledge?" he asks.

"It isn't knowledge at all, but half-digested bits, poorly memorized." Father takes a gulp of his drink.

"I've been studying the uprisings."

"Bands of marauding thieves. Now off with you, Constance."

"Which the government took quite seriously, Father, as you know."

Father pauses, tries to send me one of his own warring looks by smiling, but I pretend not to notice.

"We shall always be here, Constance. The place would be a bloody mess without us. These people don't know how to work, could never organize themselves. Great cry and little wool, I always say."

"Much ado about nothing," Mr. le Baron adds.

"Suppose it is us."

"An incomplete thought, Constance."

"Maybe we shouldn't be here."

This is when they laugh. Bubbles in their beer.

"My dear, we have squashed many great injustices."

"Yes, Father. Though I wonder if we could do that without making them our servants, our slaves."

Too-Tall boots le Baron allows his eyebrows to speak for him. The tips of Father's ears have gone white.

"A girl is as a girl was, nothing else. Now, be off with you."
He says this with dismissal because his friend is here, but I
know if we were alone, he would pull out the cane, pour out
his rage.

His rage at the death of my mother. His rage that I
survived.

This is when I remember the bangle, my shade cooling its
crimson skin beneath knickers. Father is up and calling for
Ayah, calling for the Khidmatgar to serve two whiskey sodas.
Father, who only ever has one drink before dinner, is demanding
more. My bangle spins, laughing.

$\sim$

It's after dinner and the wretched perfumed smell of the hookah
takes up the whole sitting room. I've been banished, as always,
but through this small space in the curtains, I watch as Father
takes up the serpentine tube and places the mouthpiece gently
between his lips. How strange it is to see Father like this, how
he holds onto the tube like a lover under his arms, turns to the
ladies and breathes out alternative compliments and smoke.

The ladies, they blush with him, laugh at all his pathetic
quips, inhale his fumes. Then one of them leans over and
touches his arm, her cheeks red. Father leans close to her and
whispers something that makes her smile in a bashful way, her
evening coffee cup jostling in her hand. I cannot imagine what
he tells her, it is all I can do to stop myself from running into
the room to blurt out that when she is not around, Father calls
her "Little Spin". Her sister, who has the distinction of being
called "Big Spin" is not in sight tonight. As Father uttered
before dinner, *she is bestowing her tedious spinsterhood elsewhere
this evening.*

The swing of the punkah fan begins to quicken and it seems to me that the servant who is pulling it must be watching Father as well. He draws on the rope from outside the room, Father makes sure of this, rather than letting him squat inside, in the corner, like they do in some houses. But his eyes are with mine, this I know, by the sudden jerk on the fan that flaps Little Spin's dress. She leans down and pulls at the bottom lace while Father's eyes scan their way down to the floor. When she catches him, she gives off a little giggle and Father affects shame. Another woman, a green-eyed woman, shifts in her chair.

It seems to me that the whole lot of them are bored beyond reason, as I am, and have only these small eye skirmishes with which to amuse themselves. These days are dreary, everyone agrees. Every evening, sitting in a circle, complaining of the heat. The monotony interrupted by the arrival of dinner, then coffee, then bed. Bed, where I want to be.

Safe in the cool sheets, I pluck the bangle from beneath my dress. I hold it to my nose, try to catch my own scent, but inhale instead the smoke of the hookah, the distant smell of the cardamom and ginger from the market.

"Plenty good night, Miss." Ayah is here with the candle, tucking in the mosquito net.

"Ayah?"

"Yes miss?"

"Ayah, do you think Father will remarry?"

She flickers her eyes in time with the candle.

"Maybe yes, maybe no."

I know what she is thinking, that a woman would be a fool to love Father. As she blows out the candle, I wonder what kind of fool Mother was. What kind of fool inhaled Father's fumes and let him raise her skirts from the floor?

~

At dawn the rain begins. The sky opens, dumps, curses at us, refuses to slink away.

The Indian women run out to wash their saris in the rain. Long rectangles of splashed colours, held up by dancing arms. Billowing cotton.

All day, I watch and want to get wet. I want to stand in the rain and let it collect in small pools inside me. Thirsty pockets within me that want to slurp, lick it up. Father with his eye on me all afternoon, making me read English history. Then, evening comes and the clinking glasses begins. I slip out between light drinks in heavy tumblers.

The rain, I want to be in the rain.

Bare feet on sand, mud, small red rocks. I run, under the splaying sky, water slicing over me, warm wet, hairs up on my skin.

The green-eyed woman, Father's friend, darts behind me. Her mouth is open, catching rain on her tongue. I run across the garden as rain tosses its way down my dress, soft mud squishes between my toes. The green eyed woman calls out to join me. Her white face is slapped by the rain, her thick eyebrows sleek. She swims to me through the air, water droplets on her eyelashes, fluttering.

"Quick! Let's get away." She takes my hand, skips across pebbles, leads me to the road. The smell of gin from her and the scent of chalk mud rises.

"Your Father's going to kill me!"

She embraces me in her arms, lifts me up. We are facing the house, where Father and the rest of them are standing at the door, still holding drinks, shouting at us. I laugh, she waves her arms to them, the rain our shield.

The men put down drinks, cover their heads with handkerchiefs, come and get us.

⁓

She comes to see me when I'm in bed with a cold. Caused by the rain, Father says, but any fool could tell you that isn't true. It's the boredom, and the green eyed gin lady knows it. When she comes to visit me, she brings with her a jig-saw puzzle of an elephant, its trunk around the branch of a tree.

"Constance, my rain loving girl! How are you today?"

"Bored, I'm afraid."

"Ah, aren't we all. It's our lot here."

She takes the puzzle lid off, scrambles the pieces over the table by my bed.

"How long have you been here?" I ask.

"I was born here. My parents were born here. As were my grandparents."

"Do you like it?"

"I don't know much else."

"But you've been to England? On leave?"

"Yes. But I'm a foreigner there, too. And you?"

"Father likes to go back every leave."

"That doesn't tell me if you like it."

"Yes, and no. I enjoy it here. It's religious."

"I suppose it is, though many wouldn't think so."

"You think so."

"Obviously so do you!"

I feel warmth in my belly when she says this.

"You know, no one has told me your name."

"Mrs. Newton. Nancy Newton."

"When I'm well, can we go into the rain again?"

When she grins her faux I-should-be-ashamed-of-myself-grin, I want to tell her about the dreams and shapes and colours I see when no one else is around. But I'm not sure she will understand. I want to say something about the thin ringing at night and the mali with the snake god. But Father comes in and ruins it all, fetches Mrs. Newton to play cards.

And Father, Father who hasn't brought me anything for my cold except icy stares and a few *tsk tsks*, he takes my only friend and shuts the door.

~

Ayah rushes into the house, her round brown legs leading her to the angry cries of Father. Tea on the government maps, I hear him say, splashes all over his work.

I'm glad it's her, not me. She has a way of tilting her head from side to side, banishing his voice from her brain. Pouring it out her ears, an angry stream running. But with me, it stays, the bellows caught inside.

That's when he comes back, the mali. His swish of white through the trees, around the pond that Father insists we keep, although it is more of a cesspool in this heat. Mali with dust spray around him, pointy chin. His expanse of smile, a long finger that beckons me. Of course I must go. I must because I want to watch the white cotton as it flutters over his back, even though there is no breeze.

I am behind English roses, dying of thirst so far from home. He pats the ground, folds a square of cloth and invites to me sit down. He sits cross-legged in his dhoti, me on the white cotton scarf with a sea-blue fringe.

"I tell you story?" His voice lifts up and I nod my head, yes, yes, hoping that my nodding can flatten the ringing of his voice behind the bush.

He opens the Bhagavad Gita, not the one I see him reading when he has time to take a break beneath the tree, but a different one. He turns to a page where a leaf, as long and flat as the end of an old quill, serves as a bookmark.

"Jungle tree," he says, waving the bookmark, "grows nuts." Then he begins to read:

I see in thee all the gods, Oh my God; and the infinity of the beings of thy creation. I see god Brahma on his throne of lotus, and all the seers and serpents of light.

His grey beard twitches a little and he looks very satisfied.

"Serpents of Light?"

"This is directly for miss."

"What does it mean?"

"You must think. Meaning must find miss."

"But I don't know. I want you to tell me."

"No, no. In time. You will find."

He purses his lips, hands me the book.

"This isn't the one you usually read."

"No, miss. This English. I brought for miss."

"You're not going to tell me what the passage means, are you?"

"Read."

"What shall I read?"

"You read what gods want you to read. You take and close eyes. Then think, what I need hear today? Then open, open where Vishnu bids you open."

I hold the book in my hands, squeeze my eyes. I fan the pages first to one side, then the other. When do I stop? I wait to hear it, hear the word *stop* in my mind, but nothing comes. I keep ruffling the pages from side to side, wait for a sign. But I am confused. Inside, I have a voice that says, *keep going* and one that says *here*. I open my eyes.

"I can't do it."

"What to do? Just listen."

"But there are too many voices."

"Just one."

"No, there are many, I tell you. There isn't just one. There are hundreds."

He looks off for a minute, thinking hard.

"Try again."

Again, I close my eyes, conjure up the image of Vishnu, knowing as I do that Father would slap me silly for even thinking of him. I fan the pages again, and this time, some of them feel warm, some cold. I linger on the warm ones. Then, a few increase in heat. I play with them, flick them to and fro. Finally, one page seems hotter than the rest.

"Now what do I do?"

"Find deepest voice."

I listen hard. There is no voice inside, just a phantom finger, pointing. On the left side, half way down. I open my eyes.

"Read it!" He is more excited than I.

"'And do thy duty, even if it be humble, rather than another's, even if it be great. To die in one's duty is life: to live in another's is death'."

The mali places both hands on the ground, then touches his forehead between them. He pauses there a moment, and when he gets up, there is a smudge of dirt on his forehead, like a Brahman's mark. I want to laugh. Here, a gardener, with the symbol of the highest caste!

"Very, very special, miss."

"Why?"

"You think."

"Tell me."

"No one can tell you such a thing. You think until you know."

But Ayah's voice rises frantic on the path, and in one wave of movement, the mali has swept me up from the ground, whisked up the scarf and tucked the book into his dhoti.

"God in what scares you, also."

His touch is light, so light it feels tender on my neck. But my hands shake, and in my stomach, a rolling, over and over, like a log in water.

"Constance! Where are you Constance?" Ayah's voice.

This time, I will say nothing of the mali. I will say nothing of snakes.

～

I am in a tent in a hill station. Outside, the English army are preparing to attack. I am frightened and I want to escape. I don't understand why the English are coming after their own kind, why they would choose me. I know it is time to leave when I see that someone has fired a Gatling gun and it has started a fire in the canvas of the tent.

I run to the back of the tent and try to plan my escape. I know that if I go out the front, they will see me and attack. I know if I try to make my way by crawling out the window, they will chase me. What then?

That is when I remember that I can fly. I open my arms and I fly up. I am flying, in the air, across the hills and down towards the ocean. I feel so free, so free.

～

Pigs are in mud up to their chins, a bat hangs from the branch of the tree. There is red earth all around us, and the cows, so aloof, ignore us on the road.

Mrs. Newton and I walk beneath her parasol, the sun out between rains. Back to the heat and the damp sweat that clings to my chest.

"Good day, Madam." An Indian man with a thin moustache, arms rigid by his side.

Mrs. Newton nods her head.

"I've been looking for you Madam." She stops and I with her.

"I'm sorry, I don't think we've met."

"A. Kamalakae Roe, ma'am."

"Roe. That is not a local name, is it?"

"No Madam, like Newton, not from around here."

"Ah."

"I'm here to tell you the business, Madam, the business you are to know."

"Go on then."

"Not in front of the girl."

This makes Mrs. Newton clasp her hands. She looks at me and then to the man, contemplating.

"I don't think so." And she takes my hand, draws me forward.

"I have been sent, Madam, by Major Newton."

She stops, turns. "My husband?"

"Yes, Madam."

"You have a message from my husband?"

"Yes, Madam."

"Well, go on then."

"Not in front of the girl."

This time she doesn't look at me, she walks to him, eyes on the road. He says something to her, low voice mumbling. He waits for an answer but she gives none, just turns and walks back to me.

"Was it horrible?" I ask.

"Difficult."

"Can you tell me?"

"No, no I can't."

We walk past women with baskets on their heads, past worm infested dogs with bloated bellies, past a field left fallow. I can't get Father out of my head, I can't stop seeing him in front of me.

That's when I feel it. Her touching my Father's skin. The two of them kissing, lips on each other, heat on heat.

I want to tell her, I need to tell her, but when I look at Mrs. Newton, I'm just not sure.

And the wave inside, I push it down, I push it back inside me, not wanting to lose my only friend.

⁓

Father and I alone now, him very angry. His unspoken rage hanging like draped cloth all over our rooms.

He has borrowed a microscope and pushes me down into the parlour chair. Then, the strange black object is under my nose. Father too close to my ear, telling me loudly that if I insist on a course of education, he is going to bloody well make sure it is something of import. No more Indian history.

He has placed a small fly on the slide of the microscope. It lies there, squirming, tasting its first bite of death. How excited I am to see the fly so big, but I do not like that it is still alive, is dying before me.

"What are your observations?" Father asks.

"It is so big!"

"What do you notice about the fly?"

"It's suffering."

A quick box on the ear.

"Constance, science is science. Pity is not appropriate."

"But it is suffering. Can't we help?"

Another box, same ear.

"Look again. Scientifically. Tell me what you see."

I see little legs that beat and a little body that twitches and I wonder if flies are ever reincarnated into people. But I can't say that. I can no more say that than I can tell Father that Shiva and Parvati dance together in eternal bliss.

"I still see the fly."

"How very erudite of you my dear."

"That's all I see."

My eyes still up against the lens when there is a buzz and then something new appears. It is fuzzy for a moment, until Father adjusts the side of the microscope.

"There, now. What do you see? And please, can we be civilized for a moment?"

I see a yellow flower with a big brown eye, peering back at me. The eye like the ones in the market that gleam out of the flowers piled in a perfect cone shape beside the woman who sits cross-legged all day.

"It's a beautiful flower, Father."

"What family?"

"I'm not sure."

"Don't say you're not sure. Tell me."

I am looking at the flower now, pleading with it, *tell me who you are.* And the yellow and the brown blur together and I can see the field where it is from. Wide field, dung field, field not too far away where women walk and talk together while picking flowers. And the flowers don't mind, they have agreed to be picked. They are happy and open and call the women to them.

"What do you see?"

"It's a beautiful flower, Father. From such a large field. The field has so many of them, and there are women, who gather them up."

My ear in his hand, squeezed hard. Father's breath in my face, angry breath, livid breath. He drags my head away from the top of the microscope, ear first.

"Look! I took the flower away. I took the flower away and yet you still think you see it! You think you see the field it is from!"

He shows me the table and the flower that he has dashed out from under the microscope. I look at the slide and see it is empty.

"Do you think me a fool? Explain this to me!"

"I can't Father."

"Explain your answer now!"

"I saw the flower. Then I saw the field."

"The field! Did I put a field under the microscope? Indeed I did not. I put nothing under the microscope. I took the flower away and put nothing! Do you hear me?"

"Yes, Father."

"I imagine only the cane will change your mind?"

"No, Father."

He reaches for the cane, grasps it roughly and bears it over me. He brings it down in a sharp crack against my leg. A sting of skin, red welts rising, me still resolute.

"You can hit me as many times as you like, Father. I saw the field."

His eye is red, burst blood vessel red. But he puts down the cane, walks away. Fingers dance, bangle spins. The touch of long, dark hair.

Four

Ank and Constance
London, England
1899

AT NIGHT FATHER FINALLY COMES. THE only problem is he doesn't have a body. He is all face, blurry, the contours of him smudged at the sides.

Constance has wheeled herself down the hallway between wards with a beeswax candle propped between her thighs. She is pleased to feel the small amount of flexing; sensation in her legs slowly returning. Everyone else is asleep, and the darkness is like chocolate to her; tempting, inviting, yet it has a sting if she fills herself up with too much of it.

He waits for her on a wooden chair in the corner of the hall under a half opened window.

What she notices first is his smell. Like rotting mushrooms left in the pantry too long, white souring to a slimy brown. There is a fecund feel to him as well; damp earth clings to his teeth.

At first, she cannot look into his eyes. She wishes he had a recognizable body, familiar shoes, perhaps, a favourite pair of trousers. Suddenly she longs to see his brown cardigan, one he wore after tea, the last button left undone to allow digestion of his meal. Evenings of dim light when Constance imagined a family around her. A mother, careful and doting, helping Constance wash her Father's handkerchiefs and place them near the fire to dry. A sister, someone who would scream when her hair was pulled or when Constance jumped out of the dark hall to scare her. Perhaps even a brother, older and aloof, who brought dashing friends to fuel a girl's fantasies.

But Constance had none of this; her imagination was the only diversion through those evenings when Father was not in India, but lurking about London, vying for some powerful man's favour.

Father shakes his head at her, as if he can read her thoughts. His eyes are darker now, disapproval like the inevitable yellowing of an old book. Her jaws tighten, her ears grow warm.

"Where are you?" Constance asks.

She can barely contain herself. She wants to shout. *Where have you gone?* But Father, riled by the impertinence of her questioning, will not answer. He merely disappears.

❧

Constance in bed, scrutinizing the wall. Inside the ward, it is deep black — a crawling darkness. The kind that feels like dying too soon.

The other patients are lost to sleep. They are dead to Constance, bodies without souls inside. Their spirits leave as soon as they close their eyes, abandoning the inhospitable territory of human flesh for somewhere else. But where? She would go too, if she knew, but she can't escape. Her cage is here, insomnia her curse.

Again, the rigidity of her body, the invisible ropes tying her down, arms by her side. Tight mouth, flat breath. Squashed beneath her own mind.

Then the word comes. Folded into a corner of her brain, for one, two beats before it flicks out against the wall like a lamp glow, above the row of beds across from her. Painted on by the voice inside her head. She knows what she must do.

This is her test. Each time this happens, it is a different word. A new word. Tonight, it is simple, familiar. Serpent.

It wants to live, it wants to undulate across the wall, it wants Constance to create it, here, now. She must birth it, allow it to slide from the lightless corner of her mind and embalm the ward. It must fit here, be inscribed on the walls, scratched onto the floor, invited home — only with the aid of her mind.

Constance remembers. Even prior to the accident, in the bedroom with the rose-covered wall paper that mutated into sliced hearts once Father was asleep. She knew better than to wake him and speak of her terror. She knew the words were for her alone.

The rules haven't changed. One letter per wall, until the word vibrates around her. Big letters, perfectly formed letters, taking up as much space as possible.

She begins with the wall in front of her and forms a huge mental 'S' in brilliant white. She tries to make the 'S' so big that no darkness remains on the wall. But there is too much space on either side of it, so Constance turns the letter over in her mind, writing it sideways.

The wall to her right gets the 'e', broadly written so as to fill up as much room as possible. Behind her, she carves the 'r', turning it into a capital letter to eat up more of the darkness. Then her mind dips over to the other half of the ward, to the bottom of the boot-shaped room. She continues by writing the 'p', capitalizing it also. Then on the far wall, the 'e'. She strains to fit the letters on the wall. She needs to extract the blackness. But she has only two letters left and there is one wall, the ceiling and floor. The word too short to fill the space. And it must.

The chill, the clammy sensation again. Why this awkward formation of the ward, this L-shape? Why not a box with only four walls? She must use the final space, fill it. Make the word plural, place an exclamation mark behind it, anything. Will that count?

She decides to change the spelling of the word, make it her own. She counts the walls — six. Adding the floor and ceiling, she has eight spaces. What about "Serpents." Will that fill the space?

The slithering cold fear inside. Waiting, waiting for an answer. Punishment so close, it's almost dripping down. Then the reply, from inside her: yes. She is ready to begin again, but the game vanishes, slinks away.

Replaced by another test. Letters light up the wall. Jumbled, a mismatch of vowels and consonants. She hears the voice — it clangs like a metal rod on weak pipe.

"One minute," it says.

She must make letters into words now; one, maybe two. Shifting, skipping the letters to and fro, desperate to find the sense. Breath catching, body still. A bell goes off, her time is up.

That's when the mask appears on the wall. White, with a joker's gaunt expression. A king's jester with red lips dug into an open mouth. The mask looks so happy, it is vulgar. They have met before, Constance and this mask. In other rooms.

It puts the command in her head, whispers to her, "Laugh, Constance, laugh." She cannot refuse. At first a chuckle, escalating into a belly laugh, a hysterical howl she cannot control. The laugh is much deeper than her own voice, a rich laugh that belts out of her mouth like the passing of vomit.

Then a misery mask comes pressing her to cry. It badgers her, "Cry, Constance, cry." She cannot refuse. A sniffle, some tears, then wailing.

The masks roll into each other, their mouths open and nagging, a partnership of opposites like the black and white on piano keys. They fold themselves into each other and drop down into Constance's arms.

The voice in her head returns, "Take the weight."

She tries to get up from the bed, but her legs, numb and bruised from the accident, cannot support her. She calls out to anyone who might hear, her voice a high, desperate wail. She is flailing under the burden of the weight, too heavy for her to bear. Constance needs to give this weight away. To anyone. At any price.

"What's wrong, miss?" Nurse Shoemaker, her slick brown hair plastered to her head. Her voice from so far away it sounds forced, words shouted across a large valley in painfully slow syllables.

Constance is barely audible. Sweat weaves a shiny web down her face. "The weight," she whispers.

Ank appears on the other side of the bed. He has arrived, as if by flight, grabbing the words of Constance and holding fast. He looks at Shoemaker, sees disbelief blur her face.

"Weight?" Shoemaker, never one to hide incomprehension, now wears it like a uniform.

Constance's arms are open, bent at acute carrying angles, holding onto a precious cargo that neither the Nurse nor Ank can see.

Ank leans further across the bed. "You have a weight then, Constance?" He asks.

"Yes. It's too heavy. Take it."

His voice takes on a hum. "Try and give it to me."

Constance lifts her arms a little higher. Ah, to deposit the weight, to let it go. He mimes accepting it, lies, "I have it."

"No, no you don't. I still have it. Please, please take it from me."

"Miss Stubbington, you are hallucinating."

"No!" Ank whispers at Shoemaker, then softens his voice as he turns to Constance. "Try again, I'll do my best to take it."

Her arms want, need, to unload. Ank scoops air from her arms into his own.

"I think I have it now. There, you see?"

Constance falls back, the heavy weight cradled in her arms.

"No, I still have it. I still have it."

Shoemaker sniffs at Ank, a malicious smile forming at the edges of her lips.

"Constance, one last time."

"No," she replies. "It's mine."

Ank leans over and kisses her on the cheek. She reaches up to cup his hands, holds him in place for one full minute. Then she falls into a deep, necessary sleep.

⁓

There is the mali, digging in the dirt. His fingers sift through the garden, pulling here, plucking there. Dirt moving through his hands like ghee.

I know he feels me behind him, but he goes on with his work. He waits for me, waits for me to call to him, request a story.

His hands on the rose bush, plucking off dead leaves. Fingers skim around the thorns, deft dancing.

I say nothing to him. Instead, I watch. He does not break skin, draws no blood, despite the barbs that leap at him.

The once empty bed to the left of Constance is now the lair of a hawkish woman with a twisted mouth and piercing eye. She stalks the movement of Constance's wheelchair as if she wills it to spin out of control and dislodge its occupant.

And she smells. Constance cannot place the scent; it is a blur between the faint odour of cooked cabbage and unwashed armpits.

The woman waits until Nurse Robbins has padded away. Constance pretends not to look at the old woman, noting, out of the corner of her eye, her grossly rounded spine and how the protrusion of her head, sticking out almost comically in the opposite direction, looks like a malevolent afterthought.

Constance reaches for the copy of *Punch* that Ank gave her. The woman's eyes imprison her.

"Your skin is creamy creamy, goat's milk, butter milk, thick clotted cream." The woman delivers these words like she is reading a nonsensical nursery rhyme. Constance swallows. *What on earth?* But the woman goes on.

"Not me, love, I was born with craters on my cheeks. A rat's back. A monkey's mind. Rap-trapping my way through life like the grandest insult to civility a young miss could be. You know what it was like? All the girls coming out, lacy fingers they had, plummy morsels they were, and I ugliness personified. But you, you're creamy dreamy. You don't think I'm bitter, do you? Couldn't be further from the truth."

Constance notes the tautness of the woman's eyes, how they seem to flinch along with her story, holding tight to the words like a train ride over a mountain.

"Pardon, ma'am — "

"Ah, you can leave the formalities well enough alone, dream child. Call me Jill. Jill of the hill, Jack in absentia, damn that Jack! Isn't Jill a sweet name for a ghastly old woman?"

She laughs, and instead of the macabre howl Constance expects, it is a surprising light laugh.

"I'm Constance."

"Did they tell you that your dimples are like craters? What happened to your eyes? Did the eagles pluck them out and the doctors give you new ones?"

The woman waits for Constance to smile, and when she doesn't, she looks disappointed.

"Don't mind me, I'm not nearly as daft as I am. Daft as a cat, as a rat, give me a pat on the back! Passing day, raising hay, that's all."

Constance merely stares. The woman looks curiously hurt, as if misunderstanding is a poison on which she has over-imbibed. Despite a slight sense of disgust, Constance feels drawn to the woman. Her idiocy, in contrast to the sterility of the hospital, feels almost sane.

"What are you in for?" Constance asks.

"The back. It hurts so."

"Can they help?"

"Ah, they do a bit of this, a bit of that. Gets me by."

"Did you arrive today?"

"Two weeks ago. A cursed night in the operating theatre, I can tell you. Bloody cold in there, isn't it? And all those eyes looking on, hooking on. Then they kept me downstairs one. With children, mind. What they put an old bear, an old hare, with children for?"

"Did they work on your back?"

"Did a bit of scraping."

Constance feels a knife edge run up her spine and shivers.

"Did you have Mr. Maguire in the theatre with you?"

"Who? The Paddy. God no, I wouldn't let the likes of him near me."

Constance feels like she has been punched in the mouth. She whips the sheet up and turns her back on the old woman. Jill, mimicking her movements, does the same.

"You think you have the right to say such a thing."

"Sow, cow, bovine. It's all the same to me. Not letting any bloody Mick touch my hump. This ugliness is my pride and joy, you understand? Can't be giving it up for anyone, just."

There is a long pause.

"I had my female parts all scraped out, all raped out. Age sixteen. They took them, every last shred. Thought I was an idiot, they did. Didn't want to risk it, whisk it, me having children. You still got yours?"

Constance touches her pelvis. She will not answer.

"Watch them now. They'll be coming to get you like hungry crows."

~

Crows. Thousands of crows. Descending from the sky; beaks open, gleaming eyes searing their prey. Cacophony all around, squawks and caws deafening. Then, the target.

An open chest, sliced in a vertical line down the centre of a body. Folds of skin pulled back, meaty insides plucked to the surface. Top of the head smashed, maimed brains.

Part of the face still intact. One eye, a nose too. A half-delirious, half-terrorized smile.

Ank.

~

79

Constance is seated in her chair, wheeled up to a window in the corridor between Mary and Dorcas wards. She stares at the stiff rows of dark brick lining the other arm of the building, muted light streaking across filmy windows.

"Constance."

Ank is behind her. When she twists to him, relief floods her body. His face is whole, his chest intact.

"I'm taking you out."

"But it's near evening."

She wonders why she says this, shocked at her own inculcation of hospital rules. In truth, she wants nothing more than to leave this place, escape. It has been a lifetime and more since she has been outside at night.

The evening slips around her as Ank pushes her through the front gates of the hospital and onto Newcomen Street. Constance feels delirious. Even the wood beneath her buttocks seems to soften.

Ahead on the road, a coal cart sits unsupervised by the dusty owner who squats near the ground, examining the grooves of the wooden wheels. Two children, a young brazen-faced boy and a little girl with long clumps of dark hair hold hands, dash for the cart, stop dead at the foot of it. The boy jumps up and, with a deft swing of his arm, knocks a few lumps of coal off the pile. The coal tumbles, makes a perfect arc from the top of the mound down into the deep folds of the girl's pinafore. They shriek their victory and run away.

Ank laughs too at the oblivious face of the coal man, who looks up in time to witness nothing but the children dashing off.

"That girl would be you if you could."

Constance smiles.

They make their way west, towards Borough High Street. The wheelchair dips into the long dirt gullies which have been dug out of the street. Constance is thrust forward as the wheel of her chair rams into a hole.

"Mind it, love."

"What are these holes about?"

"New tram lines. There's rakes of 'em. Tram will be right through here soon."

"It'll be the death of us." Constance says.

"Not so much as that prison there."

Constance looks over her shoulder.

"Prison?"

"Aye, you've been a neighbour all this time and you haven't met the lads then?"

Her shoulders stiffen.

"Marshalsea Prison, love. Just round from the hospital. They like to keep inmates round the same part of the borough."

Constance is sucking on her lips when she notices the smirk on Ank's face.

"Kidding you. Been closed for years."

They make their way across the rutted High Street, and Ank pauses under a lamp. He lights a cigarette and crouches down on the kerb in front of Constance. He looks at her in earnest, and she knows he is about to say something important, but their attention is diverted by a group of three women behind them, falling into each other with heavy heads and hearty laughs. One has bright red stockings that shine out loudly in the large gap between her boots and the bottom of her skirts. Another, with blue stockings and a thick brush of red across each cheek, hikes up her skirts in a bawdy display. The third, with air-fed breasts rising up from a white blouse, sees Constance and Ank and swaggers towards them.

Ank looks away quickly, recognizing the solicitation that is to come. The woman rubs her hand across her stomach in a manner that speaks of a long-time habit. She talks directly to Ank's groin.

"I'll do whatever you like."

She is standing over them with the heavy smell of alcohol raining down from her mouth. She motions to Ank, but he is distracted by the rush of a small child behind her. No more than seven, a girl who already has dark shadows beneath her eyes, runs from the open front door of a tenement up to the woman. The child winds her arms around her mother's tightly drawn waist.

"Mum."

"Get now. I'm on the job."

The other two women haul the girl away. Constance expects the girl to cry, but instead she laughs, a throaty, deep laugh that sounds like it might come from a street woman rather than a child. Constance has wide eyes, but is giving away nothing more by the careful way she has arranged her face.

The whore, realizing there is no money to be made, takes her leave. Constance can now afford to blush. She has never encountered a woman like that in London. In the city, she knew only the sitting room women like her Father's friends. All needlepoint and piano lessons and midday boredom with tea. Women brought up as sideboard ornaments, charming and frivolous.

This woman thrills her, reminds her of a scene she witnessed in India under a banyan tree. Where a woman in a brilliant blue sari sat eating an overripe mango that dripped down onto three sausage shaped layers of fat at her exposed midriff.

Ank looks to Constance and begins to say something about the prostitute, then chooses to smear away his thoughts by rushing back into their conversation.

"Few more weeks. They'll let you go."

This is a sting for Constance. She knows that the hospital staff have been preparing her for an eventual departure. For her to go home. But that is the problem. Constance has no home. Father has still not come.

"And where will I go?"

Ank sucks hard on the cigarette. "I've been thinking of that."

A hand appears between them. It is a deeply lined palm, dark with dirt and covered with small swells of peeling skin. They both look up into the face of a woman whose eyes glow white. She lacks the haughty, hand-drawn intrigue of the working women who have now made their way down to the next lane of the High Street. She reminds Constance of a mouldy blanket.

"Silver to cross my palm?" she asks.

"For the lady." Ank says.

Ank reaches into his pocket, places a halfpenny in her hand, and then folds her fingers around it. She carefully takes the coin and slides it into the top of her boots. Then she nudges Ank out of the way, grasps Constance's palm and splays her fingers apart unceremoniously.

She looks hard at the intersecting lines.

"Ah, a seer. A woman in me own image."

Ank laughs. "Constance, a gypsy?"

"No love," her voice is serious, "a truth sayer."

Bent over like this, the woman's skirt dips down onto the street and drags into a pile of dog faeces. Constance can see the black fringe of her dress, ripped in small waves all along the bottom, now tinted with a splattering of excrement.

"See this cross here, where the short line comes and crosses over the other two long lines? You look in the centre there, there's a triangle shape. Means you got the sight, don't it? You're as lucky as midnight, miss. But you pay no mind to the others, the ones who will envy you. For on my soul, there will be plenty of others. As there have been for many a year. Oh, you might have heard of them. They give parties in the city, fancy sittings with well-to-do folk believing every word they say, but that'll not be your way. You're a listener, I dare say. Many will come through you."

Constance's face reddens. Her secret, spoken aloud.

"I'm talking about your gift, see. Your abilities, if you please. You have them, you know? Or don't you?"

"Gift, you say? It's a curse, is what it is."

The woman moves too close to Constance now. Constance reels her head away from her rotten, blackened teeth. Ank interferes.

"Ta, then." He waves her away with his hand.

The woman murmurs something, then totters into the street. They watch the heel of her boot get trapped in the narrow tram lines. She curses to herself, rips her boot up and trundles away.

"Tell me what you were thinking." Constance lifts a hand to touch Ank's sleeve.

"She was telling you that you're touched."

"Ank — that gift. It's confusing. I — "

"Careful now. Don't let the mystery leave you in a huff of breath."

Constance nods, but does not understand.

"A wise woman once told me not to tell a soul about the voices we hear in our head. Just seek others who understand." Ank smiles at Constance as he says this, and in her head is the voice of the mali, swimming across continents, across years. *"Miss afraid of what she does not understand."*

Ank leans over and brushes his lips across her forehead, then straightens up, and pushes Constance swiftly away, making haste back to the hospital grounds.

"I was thinking I might help you find a flat. It might only be a tenement, though." Ank continues when they have reached the gate.

"Where?"

"Why, I've been looking. Some spots right near here."

～

It's brilliant to be out of London. Me and Father and Too-Tall boots le Baron.

And the horses, ah, the horses. What steady, massive beasts. Of course I get the smallest one, though to me, it's gargantuan. Ceylon, its name is. Could this be its real name? Father must have named it, only he would name a horse Ceylon.

Look at this beauty. A perfectly curved outline of animal. And there's father, telling me that it needs to be prodded into place, struck with the reins if necessary. How ludicrous. This is a warrior horse, a Trojan horse, a horse that could burst through walls, even the one solidly built around the expanding girth of father.

Father helps me get on. Grasps me around the waist, too firmly for my frame. His fingers dig roughly into my ribs. I hate it when he touches me, even though I can't remember the last time. There's an awful pause, a lick of a second when the air collides with itself. How many years ago was the last time? Not a pat, a kiss, a hug for so long I can't even fathom it. And now he is touching me.

The horse jerks forward. Father hits the agitated beast with a blunted cry and a smack on its thick neck. The horse knows. The horse has sensed our unease. The flash of fear that darted between us moved down into him, and he is trying to shiver it off with a wave-like motion of his taut skin. But he can't get rid of it all.

Poor thing. I wish I could tell you that you'll get used to Father. But it's not true. You can't. He won't let you.

He hands me the reins, careful now to move his fingers away from the possibility of contact. I tuck the loop into my palm like he asks, as if hiding candy. And on he goes, barking about the horse, how to control it, how to hit it if it misbehaves. So I pull that thin screen across my ears, will myself not to listen.

Concentrate on the horse, Constance. Look at that wide, flattened space between the horse's ears. Ah, to be small enough to sleep there. To sleep curled in a bed of threaded mane, safe between the peaks of the horse's ears.

Ceylon pushes air out noisily through his nostrils, then lifts his tail to permit loud bursts of gas to move through his anus. Oh Lordy, how I'd love to laugh, but look at Father, his mouth all tight like a perfectly drawn line. Laughter is unthinkable.

Still, he talks. And with the screen in my ears, he's like the cinema, the Pallidad. His graceless body hulking, teeth chattering unheard words, his pathetic pantomime.

But he moves too close and his words come to life. "Remember what I've told you."

The horse ahead is lurching forward. Ceylon is a follower, clearly. Submissive, needing very little from me. And my legs, side-by-side, bob up and down, bounce against the side of his belly. A musical instrument, both of us playing.

~

Constance's legs are in Ank's hands. He is looking well again today; nothing about him resembles the bruised mass of crow feed that remains a faint image in her mind. He hums to himself, vigorously presses her calf flesh between his fingers.

"Where did Jill go?" She asks.

"Who's Jill, love?"

"The woman who slept in that bed."

She is pointing, as if the end of her finger is a wand that could materialize the old woman for Ank to see.

"Ah, Mrs. Hommer? The old one?"

"She told me her name was Jill."

"Jill isn't likely. The name on the hospital forms is Sandra. She married into great wealth, so the gossip mill around here has to say, but her husband died. Seems she married again, this time to a pauper, and that poor lad died too. They say she was quite a beauty in her day."

"Rubbish."

"Could be true. It wouldn't be the first time the swan decomposed. And she was released only this morning."

Ank shakes her leg vigorously.

"She's gone?"

"She is. Just needed to give her a good night's peace before letting her home. Interesting companion, was she?"

"What's this supposed to do?" Constance points to her legs.

"Get the blood moving, girl. You want active blood or the stagnant variety?"

"Why did she tell me she was ugly then? I mean, when she was young."

"Perhaps she believes it."

"How was it — in the surgery with her?"

"Put me fiercely to work, that one did."

"Pardon?"

"Why, that blasted old woman would barely let the surgeon touch her. Said I had the hands of God and insisted I fawn over her. Earned my wage packet and more that night."

Constance gulps at the air, holds it in, heavily exhales.

"Do you think my dimples are like craters?"

"They're like waves kissed by the sun, what can you do about that but be grateful? Now, up then. I'm going to swing your legs over the bed and I want you to put just a wee bit of pressure on them."

As if they are unattached to the rest of her body, Constance watches her legs tumble over the side of the bed.

"You hold on good now and remember that I got you. Just want to wake these sausages up."

She grabs onto the sheets, her fingers alternately turning white and red beneath her.

"Ank, an important question."

"Are you going to be walking to the city tonight? No. The answer's no."

"Not that. Something else."

"A bit more pressure, love."

Ank is drawing Constance forward, bearing her weight so that her feet can lightly touch the floor. She knows she should be paying acute attention, but her mind is elsewhere.

"Do you feel anything?"

"Ank. Why hasn't my father come?"

Ank spends suspiciously long moments gazing at her feet. Then he murmurs something that only the floor can hear.

"What happened to him? Do you know? Have you heard anything at all?"

Constance has the open-beaked look of a hungry baby robin.

"No one about here will tell me a thing, love, not a god damn thing."

~

The next time Father arrives it is day. Constance has a long board placed at the end of her bed on which she is supposed to push her feet. The nerves in her legs are stirring, the doctors say, and she is to aid the progress, stimulate her legs, muster them awake.

This time, Father is at the end of her bed, alongside her legs, but he does not touch her. There is an impenetrable space between them. Once again, she can see his face, but this time, his arms and shoulders are visible as well. On his left hand, he has on a thin golden wedding band. She does not know if it was the ring exchanged with her mother; for she never saw it on his hand, nor in the top drawer of her old vanity. Constance peeked in there once, prowling for signs of her mother whose time on earth seemed to have been wiped clean. The trail of her presence in the world was alarmingly thin; just a name, Wanda, and a small painting that Father kept locked up.

Father leans forward and smiles at her. His upper lip lifts high enough to reveal a slightly browned gum line that was never there before. Thin black lines that outline the top of his front teeth, too, capping each tooth along the ridge of the gum, as if drawn in with a dark pencil.

He folds his arms and waits for her. She lingers in the staring silence for a moment, almost reluctant to speak. When she does, she whispers.

"Where are you?" She does not know if he will answer. If he *can* answer.

Constance pauses, her breath held deep in her chest, fearful to let go of it and hamper the moment, the focus she has on him. Finally, he opens his mouth, and out come three perfectly blossomed red roses. They are floating in the air, and just when Constance stretches forward to touch one, Father's tongue vanquishes them with a flick. Then he extends his left hand, flaunts the wedding ring, and is gone.

Constance is confused, angry. Her right leg makes contact with the board and she strikes it hard enough to feel it. *Thump!*

⁓

The nurses fall into two camps, two enemy lines. In one trench are the matrons, armed with verbal weapons and pugnacious intent. On the other side, and slightly more problematic in Constance's mind, are the younger ones, just slightly older than herself. Since hearing the news, they look at Ank like he is Father Christmas, and they are queuing for their presents in turn.

The doctors murmur Hippocrates name, invoking their tongues to lash Ank for his less than professional decision. The matrons are scandalized; after all, she is a patient, and a half crippled one at that. The young Nurses smell blood, and gather round for a kill.

Constance leaving the hospital in just over one month. Marrying Ank Maguire.

Private Nurse required for home-bound young woman. Attributes required include experience with skeletal trauma, an excellent bedside manner, and a good sense of humour. Please make application care of Ank Maguire, Guy's Hospital, London Bridge.

Constance herself added the point regarding humour. She wanted a dance partner, a quipster, a clown. She'd go mad, she told Ank, if she was stuck in a house with the likes of some of the miseries she was bound to in here.

Nurse Shoemaker approaches the bed just in time to hear herself described. Her fleshy throat ripples, her lips purse. Both Constance and Ank watch as she batters the floor with her heavy walk and reaches up to open the window. As if to let the demons free. Then she spins around.

"Mr. Maguire, I believe you are wanted elsewhere."

"Indeed? Where might that be, Miss Shoemaker?"

"Perhaps in the theatre?"

Ank grins at her obvious disrespect. He watches her turn abruptly around, the sight of her considerable buttocks redistributing shores of fat as she leans over to pick up a blanket that has fallen on the floor. For the moment, he will permit her condescension, if only to enjoy the show she is intent on putting on for both of them.

Constance chokes back a laugh as Ank's eyes widen with the sight of the nurse's behind. His irreverence thrills her. She feels, after all, like she had been passed from her father's bloodless hands into the hospital's sterilized arms. Ank's maniacal streak slaps her out of the numbing.

"I beg your pardon sir," Shoemaker is standing up, her hands on the ledges of her hips, having antennae, developed through years of experience, which inform her when people are mocking her.

"Pardon graciously accepted." At that, Ank is treading down the ward, leaving the gaping mouth of Shoemaker and the barely contained Constance behind him.

As soon as he is out of sight, Constance knows she is going to feel Shoemaker's wrath. The nurse has a darkness around her eyes today, a gravitational pull of her eyeballs deep into the socket.

Constance wills the assault to come so that it will be over and done with. But Shoemaker stalks her, sniffs her out, waits for the precise moment to strike.

When it comes, it is not what Constance expects.

"You'll never give him what he wants."

Constance has to pause before responding. She forms her words carefully. "What do you mean?"

"You know, Constance, because of the accident. You're incapable."

'Incapable' is drawn out, a lengthy rug rolled out for graphic inspection. Constance swallows hard.

"Incapable of what?"

Shoemaker seizes her eye, and spits out the venom. "Children. You're incapable of having children."

Her voice has a sting to it that moves into Constance and scars her inside. Inside where no one will ever see it. Where there are no witnesses. Constance sputters, breaks into a cough. Her face is white, then flushes to scarlet. She is locked in a reaction, not knowing whether to feel shock or anger.

"I suppose we should have told you before, but no one really had the heart."

The word 'complications' comes back to her and splatters across her mind like blood. She remembers the voice in her left ear. 'Let the nurses tell her.' Tell me I'm incapable.

Shoemaker sees the turmoil play out on Constance's face. Her voice is shadowed with defensive guilt.

"I'm sorry, Miss Stubbington. Perhaps that wasn't the right way to tell you such news. But you and Mr. Maguire pushed me to it. The chiding, the relentless teasing. It's really not very fair."

At this, Shoemaker bursts into tears and hurries away. The lisped voice of Jill comes into her head.

Watch them now. They'll be coming to get you like hungry crows.

$\sim$

Nurse Robbins pushes Constance through the shadowy corners of the hospital colonnade on her way to the park. The chair crunches towards the grate, where thin black metal poles stand guard against the brilliant sun that bursts through from the outside world.

Robbins pauses for a minute. "I've clear forgot something. Wait, please."

She abandons Constance three paces from the Porter's Lodge, where a tall man blocks the entrance. His black top hat catches a bit of light, but his face is in shadow.

Constance waits for him to step forward, but he doesn't move. He lingers in the doorway with dark wood on either side of him, his body immobile. She is unnerved, her chair an island in an unknown sea. Constance steals a look behind her, searches for Robbins. The man's eyes are still on her, scrutinizing.

Constance fumbles for the wheels of the chair, tries to spin them forward, but she knows she won't get very far. He stands between her and the exit. The colonnade behind her is long. If she turned back, it would take too much time. Whoever it is, he would watch her, eyes piercing her back.

"Miss Constance?"

She has heard this voice before. He removes his top hat and Constance sees a shining bald head.

"I have something for you."

Roger le Baron. He hands her a letter, offering a perfunctory smile. Her body still vigilant.

"Mr. le Baron!"

He merely nods.

"My Father?"

He points to the note.

"From him?"

The fastidious curve of Father's handwriting across the envelope. Just her name, *Constance*. Tight, controlled letters by a hand that draws lines on a map, carves up a country with an unwavering hand.

"Is he due here shortly?"

With this question, Constance is ready to banish the dark thoughts she has been having about Father. She quickly promises herself that she will make amends, that under no circumstances will she ever think ill of him again. Guilt crests at the back of her throat, an arc of shame.

She wants to read the letter, devour it immediately, but a pasty taste glazes her tongue. She is afraid of the letter's contents, of what harsh words her father might have. Perhaps he is angry over the fall. Perhaps he blames her. She needs to shield herself from the voice that may leap from the page, slap her. She wants a messenger to edit his reproach.

"Where is he? How is he? Please tell me what you know."

"He only asked me to give it to you. Glad to see you are recovering. Now, please excuse me."

Constance hears Nurse Robbins's clipped footsteps at the other end of the colonnade. She watches Mr. Le Baron amble confidently down the steps.

"Wait!" Constance calls after him, but he is gone.

Instinctively, she slips the letter into the folds of her skirt. She wants — needs — to read it alone.

"Who were you calling?"

"The Porter," Constance lies.

"Where is that man?" An impatient huff.

Robbins doesn't wait for the porter but unlatches the gate herself and pushes Constance through, easing the wheelchair down the wooden incline.

Outside, Robbins wheels her near 'The Bridge'. The huge brick archway, looking like a half loaf of bread with its centre eaten clean away, is a piece of old London Bridge.

Four men sit in a semi-circle, smoking and swapping convalescence stories. There is a malodorous cloud about them. One has a black patch over his right eye, his face betraying the creaseless skin of a mere boy. Beside him, looking as if he may have nipped a few drinks earlier in the day, is an older man with a ragged top hat propped on his head. Another man with a bandaged arm slouches forward, his cigarette hanging precariously close to his chest. At the end is a man with a full beard that encircles a diminutive mouth from which a pipe pokes out. They all look up at her as she is wheeled past, and the conversation pauses.

The nurse nods at them but keeps moving. They are not looking at Robbins though, they have their eyes fixed firmly on Constance. The thin mouthed man mutters something under his breath and they all let out a guffaw.

Robbins stops and arranges the chair so that Constance is staring at an oak tree. Then she drifts off, to pick some flowers for the ward.

Constance is anxious to get at the letter, but she must do so unseen. She wants time to think about his words before the whole hospital comes to learn of the reason for her father's absence.

The eye-patched boy is behind her.

"Aye, you're Constance, that so?"

She nods.

"Me mates and me were just wondering — you don't mind us wondering about you now — but we wondered if you might tell us how men such as ourselves could catch a wink from the likes of a girl such as yourself. You know what I mean, then. You know what I'm after?" He beams at Constance; the men behind him start to snicker.

"I don't know what you mean. Now please — "

"We heard 'bout you. We'd like a piece for us, is what we'd like. We thought you might be giving turns."

The men break into laughter.

Constance puts her hand down to the wheel, tries to escape. But his hand is on hers, greasy palms capping her fingers.

"Move your hand please."

"Ah Constance, we love a bad girl, we do. We heard 'bout you. We just want a fair go at it. Maguire can't get it all."

Robbins is suddenly behind him. She clutches his shirt, heaves him up to face her.

"Young sir, you will step back and leave my charge alone. You will sit down there and you will not attempt conversation with her ever again. Is this clear?"

The muggy face of the boy twists into a pout and he backs off. The men continue to laugh, slap him across the back when he returns to the Bridge.

Robbins begins to stroke Constance's hair, but she snaps her head away, unwilling to be comforted. The nurse frowns at her, rejected. She wheels Constance to the other side of the quadrangle.

Now she hovers around Constance, not willing to allow another such encounter. *Just go away*, Constance thinks. *Let me read his letter.* Constance stalks the nurse's every move, as if her eyes could lure the nurse away. The moments creep by until a patient hails Robbins and Constance finally has a moment to herself.

Gingerly, she draws the letter out from under her skirt. She ferrets her head in all directions, ensuring no eyes bear witness. The men are once again immersed in their conversation, flicking their cigarettes, laughing in ribald unison.

Constance digs her fingers under the flap, rips it open. Again, she pauses, looks in the direction of Robbins who helps a young man with his crutch. Her heart speeds up, thumps in 2/3 time. Her mouth is dry, heat rises from her cheeks. What is it, Father, what is it that has kept you away so long?

She fears the worst. He is not ever coming. Or perhaps the worst is that he is coming. She no longer knows which she dreads more. But how will she tell him about Mr. Maguire?

Constance opens the envelope, draws out a paper that is neatly folded into three, with a lump in the centre. She only hopes this isn't a scathing letter, a reproachful letter. Oh God, just once, let him be kind.

She unfolds it. Then she stares, her eyes hardening. This is not at all what she expected, not at all what she feared. She couldn't have imagined this.

The paper is blank.

But inside, wrapped in a torn piece of blue silk, is her bangle. Blood red, with little white stones.

⁓

Constance has been musing on it all night, though it refused to supplicate her by coming into her dreams. Just the words, floating. Feet. Floor. Walk to the door.

She wonders what her feet will feel like when they are asked to meet the floor. The flesh on her toes, her heels, is so soft, so pink, she cannot imagine that they will submit to the weight of her.

She wishes it were a surprise attack. Not all this build up and excitement into a crescendo, as if she is a baby about to take her first step to the sound of crashing drums. Her anticipation has been usurped by embarrassment, and now she wishes so many people weren't going to be there.

When the nurses come in to get her, they wear wide smiles freshly painted on for the occasion. They fuss and hum like insects around a newly opened flower. Constance suddenly craves the clammy flatness of her father and his dour, disapproving glare.

The nurses have outfitted her in a conspicuously clean white dress. The material scratches at her skin, cotton that bites as if just plucked. The whiteness, too, seems an enemy, deflecting any chance for a last minute retreat from the show of which she is the star. They wheel her down the hall and into Bright Ward, a sitting room of sorts, and as Constance enters, it is as if she has left the hospital, has entered someone's parlour. A longing comes over her, to be inside a house, encircled by domestic ease.

Ank sits in a wicker chair beside the upright piano. There are two other interns as well, one on either side of the stone fireplace, which has been lit and crackles a hello to her entrance. Doctor Watts sits directly in front of a vase of carnations, which look like they are blossoming out of the back of his skull.

Constance nods to doctors, but they do not pause in their discussion about the curriculum of Guy's medical college. They merely nod at her. Ank sends her a furtive wink, intercepted by Shoemaker, who issues a disapproving snort.

Now she wishes they had let her eat breakfast first. Her stomach feels hollow. But she knows they had fears of mopping it up, as if the mere act of standing would cause her to heave the contents of her stomach all over the rugs that pattern the wood floor.

Ank and the two housemen nod at Watts. He clears his throat, signalling an end to the conversation. They turn to Constance en mass, a Greek chorus heralding the beginning of the play. Shoemaker stands beside Constance, her hand leaning on the wheelchair, blushing as she addresses the Doctors.

"As you know, we have waited for this for a long time. After considerable care, we believe that Miss Stubbington is ready to attempt what once seemed an impossibility. Gentlemen, please note the progress you witness. I believe you will be impressed."

Shoemaker's voice is shaky, and her normally generous legs buckle slightly under her. She's using me, Constance thinks, I'm her testimonial of competence.

Nurse Robbins and Nurse Shoemaker descend on her, sidling up on either side of her chair. They seize her arms, their fingers cupped into the sweaty curves of her armpits. Constance imagines herself a worm being plucked from the ground. She wonders if she might just fold in two.

She feels a sharp pain down the back of her legs. The doctors nod their heads again. Nerves. This is a good sign. She feels something under her feet, something hard and unrelenting. Then a snap in her hips, a suction sound, a popping sound.

Blood rushes to her head. Why my head, she wonders, shouldn't it be my feet? But her eyes sting and have to tear themselves in order to see. A slap of fear shifts down into her knees, locks there. She feels, too, her roots, for so long grounded in the soft flesh of her buttocks, struggle to relocate. The centre of weight sways inside her, a pendulum swinging, seeking a place to relocate. She feels emptied, a rush of water that flushes inside her, waves that unfold down her legs.

Constance sips at the air, careful not to take in too much at once. Her weight, which rested in her pelvis for so long, now lengthens away from her, stretches out of sight.

She is up and the fingernails of the nurses are her lifeline. Nail me to a cross. Puncture me, just don't let me go.

Ank stands in front of her. He has a look of pride in his eyes. Constance wonders what it is that he has to be proud of. It isn't him who is up and tilting forward like some leaning tower.

He holds out his arms. She feels the Nurse's clutch slacken. She catches sight of the soft skin that dips into a valley between Ank's thumb and forefinger. Lily of the Valley. Soft grass. Is there scotch broom in here?

It is Ank who catches her as the stem below her buckles and she sinks out of the grasping hands of the nurses. As she crumples before him, Ank forgets about her legs, disregards the other doctors, and abandons his medical duties. Instead, he plants a wet kiss on her mouth.

～

"'Tis time. Are you ready?"

Constance feels her insides pitch forward, shakes her head yes.

Ank wheels her to the chapel where a priest is waiting. Dr. Watts waits too, with an awkward smile that looks as if he is holding in something; a loud burp, a violent cough, an inappropriate joke. There are flowers in a vase near the table where the priest stands. They seem slightly wilted, as if moments ago they were beside some patient's bed, seized quickly, and put into a new vase for this ceremony.

"Are there any other witnesses?" The priest inquires.

They all look around them; no nurses, no patients, no other doctors. No one else has come, despite the invitations.

Ank bows his head for a long moment, makes the sign of the cross, and then signals with a nod of his head that he is ready. Constance sits in her chair, thinking this to be the most unromantic wedding she could ever have imagined. The fact that she is being married by a priest prickles heat over her face, a sensation all the more immediate given that her father is lurking around. How he would rage at this. How he would go on about the bog-trotters and their uncivilized ways. Catholics and Irishmen and you might as well invite the devil into your bed.

The priest begins to read a passage from the Old Testament, in Latin, so Constance barely listens. Instead, she studies one small bead of sweat that has formed on Ank's brow, and she watches it slide down his cheek, pause, then drop in a perfect wet dot onto his blazer.

"The rings?"

Dr. Watts steps forward, his mouth finally relaxing. He hands Ank the rings. As Ank places hers on her finger, Constance can't help but think about her Father and his new wedding ring. *Is he married?*

"Please, Mr. Maguire, you may now kiss your bride."

Ank bends down and kneels before Constance's wheelchair. He awkwardly drapes his arms around her back, and once again gives her a full, deep kiss.

"Mrs. Maguire?" He asks her, trying it out.

"Indeed," She replies, imitating Ank, "Indeed."

~

This horrible hat, a gust of wind, the bow under my chin unravelling. The hat lifts off, creeps away. A smear of white, an outline of pink, smooth rounded curves of cotton floating past. I reach out to catch it, but I'm unbalanced. Falling sideways.

Finally, some freedom to my legs, though this is not what I wanted. My legs feel splayed apart, ripped in different directions. And a sharp pain in my groin, a sensation of tearing.

The heat, I'm overcome with the heat, the dryness of my lips, the salty taste of sweat as it dribbles into my mouth. How did this happen? Did I kick the horse, make it gallop?

A breath, a beat in time. Ceylon snorts, some kind of panicked cry that sounds like a grown man's yelps. A waft of lily of the valley, a smear of sharp light scorching my eyes, then the dirt of the trail bathes me.

Now I feel something I have never felt before. Dead, my body feels dead. I can even look at myself, because I'm all afloat, lingering in the air. Watching myself fall to the ground.

Ceylon's good and spooked, his legs recoiling. I see my right arm bounce off the hard ground and fall across my open mouth. My hair is entangled in a patch of broom, the edges of it scrape my skull. Bony hips tilt heavenward in a wave of motion, then are slammed down with a crack against the ground.

That's when he does it. His strong, brown legs only inches above me. He almost pauses in consideration, then comes crashing down.

His hooves crack my pelvis.

A relinquished shell like a giant walnut wrenched apart on Christmas Day.

Five

~

Ank
Victoria, British Columbia
1889

CAN SEE YOUR BODY TRAPPED IN *the bed. Your half curled hand, fingers waving in a slow dance like couples in a late night embrace. I near it, reach out to touch it, but your hand disappears. In its place comes a small child, white-faced, and dead. Did I say dead?*

I'm about to say hello when it changes. Multiplies like. The one child becomes two, then four, then eight, until the whole cabin is filled with the bodies of dead children, looking at me. Dull eyes like those on discarded puppets, torn at the edges like tears. And the whole lot of them, one atop the other, piled up to the burning rafters.

It's then I notice, I can't stop the screaming coming out of my mouth. But it makes the cabin disappear. The eyes too.

Now I'm on this thin plank of wood and some man is telling me this is the ship that will take me to Victoria. My legs hugging the wood the way they are, my fingers blistered from the water, bloated and red as they clutch the plank the way they do.

The man's cracked altogether. This I know as I know the curve of your hip. The Atlantic is too big, too fierce. How's a lad like me to get across it on just a single piece of wood?

That's when Mrs. Brennan comes. Touches my face, her powdery kitten fingers. Waking me up and stroking me and the smell of smoke already gone.

I want her to keep holding me.

⌒

Mrs. Brennan's shoes are grounded, flung onto their sides just beneath the sofa, tilting boats on the beach. All the while her thumb and forefinger rub at her toes. Long white fingers that dig and shift and buff till it makes me want to howl with the teasing of it all. Pretty hands, she has. Grand toes, too, if the truth be known. And know it she must, because she keeps on with the rubbing, like she's in her own private garden with white gloves on.

I got my one eye on her. The other keeps wandering, like I can't control it, see? It's her underclothes, all that white that I'm not supposed to look at, all of it in plain view. Drying on the sideboard. Petticoats and knickers just singing to me. 'Tis my new home.

"God forsaken ship it was."

"Oh?" It's all I can think of to say.

"Bride's ship. Fool's ship."

I swing my legs back and forth under the chair to keep my one eye off her lovely toes, the other off those white underclothes.

"Ah, Ank, marriage was the death of me."

I clear don't know what to say about that.

"You should have seen him at the docks, Ank. Looking beaten by the Master he looked. I come all this way to get married, but a year apart and he'd gone cold."

She's forgotten the fire again. Never met a woman before in my life who forgets the fire. 'Tis a Model cook stove, one like you never set eyes on in your whole short life, Ma. You'd have laughed this way sideways to feed the thin wood wedges into the small compartment at the side. Wedges I split out back early this morning. You wouldn't have believed that either. Mrs. Brennan up and taking herself for a walk before lighting the fire. Me left to crank up the house for morning, like a woman.

"Brought a sorry lot of brides to this god forsaken place."

I feel my face go red the way she forms that word in her mouth. *Brides*. She says it by lowering her voice, stiffening her tongue.

Talking about her husband, Ma, your brother, but I've got to say he doesn't sound a thing like you've said. In your stories, he was a man so funny, he could make the dead laugh. She seems to be talking about some other man. Some awkward man. A man who never saw the inside of a laugh in his life.

"There I was stinking from the ship. Just wanted the baths, I did. And he comes at me, breath hot and salty."

I light the fire. Draw it out, blow into it.

"Christmas eve, it was. And he leads me through dirt streets in a pathetic town where a bunch of the Indians are squatting. They wave at us, selling blankets I think they were."

A blaze. I'm cramming the wood in, promise I am.

"I went to the baths, hoping he'd do the same. But oh no, there he stood, outside by the lamps, beating a line with a bunch of Scottish miners who didn't have the head to go home ten years ago. So I got clean and out I come, must have smelt sweetly cause an old Indian woman walks up to me, she did, baby in her arms. Now you've got to believe me, was a newborn. Ten days, maybe two weeks only. And there she does it. Tries to put it in my arms. Offering that baby for a price."

Her legs out in front of her, dress sliding up.

"What was I to do with a baby? A wee Indian baby at that?"

She even coughs without covering her mouth.

"You didn't buy it, I know that."

"My husband, Desmond, gave her the wave. Told her to be off. First laugh we had since I arrived."

I hope that she's going to laugh now, break up her story some, but doesn't her face sour. That's when she sits up, drops her feet to the floor, beside the tilting shoe ships.

"When did you feed the fire?" She asks me.

"Just now."

"When I was talking here?"

"The same."

"Didn't see that, I didn't." And she looks right confused.

You got to believe me, I try hard not to look surprised. And on she goes, about the Boomerang Inn, where the wedding took place, white candles and holly. But she doesn't stop there.

"Rain and snow at once. Big hint I'd arrived in hell. And the room Ank, well it was small enough, it was. Little flowered bedspread looked like it was torn from someone's old bed clothes, lavatory down the hall dirty as a miner. And he says to me, says, 'Take your coat off, love.' I clear was wanting the next ship out."

"Mrs. Brennan. I have chores to do."

"Auntie Bree, it is to you. And stay one, will you."

I don't want to hear this. You wouldn't want me to, would you, Ma? I'm just a lad and it seems like this part of the story isn't for lads. The underclothes are still in the room, lolling about the way they are. I won't touch them, but I'd love to. Smooth my hand all over them. Smell them. What do the underclothes of women smell like?

"Shall I finish the dishes?"

"No, mind, sit."

So I sit. She is finished with her toes but by god she starts rubbing her neck.

"Then he said, 'I must tell you something, now you are my wife. I must tell you about this'. And he lifts his shirt up and there it is, a long puffy scar hugging his heart. Looking like a slunk snake, all the way from his collar bone down his left side, still oozing puss, it was. One of them scars you know was made by the drink."

"What do you mean?"

"Rough hands, hasty hands. Thick with drink."

Her fingers move down her own chest, moving over whatever is down there. Whatever pink skin she has in there. Under that dress.

"No one could have prepared me for that. Any of it. Alone with a salty man in a hotel room on my wedding night. Alone in a foreign country, none of my sisters or brothers near. So I waited. Knowing of course that it was a wedding night act expected of me. Now don't blush Ank, you've heard it from those snickering lads at home. The act, it is."

"Yes, ma'am."

"So into those cold sheets we went. There I lay, waiting for the man to begin. And he does, slips his arm under my neck, uncomfortable it was, but what choice does a woman have? Expecting the act and all."

I am up and stacking and re-stacking the wood and I don't know what got me here.

"Got to get to the chores," I say.

"Don't let it mind you."

"Got to get to the books."

"This isn't a school, boy."

I need to go outside. I need to get to the door. But her hand is on mine. Caught. Her fingers slide through mine, all slippery, pulls me back.

"It's just a silly story. Be a warrior, will you Ank? So, there I was, lying in the bed next to Desmond, who god knows has fallen asleep. Can you believe it Ank? The man's asleep, not having barely touched me. I didn't know whether to dance or cry! So there I lay, awake for a long time, staring out the single paned window, out into the rain. The ocean just a few blocks away. That cold world just waiting for me."

"The both of you."

"Indeed, the both of us. And in the morning, wasn't Desmond dead. His heart, dead from his heart. And me a virgin widow."

"Dead?"

"Aye. Dead. Just like I'm saying so. Come all this way to this new country just to have him dead."

It isn't no way for a woman to speak of her dead husband. So cold she is. I look to see if she is going to cry or the like, have the regret like I have over the dead, but her eyes are clear. She's stopped the rubbing of her neck, and has moved on to her ears.

So my head is down and I look hard at my shoes for something to do and I notice the dirt on them and how the old leather is spotted, like a wet dog in the rain. I can't think of a word to say. I want to tell her that I don't think her story was very suited to the likes of me. It was for an older boy. Or maybe not even a boy at all. Another lady. Or a diary maybe.

She flickers a cat grin when I ask to go. Stretches her legs and slides them onto my chair the minute I'm up. And all I can see is the shape of her calf, dipping in and out in a perfect wave.

Wondering what it would be like to have a scar.

~

In salty water, swimming down to the bottom of the sea. Can see the layered ocean floor, the sand, the flat fish scanning around for food. 'Tis funny, I can glide easily, press through the thick blanket of water that's all about me. Like I'm floating on clouds at the bottom of the sea.

A line in the sand. 'Tis a long deep scar, slicing the ocean floor. I reach out to touch it and my fingers slide down into some kind of dip, some crevice, like the scar on Desmond's chest.

'Tis soft. Tender. I let the edge of my finger play with it, run over it again and again. A lamb's soft belly. The droopy ear of a furry dog.

But I push too hard. The slice suddenly opens, barks at me, snaps its jaws. The ocean floor cracks and sucks me down.

I can't get out.

~

Douglas Fir. Sequoia. Garry Oak. Birdcage Walk. Menzies Street. Niagara. Dallas Road. I'm learning, I am. Understanding the place. Knowing the names of the streets, the names of the trees. In this Victoria.

I put my nose to the ground and breathe in. If my eyes are closed and my nose open, I can leave the Garry Oak and Sitka Spruce and the Arbutus — the funny one with the red skin that peels — behind. Leave and go back home. Back home.

This isn't home, that much is clear. But I'm here for the time being. Don't know how much time. Just time.

I'm thinking that maybe if I can keep my nose to the ground, your voice will return, Ma. Put my head down and pretend it's Galway not Victoria, and you're alive and talking to me about the chores. And I'm not listening, I'm being a lad, and I'm all a' search for bugs in the ground, which all lads know is better than the chores. And I pretend you're talking to me, you want me to get up, promising the stories if I stand up and get away from the bugs and help you some.

But there is something in my throat. A small clump of mud, half way wiggled down my throat and lodged there. And it isn't Galway dirt, no. This is Victoria dirt if I ever tasted it.

I got to get the dirt out of my throat and get back with my head to the ground and then maybe you'll talk to me. I leap up and pound my chest. Lean forward and shake my head. Nothing happens. The dirt only slips further down, out of reach. I know I can't get on my knees again, I'll choke, I will.

Walking is the only thing that's going to help. No more wet dirt and tall trees, I need to get myself to drier ground. Maybe that peak of the hill will be good, see those mountains cross the water there, watch some boats go by.

But 'tis a hand that stops me. Oh no, not what you're thinking at all. Not a hand that smells like socks. Not the hand that held me and kneed me in the back and took a piece inside of me, not that at all. This hand, well, it's soft, and small. Smells of mint, and it reaches around me from behind. Girl hand, I decide.

"What were you doing down there? Looking for bugs?" I like her immediately. Knowing about the bugs as she does.

Her hair is blonde and the whole lot of it is brushed back on her head with some kind of hardness. I can see her Mother must have done it, no girl would brush her own hair that way, but springs of it leak down near her cheeks. And doesn't she have an army of freckles on her face, dotting her skin. Anyone with freckles must be a friend.

"Who are you?" She has a funny accent. Like so many of the people here.

"Ank."

"The Irish boy with the silly name?"

"Aye. 'Tis Egyptian. And a mistake, too."

"What on earth do you mean?"

"'Twas my Da's idea, the name, but Ma made a mistake in the spelling. Who are you?"

"Emma. We're from England and my Mother hates it here."

Emma extends her hand to me. I don't know if I should kiss it or not, like the grown up men do. I just look until she drops it.

"What's your name mean?"

"When it's spelt right or when it's spelt wrong?"

"You're peculiar."

"When it's spelt right, it means life. 'Tis a life charm. A good luck cross."

"Well, you must have used your good luck up, Ank, because it's right bad luck to be on this hill all alone. Didn't anyone tell you?"

"I'm new here."

"I already know that." She twists her mouth around and looks for a minute like a grown lady.

"Everyone knows that Mrs. Brennan isn't your mother."

I don't think she likes that. That Mrs. Brennan isn't my Ma. But I don't like the way she said that and how she got all important and everything. She's half turned and she rubs her hands down the front of her dress and she looks like she is going to run away.

"Ow! Let go of my arm!" She calls out so loudly, I drop her arm quick.

"Tell me about the bad luck".

"Not here," she whispers, "Follow me!"

She runs down the hill some and I can taste the dirt in my mouth again. She waves her fingers at me, like a fancy lady calling for a carriage, but I go to her anyway. She has freckles after all. When I get to her, she hugs the trunk of a Garry Oak, its crazy jagged branches leaping into the sky.

"Want to see my secret hideout, Ank-with-the-name-that's-a-mistake?"

"Why wouldn't I?"

Emma lifts up her skirt and runs again. I follow her, and we scamper out of the trees, through the grass, across the road, to the edge of the cliff. Emma pauses, then proceeds down the sea cliff at a roaring gallop.

"We're not supposed to go down there." Doesn't she know that?

"Who says?"

Emma is clipping her way down the hill, she really is. Her body is weaving with what I know they call the switchbacks that go all the way down the face of the hill. Down she goes and slides on her behind when it gets too steep, but then she's up again, arms out to the side, as though she can fly. And she can, she very nearly can.

Near the bottom, she brambles right through a spiky bush and jumps down to the rocky beach. She dashes over those stones like she was born atop the whole lot of them. And I am behind her, still, hoping she doesn't turn around and see the awkwardness in me. Galway had the cliffs, yes, but I was there with Eoin. Boys running with boys, mostly in sand. Emma being a girl and all makes me slower. 'Tis what Da would say is the element of surprise.

Now Emma is gone. I see a big pile of logs, a small hut, built right up against the cliff. Temporary like, but strongly built. She wouldn't go in there, would she? Looks like a place for madmen and murderers you'd say.

But when I look in the opening of the wood, there she is. Her legs splayed apart, fanning herself with the bottom of her dress. The running has put a red glow to her cheeks, and she laughs because she beat me but good.

I creep under the log and into the hiding place. Has a musky smell, it does, like someone has slept here a long time without taking a bath. The ground is damp with the sea spray that spits in, too, but still, the smell is all around us. I think we're in danger here, I do.

"This is my secret place; I come here all the time. I showed it to you and now you have to keep the secret."

"I will."

"It's your first time here," she says.

"'Tis."

"Then you need to be initiated."

Emma scoops up a bit of leather strap from a secret fold in the corner.

"Ten lashes."

Ten lashes! "Not on your life."

"It's the ritual."

"Not for me, it isn't."

She twists her mouth in that grown up way again. I decide I have to leave. What if Mrs. Brennan knew I was with some English girl in a log hideout on the beach?

I'm up and leaving but she grabs my arm and pulls it. Then she pats the ground beside her. Like you used to do, Ma, when you told me the stories.

"Why did you say 'tis bad luck to be on the hill?" I ask.

She begins in a whisper. "Because of the Hill Spirit. It's been there since long, long ago. I couldn't tell you out there, because he would have heard me. And he doesn't want anyone new to know."

I watch her mouth as she talks. It is pink and thin, and her breath smells like boiled carrots.

"Who's he?"

"Wait, will you? That's the story."

Emma pauses, and her green eyes get grown-up narrow. "But first, before I tell you, you must swear that you will keep this secret until you die."

Die? I cannot imagine dying. Dying is something that happens to other people; to you, Ma, to Da, to Eoin, to Uncle Desmond. If I didn't die on the ship on the Atlantic, I'm not going to die for a very long time.

"I swear."

"Until you die?" She looks stern.

"Until I die."

Emma leans closer and my ear twitches and tingles as her breath blows inside.

"An old Indian lives in this hill. Once, he was free, and he would fly over the ocean, land here, then fly away. Until one day, a huge wave caught him and buried him in the ground at the top of the hill. Now he's caught forever. So he listens. For boys and girls who he can catch and keep with him. So you mustn't pause at the top of the hill, or he'll catch you and keep you for eternity."

I smile at Emma.

"That's why I hide down here. He can't see me."

I know Victoria will be alright, now that Emma's here.

"Friends for life?" I ask.

Emma considers this like a lady might, then smiles like a girl. "Yes, friends for life."

As soon as I open the door, the heat leaps out and strikes me across the face. The cook stove blazing, crammed too full. Bubbles of red on the surface of my cheeks.

Bree at the table, of course, not up and working like you would have been. With her head bent over, she rubs her temples like she's kneading bread. God help me, the rubbing again. Toes, neck, head. Don't understand the need for the all rubbing, I don't.

"You're flushed, lad."

She lifts herself to standing in that sly way of hers. Caught me staring, she did, her sneaky eyes on me and I'm latched. 'Tis the way that her dress chafes against something that I'm looking for. A crinkle, a crumple, some whisper coming up from under her skirts.

'Tis bold of me to even think it, I know. Not proper, I know that too. But I can tell she likes it when I peer so. Can tell by the way her fingers reach down, stroke her legs, slow-like.

"Tea, then?"

"Thank you, Mrs. Brennan".

Maybe I should have said no. I love the tea, I do, but the making of it is pain if a lad has ever felt pain. Besides the clinking of china, there's the silence. A kind of silence like both of us are wanting to sleep and not able to. The tossing and turning kind of silence. The agony kind of silence I always want to fill.

And I'm stone frightened of the kettle. I know it's mad altogether, but there is something that happens with the making of the tea. A kind of laughter that isn't on the good side. The kind that's on the teasing side.

When she lifts the water, that's when I hear it. The jeering noise. The way the kettle talks to me when the fire is too hot below and Bree has made the crumpling noise with her dress.

I am pretty sure she can't hear it, but maybe she's pretending, to save the face of me.

"*Tssh*," the kettle hisses.

I wiggle in my chair to cover it. Make it seem like me. But she looks and half of her mouth is raised again. She knows.

"Hiss!" it splashes.

So I laugh. To cover the kettle noise and the jeers. Oh how I would love to sod it off and take my fist to its hole is what I'd like to do. But a lad can't fight with a kettle, can he? So I tighten my legs and wait for her to be done with it. Done with the tea and the silence between Bree and me.

"Ank?"

"Yes?"

"Tell me about your mother."

My fingers in the circular knots of the wooden table. "But your husband must have told you some."

"He died."

The rain yelling down and I so want to be in it. Feel the wetness soak through and into my skin. Like Galway, the endless days where the sun never graced us, the clouds shouted out of the sky. You said the rain was the tears of angels.

Angels. Playing with balls in the sky, thunder their laughter. And there was me, seeing the angels in my mind with strong arms busting out of frilly night dresses. Always wondered what God thought of this ball playing, this mirth. Figured he was just too damn busy to care.

"She believed in guardian angels."

But I shouldn't have told her that. You may not have wanted her to know. So I go through my head and find something to take the talk of you away. Think too fast I do, cause what comes out is a surprise. For both of us.

"Why do you hate it here?"

I didn't mean to blurt it but I did. She finally pours the water, gulping noises from the thirsty pot.

"Because it isn't my home".

This is the first time that I think it. That maybe we're more alike than not.

~

The mud flats at low tide. 'Tis a swampy, murky mess.

Between the chipped bottles and discarded wagon wheels, I'm honing in on some of those goose neck barnacles. Grasp onto the rocks, they do, hide out among the stones.

Ah, 'tisn't the Atlantic, that much is true. A walk in Galway would have brought up so much more — remember the leprechaun skis, Ma? The long shells you used to collect and place around the mantle for luck? None of that here. Here, 'tis a much different body of water. It's tempered in. Like a too-good boy scared to ask questions of the Master and so he doesn't learn a thing.

Someone is watching now and I know it isn't the likes of you or Da. She's on the embankment, a woman in a funeral dress. What's she thinking wearing a black dress like that so close to the mud flats? She's even got short hair, she does. Tight curls all round. 'Tis a different sight. A woman wearing her hair like a man's.

So I come at her, wait for her to acknowledge me. Her face stern and quizzical all at once. A long nose and deep set eyes. Don't she look severe. But there's something else, something nice. A glint of sweetness in one eye.

Come on then, ma'am, speak or turn away, what's it going to be? But she doesn't do a thing. Stares she does.

"Ma'am?"

"Son."

"Name's Ank Maguire, ma'am."

"Mmm."

"You were looking at me, ma'am."

"Come with me."

Something about her smells like fire. Not sour, hair-burning fire. But warm fire, cabin fire, bread baking fire, so I follow her. Hope I didn't make up the sweetness I seen in her eye. And doesn't she walk, clipping along she does, all the way up Government Street, past Union Hook and Ladder, the Undertakers, the Bank of British Columbia, the London Bazaar and the Billiards, all the way to the corner of Johnson. Up one block, to a dead stop.

Photographic Gallery. Boots, Shoes, Leather & Shoe Findings the sign reads.

Then another: *Mrs. R. Maynard, Photographic Artist and Dealer in all kinds of Photographic Material. Stereoscopic and other views of British Columbia and Vancouver Island for sale.*

"Are you having your portraiture today?" I ask.

"Certainly not."

"Are you visiting this Mrs. Maynard?"

"Certainly not."

"Are *you* Mrs. Maynard?"

"One and the same. Step inside." She opens the door.

On the second floor, there's a chemical smell. A high-pitched scent that freezes my nose hair and splats against the back of my mouth. Makes me feel like I've licked old coins. Like Mrs. Cleary.

Mrs. Maynard's studio is crammed full of all kinds of things she has to tell me the name of. Things dangling from every blasted corner. She's got a bay window with a broad-leafed plant called a dieffenbachia. Beside it is a large wooden camera on a tripod, looking so much braver than our three legged stool at home. And it has something no stool I seen has ever worn: a black cape hanging down its back like some girl's freshly brushed hair.

And that's not the all of it, either. A half staircase with an elaborate banister on its left side and only four steps that go nowhere. A stuffed blue heron, some large pitcher she calls an urn, and a chair with a hole in its back.

'Tis the holey chair I'm staring at when it's come on me again that I'm being watched. But this time, it's not her. It's the photographs hanging on the wall. Babies mostly, young children — all of them looking at me. Some of them relaxed like, dangling all about rather than sitting up straight like a person in a portrait should do.

"My gems," She says.

I want to acknowledge her, let her know I heard her, but the photographs won't let me. They're the strangest things I've ever seen. Filled with children, hundreds of them, packed all together and calling out. Far too many of them to be in one portraiture, so they spend their time fighting. One on top of the other, they shove arms into chests, knees into thighs. Pushing and curling in and out, jamming chest to head with not enough air to breathe.

I feel their tightness and I can't do a thing about it. It moves into me, their tightness, right into me, into the space between my ribs. Making the shadow in me bigger.

"My photosculptures I call Living Statuary."

It's the ones at the front. The ones with more room, they reach out and place their tiny fingers around my neck.

Mrs. Maynard takes my elbow, pulls me towards a portraiture of her. Except there are two of her in it, staring at each other. 'Tis creepy.

"How do you like me?" She asks.

Can't answer her, won't answer her. Don't like her dress in the portrait, on either of her. Dark, like all the ladies wore to the funeral for you and Da and Eoin. Same look as they had, same locked-in-a-coffin look.

Mrs. Maynard points to a tombstone that rests against the wall. Grey it is, and looking old, though I can see it's been painted over in blotches. I want to touch it. I want to ask her whose tombstone it is, but the children's fingers are still on my neck.

Can't a lad talk, then? They murmur among themselves, decide to allow me.

"Why this?" My hands on the tombstone.

Mrs. Maynard has plopped herself down into a red chair with tassels that hang down from both arms and the bottom.

"How wonderful." She says.

"The tombstone?"

"To watch and see what people care to comment on. What inspires whom."

Well now I'm feeling pinched. There is so much I could have asked about: the chair with the hole in it, the piled up children, the photographs of Mrs. Maynard glaring at herself. But she's right. I didn't ask after a thing until I saw the tombstone.

"I had that sense about you," she says.

"Sense? What sense?"

"*That* sense."

She seems happy, beaming like. Doesn't she know the children have their fingers on my throat?

"What's the hole for?" I try to concentrate on the chair, not feel the skin of finger tips on my throat.

"Ah, backing down are you?"

"What are they both for? The chair and the tombstone?"

"Which first?" Why won't she just answer me?

"You choose, ma'am."

"No, your youth demands it." She laughs.

"The tombstone then."

"The hole in the chair is for babies — their mother's hold them with their heads poking out. You see? A delight."

"I asked about the tombstone."

Mrs. Maynard gets up and strokes the cape of her camera. "This beauty just arrived from England. I had an old one with me in Ontario, but this, this is my newest prize."

"Are you going to tell me?"

Mrs. Maynard sidles over to the tombstone and runs her fingers around its arched top.

"With whom do you live?"

"Bree Brennan."

"Irish?"

"That so."

"Are you willing to sit?"

"Have my portraiture, you mean?"

"The same."

"I haven't any money."

"That is quite evident."

"Can I have the tombstone behind me?"

"I had that sense about you."

Then she disappears behind a curtain. That's when their fingers tighten. The children stare at me, hard at me. When I try and look away, I feel them. They leave the photographs and come into me. They get in my eyes first, make my eyes all foggy. Then a few of them get in my ears, one even goes up my nose. I think they want inside me so they can see from the inside out.

Then they start to laugh. From inside me. All the way inside me and daring to snigger at me. Tiny taunts, squeaky laughs rusted like the old chains 'round the cemetery gate.

Now too many of them are talking at the same time. Too many inside me now, and I didn't ask them to come in. All a' whisper, saying something about Eoin. And that's when they do it. Close their eyes, all of them at once. Then they open them, and yell his name.

"Eoin!"

I run to the wall and try to push them out of me and back into the photographs. They are laughing, letting me know that it can't be done. So I press those walls, my hands all over the photographs, all over my own body, trying to pluck them out and push them back.

They're mad as hell at me now. But I have to find him.

In the photographs, I see blonde boys, open faced boys, but they look all white and waifish, when as you always said yourself, Eoin was ruddy and strong. Faces, gleaming at me. Faces laughing at me. Children making fun of me.

Where is Eoin?

They're howling at me now. Still snickering as I pick them out of me, fling them all against the wall. Push them back into the photographs. And still Eoin is not here.

Their noise is too loud now, the pitch is shrill and the sound breaks up near the ceiling and pierces my ears. Ringing, singing, playing, keening.

I have to get out.

~

Back home and Bree's not in sight. Again. Often come back to find her gone, god knows where. Should be home after her job serving lunch at the hotel, but sometimes she doesn't show up for hours.

'Tis a mess, too. Dirty dishes piled atop the sideboard, clothes strewn over the chairs, a mason jar overturned on the table, two pieces of silver all that is left of the coins it once held.

I know you'd tell me to make haste and clean up like a good lad, so I set to it, try for the humming in my head to banish Mrs. Maynard's photographs from my mind. In Bree comes just then. Her eyes half-shut, her hair dropping down like an unmade bed.

"Ank, sweet Ank. Help me, would you?"

Her knees seem to fold beneath her and I catch her arm just in time. Her body like porridge slipping to the floor.

I help her to the chair. Wishing, I am, that I could tell her about the children in the photographs and Mrs. Maynard's invitation to have me sit. But Bree is not one for my troubles. Her talk an unfinished bridge.

I decide to fetch her water and am pouring it from the pitcher when she calls me. Put it down, I do and turn to her. She's unbuttoned her blouse, the white skin of her bare bosom all aglow. I feel my face go red like a cabin on fire, but Bree laughs. Pink orbs on white knolls staring me down. Staring me down.

Six

Ank and Constance
London, England
1899

THE CHILDREN ARE IN RAGS. A knot of them bob alongside the wheelchair as Ank steers off Great Maze Pond and onto Snowsfields. Constance sits rigidly, her body heaving from the pock-marked street. The silhouette of the hospital fading behind.

Both of them silent in the shadow of a quarrel. Constance was adamant that she could walk, slowly, with two canes by her side but Ank, who slipped his doubt behind celebration, insisted that she be piloted by his own hands. In her defeat, Constance slumps into a mute cloud, allows the faces in the street to smear the images of her departure.

She had anticipated a tumultuous withdrawal from the hospital, but instead, it had been deadly cold. Shoemaker busied herself down in the swimming baths. Dr. Watts was in the operating theatre. Patients abandoned the colonnade and the quadrangle, leaving a vacuum for Constance to take her leave. Only Nurse Robbins said goodbye; a hasty, awkward peck on the cheek as Ank pulled Constance away from the hospital for what she hoped to be forever.

Constance hasn't spoken, but Ank can clearly read the hurt on her face. Those walls, which housed her for several long months, merely opened themselves and dispelled her. A discoloured bean discarded from the pile.

A girl of no more than five hops alongside the chair, her black ruffled dress stinking of cheap cooking oil. On her feet, small booties open themselves to the air in holes that look like gaping mouths. Her cheek bears the streak of black coal, and on her neck, just above her collar bone, there is a bruise in the shape of a large thumb.

A boy steps in front of the chair, swelling up before Constance like a log in water. His eyes are black, and stare at her with a hard knowledge, an understanding that appears many times older than he. He puts out a hand, cracked and chapped, begging.

"Go now, be off with you," Ank says to the boy, who stone faced, begins to back out of their way. The boy permits the movement of the chair forward, but tracks it, clinging to the event as if it is a life raft.

The crowd swells by the time they have reached the tenement. A woman who has hurriedly thrown a dark shawl over her grey dress has joined in, along with an older girl who wears a hat made of layers of material cut into triangles, which gives the overall effect of badly decorated Christmas tree. Constance looks at their garments and sees age in the creases, despair in the torn seams.

"She's the one, she is. Heard 'bout her."

"Aye, and he is a dresser down at Guy's, if you please."

"Heather, move will you now so I can get a better look at 'er."

"They say she's spooked that one."

"I thought she'd be younger. Or older."

The commentary continues as Ank parks the wheelchair at the front door of the flat. Just as Constance prepares to thrust herself to standing, a little girl with alert, pleading eyes places her hand on Constance's. The girl opens her mouth to speak, but a phlegmatic cough is all that escapes.

Ank moves towards the girl, ready to gently back her away.

"Wait," Constance turns to the little girl. "What is it, then?"

An eight-year-old mouth widens with anticipation. Her tongue curves to form a sound, but a deep, rattling cough usurps the words. Behind her tiny frame, Constance notes how the dilapidated buildings tilt, their corrugated roofs threatening to fall inward in an implosion of metal. But there is no crashing, only a few seconds of complete silence as the crowd waits for the words of the girl.

Finally, a whispered voice, squeaky with shyness. "Can you give me a present? From Guy's?"

Constance surveys the crowd, knows that one gesture on her part will incur a sea of grasping arms and protesting voices. She has an image of them tearing into her like birds of prey, carrion birds like the ones she heard about in India, circling above the Towers of Silence, where still warm bodies are laid out for the vulture's meal.

The little girl's burning breath blows across Constance's face. The child is now so close that Constance feels her eyes blur in an attempt to focus. All she can see is the moistness of long eyelashes in a fuzzy blue sea. Constance draws back and inhales a wave of innocence for one lucid moment before the force of the girl's cough stings out. Constance shields herself with her arm.

Lifting a shawl up from her shoulders, Constance covers her mouth, whispers in the girl's ear. "Here's your gift. If you come by next week, I'll tell your fortune."

The girl giggles, aware that what Constance has promised is special, but her eyes belie her ignorance of what a fortune might be. The others, not having heard the whisper, are stung with jealousy no less, and pounce upon the girl, beg her secret. She laughs and hides her red face in the dirt-creased sleeve of her dress.

Constance takes advantage of the commotion to hoist herself out of the chair, clutch Ank's arm, and step inside.

She cannot hide her disappointment. The flat consists of three small rooms. The sitting room has a doorway that leads to the kitchen, which houses a blackened cook stove and a tilting table. Beside the stove is a large jug for collecting water, which comes from a corrosive copper tap on the landing. The walls are bare, exposing peeling paint where cockroaches and spiders lurk. The bedroom is crammed in the back. A dank, dark burrow.

"Lavatory's out back - there." Ank points.

Constance follows Ank's arm. The roof from the building next door is hanging down, a huge lip open and ready to discard the contents of its mouth. The crawlspace between the tenements teems with garbage.

Constance sees the joy on Ank's face. She tries to smile at him, but she cannot hide her shock.

"Don't faint dead away on me there, girl. The nurse will help with setting up. She'll distemper the walls right enough."

Constance manages a perfunctory smile. Ank pats the second-hand settee he bought, encourages her to sit. He pulls a chair from the kitchen, draws it right up to her.

"It's dreadful. I know, love. On my wages, what with hiring a nurse and all, there isn't anything left. Why do you think we live in the rooms at the hospital?"

The rooms at Guy's where Ank lived are little better than this, Constance knows, but they are men's rooms. There aren't any women to feel shame for, no one but other men, who do not rate an effort.

"I'll grow used to it."

"It's a cry from your Father's last house, I expect."

The house in the city, the house before the return to India. Wide rooms with polished wood and paintings on the walls.

Ank slips his fingers through Constance's hair. She feels ashamed of her reaction, like a spoiled child.

"It's ours. I like that." She tries to believe it when she says it.

"The nurse will come soon enough. I'll do what needs to be done until then."

Then Ank leans over and kisses Constance.

"Do it again."

Ank pauses. The words, "do it again" float toward him through a long tunnel. A gateway to Emma. He quickly kisses Constance again, hoping to banish a slice of sorrow that moves through him when he thinks of Emma.

Constance looks serious, almost dour.

"What is it Connie?"

He has never called her Connie before. She thinks about this for a minute before she speaks.

"I have an idea."

Constance can't bear to be on her back. Ank insists that this is how it is done, though he sputters that his knowledge is largely intellectual, and not garnered by experience. She suspects there is a lie to this, but cannot concern herself with its depth. Instead, she sits up on the bed, hugs her knees to her chest.

Ank has neatly folded his trousers and draped them over the back of the chair. He stands in his yellowed long johns and nervously toys with his moustache, tasting the right end of it by pulling down the hairs and flickering out his tongue. Constance has unleashed herself from her garments and has a thrown a quilt around herself. She doesn't know if she should look at Ank or if she is supposed to shyly avert her gaze. She considers lying back on the bed, but thinks that it would look too wanton, so she remains sitting upright. She gazes at the lamp pleadingly as if it might tell her what to do.

"Put it out, shall I?" Ank gestures to the lamp, and Constance realizes that he doesn't seem confident either.

Constance nods, then just as Ank reaches for the lamp, she blurts out, "No! Leave it on."

With the light on, there is less chance that Father will come and ruin everything. She can almost feel him now, his disapproval, his readiness to reproach her. An invisible voyeur.

Ank fumbles towards the bed. Constance clutches her knees tighter. She can think only of the scars that ripple across her abdomen, engraved like worry lines around her pelvis. She knows it is ridiculous to fret about them, Ank witnessed the surgery, after all, but this is so different. Here, she is certain that she is expected to be whole, somehow, unblemished.

Ank, on the other hand, wishes they were in darkness. The light bears witness to the squalor of the room; the matted bedclothes, the rough wood on the floor, the greasy windowpane.

On the bed, two worries meet. Constance changes her mind.

"Can you turn out the lamp?"

"Indeed. Will, love."

Constance is frozen in the darkness with the sensation that Father is near. She realizes that she must make a choice — it is either the criss-cross of scars on her abdomen or the presence of Father. Aware that Ank is waiting, she wonders if he is disappointed in her, seized as she is by indecision.

"Turn on the lamp," She says.

Ank hesitates. It was just a rip in time, but Ank found himself tumbling back in the darkness. In Victoria, listening to the jeers of the tea kettle on the cook stove, with Bree's hungry eyes on him.

He eagerly lights the lamp.

"Lie back."

Constance remembers these words, Ank spoke them to her once before, just prior to the surgery. Then, she was in a grizzled fog, most of her absent, floating above her body, watching. Not inside herself, not like now. Now she has a body she can't escape even if she tried.

"You need to relax, Constance. Lie back."

Ank's voice has a measured smoothness to it, a soft paddle away from an impending wave. Constance finally concedes and lies on the bed. Lying supine as she is, with her knees bent and breaking the space between them, his face looks huge. Not the usual thin, slightly ruddy complexion of Ank. Her insides go icy and where she thinks she is supposed to be moist, she is cold dry. She is certain he must regret bringing her to live with him. He is resolute that, no matter what, Bree must not reappear.

"I feel scared."

"Relax, love. It's normal to be scared."

"Is it normal to want to slap you?"

Her body braces up to sitting. One arm hugs her knees into her chest, the other pushes him away.

"Jesus died, give me a reason to be, woman."

Ank rolls awkwardly off the bed, his hand covering his chest in an act of protection. In this moment, Constance thinks she can see his black hair spark, eyebrows following suit.

"Can't I turn around or something?" she asks.

"Around?"

"Yes, so you're not over me like the horse. You were coming on top of me like the horse did. I was afraid you might press down on these hips, and — "

In his head, Bree is smiling at Ank, her lips parted as if she is going to say something. Ank wants to yell at her to go away.

"I can't."

"Why not?"

"I just can't."

There is a long pause as they look at each other and both wish they were not attached to the awkward bodies that form a fence between them.

"Even if we turn out the lamp?" No sooner is this out of her mouth than she imagines Father, lurking in the darkness.

Ank thinks he hears Bree laugh, thinks he hears her scowl, *Be a man, would you Ank.* He wants to escape from the room, from the flat, from Constance's furrowed brow, but he is not sure he can tolerate the dark. Bree is sure to be there, jeering at him.

"Let's leave the lamp on," he says.

Constance draws the covers up to her chin. Ank rolls onto his back. Side by side, in utter silence, they observe the movement of ants up the wall and across the ceiling. He wonders how he might kill the ants, how he might kill the image of Bree that is budding in his mind. She wonders how to manage Father.

"Why don't I turn around or something?" she insists again.

Her voice breaks the hypnotic spell of marching black ants. Her suggestion is forced, she knows this, but she doesn't know what else to do. Perhaps if she shocks him enough, Father won't look.

Ank can only wonder where Constance got this idea.

"No."

"Ank, why not? Since when did you turn into such a plumy gentleman?"

"I just can't."

In his mind is Bree's smooth round buttocks pressing against the fabric of her tight blue dress. He reaches for his pants.

"Come back here, right now, or I swear to you Ank Maguire, I am going to stick my head out the window and scream at the top of my voice that you're afraid of women."

"Wouldn't matter around here, would it?"

"Not on Snowsfields. They'd likely take up the challenge."

Then they laugh. Both of them, imagining the neighbour women, blackened hands and eager eyes, at the front door of the flat.

For a moment, this gives Constance relief. Then she remembers what she is about to do and her relief dies. There is a sticky pool of sweat behind each of her knees. She wants to curl up under the covers and plunge into a run-away sleep.

"Can we start again?" Ank's voice is calmer now.

"Love, yes. But you have to mind these hips."

"I will."

Ank looks at her seriously for a moment and then gives her a deep kiss. He pulls her down to the end of the bed, and helps her roll over onto her knees.

He shunts the image of Bree away, and wills himself to see Constance's face in his mind. He drums up an image of the first time she tried standing, her half terrified, half joyous face sinking into his arms. He lifts a thought of her as she described an afternoon in India when she read Rudyard Kipling beneath a banyan tree.

For Constance, there are no such images. Just a pale blue glow inside her head. But her head is heavy, thick. Stuffed to overflowing.

Now he is sliding into her and he has not thought of Bree once. Until Constance lets out a sharp cry.

Tears roll down her face. Her knees are sore from where they push into the bed and her buttocks are icy cold. She screams in her head at Father to go away. They both collapse on the bed, unfinished.

For a long time, they lie there with the lamp on. Ank hugs Constance and begins to breathe his slow, deep breaths the way Ma showed him. He craves Ma's voice, craves company in his head, anyone but Bree.

He has his fingers in the slow dip of Constance's hip, her skin warming beneath.

Constance gives off a sigh and Ank responds by kissing her neck, his tongue following the line of her collar bone, the curve of her right ear.

Then, he inches his hands down towards the scars that lie like a rugged map across her abdomen. He traces the lines, a hand guided by the scars like a sailor adept in the waves, fingers rising and falling in the sea of her wounded flesh. He glides across her hips, her pelvis, her breasts. He lingers for a moment in one deep crevice, and with the pads on his fingers, he fills it, flushes it, smoothes it over.

In her mind, the scars, the lines, the wrinkled skin aren't so ugly anymore, can't be so ugly anymore, not the way he strokes them. His mouth finds the scars. A smooth lick, a nomadic tongue that caresses, buffs, laps its way across her abdomen, around her hips, down the centre of her thighs.

Constance feels the heat everywhere now, a heat that burns out the image of Father, burns out the fog, burns out the shame of her scarred body. Ank's tongue laps up her fear, sucks up shyness, leaves his strength in small pockets up and down her body.

When she opens to him, he fills her, garners in her heat. In his mind, Bree is slipping away. Sleepy Bree, becoming a cloud, a fuzzy cloud evaporating. Father has disappeared too, a long lick of Ank's tongue and he has been wiped away.

There are only two of them now. Front, back, side.

~

Rain knocks at the window, but Constance refuses to answer. She is in bed, the blanket tight against her chin. Ank at the hospital and the night outside wants in. Darkness inhabiting the flat.

In the hospital, she was never alone. She always had the moans and coughs and soft cries of others to keep her company. She turns her head away from the window, forbids herself to look. Ank will be home soon, Ank will come in soon.

Constance tries to relax, let the weight of her head release into the pillow, but she cannot let go. The muscles in her neck are strained, her ears cranked for noise. She is on guard and unable to let down her armour.

An hour passes. Then two. Sleep still has not come. Ank has not returned. Then the thought strikes her: What if Ank never comes back, like Father? What if he vanishes forever?

On the ceiling, shadows dance for her. Then a flicker of the gas lamp outside and Father's eyes take shape in the peeled flakes of paint. His eyes are open, a rude gawk, scrutinizing her. Constance flips to the side, faces the wall. His eyes appear there too. She wants to escape him, but the window raps for her. She knows he wants into the flat. Wants into her mind.

No, Father, go away.

Constance places the pillow over her head. She can smell her own hot breath. It smells like fear. There is a sound here too, that fills her ears like rushing water, swamps her silence. The sound of being trapped under water, liquid deafening her. Eyes puff from the memory of salt.

She hears Ank outside the front door. She waits, the pillow still over her head, listening for his hand on the door handle. But he is not there. He has not returned yet. She is alone.

~

This is the place where no one has a body, they are all just shapes. Not shapes of a body, not outlines of their physical form. No. This is the place where everyone is the shape of their thoughts. Their thoughts have formed them. Hold them here.

And sometimes, the people behind the light, on the other side, they ask me to help them. They ask me to gather the shapes and knead them, fold them together. The people don't need them any more.

The mali is here. He is a complex shape, so many contours rolled into one. So much knowledge.

He is showing me a well-furnished room, it is very beautiful. There is a dark table made with deep, brown wood. It is Father's room, his study. But he isn't here. He is gone. The mali won't tell me where, but I know for certain, Father's shape won't change. It doesn't budge.

~

Constance has insisted they walk to the river. Without realising it, Ank talks to her hips, addresses his concern to her pelvis, her legs. They are the ones who restrain her, and he articulates to them carefully.

"It's a long way, love. Why not a shorter distance?"

"It's not a long way at all. It would take you ten minutes."

"Yes, and you, it would take thirty with those canes."

Constance grasps a cane and playfully shakes it at him.

"Take me or wear the scars for eternity."

Ank acquiesces. He feels guilty about her late nights alone, when he is called to duty at the hospital. She needs to get out, breathe some air. He feels ashamed for suggesting that a trip to the Thames might be too much for her.

As soon as they are out on the street Constance turns to Ank, her moon face tight into his.

"You haven't mentioned what you think of my idea."

"Idea?"

"To have a baby, Ank."

Ank swallows a wave. "Connie, you know now that isn't possible."

"Why not?"

"Because of — the physical problems."

"Ah, yes, the complications." She drags out the word in mockery.

"To be sure."

"I say bollocks to that."

Ank cannot hide his surprise, breaks into laughter. "Bollocks?"

"If those men at the hospital can say it, then so can I."

Constance smiles too. She likes the way the word came off her tongue. Like a dart thrown with precision. *Bollocks.* She wants to say it again. *Bollocks.* Like the men in the quadrangle who smoked all day and whispered ribald secrets as she was wheeled past them. Bollocks to them, too.

"Connie, bollocks or not. It's impossible."

"No it isn't."

They near London Bridge station, and enter a tunnel to take them to Duke Street. Constance listens to the rattles above, and wonders, just for an instant, what would happen if the beige brick above her began to crumble, trap them both inside.

"Constance, the accident — it didn't leave you with that ability."

"Bollocks again. I can and I will."

The light in the tunnel is dim. The air is cooler too, and Constance breathes in a huge mouthful of it. She can tell that Ank is on a search for words.

"You didn't see the records, I did. You can't have — "

"Yes I can."

A snort comes from Ank. He stops and holds her face with both hands. "Constance, listen to me. You cannot. You cannot physically carry a child."

"I think you are wrong."

"Jesus, Mary and Joseph. Why are you so obstinate?"

"Because I know."

They are at the end of the tunnel and on the street. Their voices have echoed, drawn others to them, created an audience. Ank sees faces gawk at him and lowers his voice. Constance is still loud, allows every word to carry to awaiting ears.

"That horrible Shoemaker just needed poison against me."

"No, Connie, it wasn't just that."

"Watts doesn't know either."

"Of course he does, he did the surgery."

"And you watched."

There is accusation in her tone. Ank remembers how crowded the theatre was, how Constance was laid out, her injuries a teaching aid.

"That's what is done."

"And did Watts draw the others attention to my crushed femaleness?"

"Constance — "

"And did you all examine it? Did you?"

She is half screaming now, but Ank decides to let her. Perhaps, he thinks, this is her way to understand. He gently nudges her over Duke Street and onto Tooley, away from the keen eyes and upturned lips.

"Well, I'll tell you one thing. Dr. Watts doesn't know anything about my capabilities."

"He's a medical doctor."

"He's a coward."

This is painful for Ank, to hear Watts spoken about like this.

They are almost at the entrance of St. Olaves Dock. Ank stops and indicates with a sweep of his arm that he wants Constance to walk ahead of him. They walk without speaking away from the street, onto the stone path alongside the church, past the disused cemetery. The walkway veers to the left, slides along curved brick buildings. They reach the wooden gate where they pause, lean over the busy water, watch as barges and boats and ships below them wrestle for room in the murky river. Neither of them look at each other for a long time.

"When you are gone at night, I have this need to get out of bed and check on the boys."

"The boys?"

"Our sons."

Ank only swallows in reply.

They both look across the water, to the Northern Gate. Constance catches sight of St. Magnus the Martyr church, with the Monument tower proudly behind it.

"See the monument? How many steps?"

Ank thinks for a minute. "Three hundred eleven."

"Not only will we have children, but sometime soon, I'll run all the way up those steps and back down again."

Determination is splashed across her face. If anyone else had said such things, anyone else who had been through what she had, he would decide they were quite mad. But this is Constance.

~

When she arrives, Ank makes a hasty introduction and excuses himself on an errand. He bolts from the flat, and only when he is clearly out of sight of the tenement does he stop, breath, think. *It's like bringing Ma to her.*

Constance's first impression is that the woman and her look alike. They are both young, but the woman is softer somehow, the lines on her face rolling outward in a more fluid movement, her skin pink without the red blotches. Like Constance imagines herself before the accident. Whole.

She wants to be called by her first name, Bridget. The same name as Ank's mother, both born on Candlemas, and Irish too. No wonder he hired her, Constance thinks, despite the fact that she isn't a nurse at all. But Bridget smiles a row of perfect teeth and strokes her hand over Constance's. An animal demonstrating friendliness.

Bridget's first order of business is to clean the flat. Constance is allowed to help, but there are strict rules about tiring. From her place on the settee, Constance assists by telling Bridget where to wipe the walls, where spiders still lurk. As they work, Bridget talks, Constance listens.

"Ma taught me to distemper, she did. You would have loved her silly, Constance. See, Ma wasn't like other Irish women. She followed the old religion. The Irish religion. Oh, I can see you think I'm talking about those Catholics, aren't you? No, that isn't the Irish religion, that's the one St. Patrick brought over and stuffed down our throats. People were so bleedin' poor and miserable, they had to believe him. They would have listened to him if he had told them to follow him clear to Africa. Anything for a bite of bread, you with me now? But no, I'm talking about the women's religion. The old Goddesses. They lived on the island, there. You never hear much of the goddesses, no. It's all men, men. Has been since Jesus died on the cross and all that foppery. Ah, don't get me wrong, no sacrilege intended, just sick of the way it's always men. See, with the old religion, the real Irish religion, there were women who were heading up the people. Ladies with sacred knowing. Women who knew how to cure each other from the wet diseases always haunting the Island. Sounds strange, don't it? But many a woman followed it, even going to the church on Sunday and saying all that hail Mary full of grace yarn. Indeed, women out walking the cliffs, some of them remembering the old rites. I was named after the original Bridget, you know of her?"

Bridget poses the question but doesn't look at Constance at all. As if she has asked no question at all, she rambles on, wiping the walls.

"Ma had the wind in her lungs. Couldn't stay too still, that was her. Before I was born, every now and again she lifted up and carried herself away to a different village. She had a knack for telling stories, and singing songs, and made a fist full of money, if you please. That was until her demons came. See, she was near Cork when she woke up one morning and her voice had vanished. She was ruined, to be sure as I'm standing in front of you, and was sure she would die without the use of her voice. It was how she fed herself, after all. That day, she walked around the shrubs, and pulled berries and plucked grasses, and decided that she was going to make some kind of concoction that would ease her throat and restore her voice. And it was when she was under a tree that she met my Da. He'd just killed a rabbit. She was frightened by him, the look of death still fresh in his eyes, and his hand holding up the bleeding body of the dead creature. But when he called her, she went to him anyway. She said there was something about the way his eyes demanded it, she couldn't say no. He cut off the rabbit's foot and strung it around her neck. Wore it for three days before the stinking limb near drove her mad. But in that time, she got 'up the flue' as he said. Pregnant with me. I was started when that rabbit's foot was pulled tight around her, decomposing on her chest, 'tisn't it so? My Da brought her to his cottage where he lived with his brothers. None of them had wives, see, but all of them hunted. Ma said the cottage was filled with the smell and blood and fur of dead animals. And the men all smiled when they realized she couldn't talk. But with time, her voice came back, slight though. Not like before. She never could sing again, but she could whisper in a soft voice that kept people with their ears pressed near her face. When I was born, my Da held his head so close to my mouth that I almost died from inhaling his hair. Guess he figured I'd have a soft voice too. But it wasn't meant to be. There were gifts for my Ma, though, because she couldn't talk like other people. When her voice got bad, her eyes got better. She could see things no one else could. Like you, from the sounds of it."

Constance hadn't dared to interrupt before, but now jumps in.

"How do you know about that?"

"I know. See, we can see a ghost where I'm from, and it's plain to see Mr. Maguire has a couple in his eyes. Figured you did too. Then I met you, and sure as the moon rising, you got 'em too."

Bridget pauses and takes a deep breath.

"I think I can get you a picture to put there." She points to a vacant wall. Constance ignores the wall, presses her.

"Well, what happened?"

"Da shot himself by accident, or his brothers shot him, we never did learn. And Ma died."

"How?"

"I was thirteen. Tired, I'm telling you, of sitting there when she saw. Of an infection. Animal bite."

Constance sees a huge rabbit in her mind, tearing the skin off the woman. "Rabbit?" she asks.

Bridget laughs. "No, silly Constance. Sick dog."

~

Morning. A drizzle descends as Constance steps out of the flat onto Snowsfields road. She has only one cane today, a gift from Ank who in turn received it from some hospital benefactor. It has a perfectly carved handle with tiny imprints for fingers, and a gold cap on the top.

She hides the gold end in her palm, for on this road, such a sighting is likely to invoke a riot. Constance feels embarrassed by the richness of the wood as well. What overfed gentlemen used to walk with it, tapping the ground haughtily as he strolled?

These thoughts are new for her. As a girl, with Father, ideas like this never entered her head. But everything was so different then. She had never crossed London Bridge, had never even wondered what life was like south of the river. Anyway, Father forbade it, which was unnecessary, as she had no cause nor enticement to go. The East end was also out of bounds, the whole lot of them scoundrel foreigners and untrustworthy crooks in Father's eyes. He lectured that their poverty was the result of moral debasement, evidence of wicked intent. It would have never occurred to him that if given the chance, they would have gladly traded him places. But in his eyes, his position in life was based not on a lucky birth, nor on educational advantage, but on his fortitude and diligence.

Constance laughs aloud.

Ah, father, the rats here have more fortitude than you.

She instantly feels shame for this thought. And fear. With father so close these days, it is ill-advised to think in this way. For all she knows, he is curled up in her brain, listening intently to every thought she has.

A street sweeper in his open vest and greying white shirt stares at her with slit eyes. She has muttered aloud. He has a mug face, dirt darkened cheeks. His down-turned mouth doesn't lift an inch as he turns his back to her. Constance reminds herself to keep her lips tight.

The street is busy today; dock workers en masse make their way to awaiting bundles of hops, a few men clip to the trains at London Bridge, women exchange small food items with their neighbours. And horses too, led by large-armed men. Constance smiles at the horses, friends of Ceylon all, who this morning choose to ignore her. There is even a Tilling's hansom cab with a stone-faced lady inside, who peers out the window. Constance's eyes move from the woman's hollow stare to the whip in the holster at the side of the cab, where its long knotted braid vibrates in the wind. She has the urge to steal it, an impulse she cannot trace.

Children scamper into the streets to follow the cab. A boy picks up a rock and throws it at the driver. The rock misses him, hits the large right wheel, makes an insignificant plunge to the street.

Constance scours the crowd of children. *Where is she?* The children recognize her, a boy with a pug nose calls out. "Morning Mrs. How's the legs then?"

Constance waves, distracted, on a search for the girl to whom she promised a fortune reading. The girl never came.

"Excuse me, you, there, with the suspenders falling off. Do you remember me?"

"Indeed, ma'am. You're the one from Guy's if I'm right."

"Yes, that's me. Were you here when I came home from the hospital? You recall that, don't you? There was a whole lot of you."

"I was here."

"Do you remember the little girl who asked me for a gift? And I whispered?"

"Yes, ma'am."

"Where is she?"

The children turn to each other, and as if led by an inaudible call, they turn and scamper away, a flock of birds scattering.

"Wait! Where are you off to?"

Constance hobbles after them. She follows them for three blocks, as they dart over to the right and down a lane. Her breath is tight and shallow by the time she makes it to the entrance of the street.

There she stops dead. Two hundred faces stare back at her. A mass of people lined up on either side of a narrow alley, all looking out to the road, where she stands alone. People huddled together amongst large grey sacks.

Despite the number of people in one place, there is silence. The children take their places alongside their families. Her laboured breath is the only sound to be heard.

Faces glare at her. Mothers with stained aprons over their dark dresses squat on rolled sacks of clothes and household items. Boys of twelve or thirteen have their arms around younger children, hands on their shoulders in restraint and support. A little girl with a bluish tinge to her lips sticks her finger into a baby's open mouth.

Constance can't find her voice. She wants to say something, but her tongue has vanished. She even wonders if she has any teeth. What on earth are all these people doing, sitting about in the rain?

A boy with eyebrows that meet in the middle steps forward.

"She ain't here."

"Thank you. Would you happen to — "

A woman with dark caves beneath her eyes stands up, hands on her hips.

"She's dead, miss."

Constance lets out a bleep of air before she can control it. The boy with the pug nose holds his sister's hand and leans forward.

"Dead of the cough."

Constance backs up, afraid of these people. Fearful of their need, their loss, their collective misery that echoes through this lane way and ricochets off the wall onto her chest. She feels suffocated. Can't draw in a deep breath. Constricted.

"Go on home now," The woman says.

This is emphasized by nods and gnarled lips. Constance nods back at them, not trusting herself to have anything at all useful to say. Her eyes hold on a woman with short hair, snipped haphazardly into differing lengths. The woman wears a dress with short sleeves, her arms reddened by the rain. She is sitting on a pile of grey clothing, her outstretched legs propped on a tattered leather case. Beside her, tumbling out of a worn basket, is a blackened kettle and some chipped mugs.

"You still have a home, go back and sit inside. Don't worry 'bout us."

Constance turns to see the only adult man present bleat out these words.

These people, so stony, their belongings rolled up beside them. She turns, grabs the gold on her cane, and hobbles away.

～

There is no blood.

No ache either. No hot bites that feel like electric shocks deep inside of her. No bloated abdomen, no quicksand bowels. Just a throbbing tenderness on the outside of each breast.

This absence is so unlike the river of blood that once poured from her. The blood of complications. The blood of being incapable.

At that time, blood was a vehicle through which she lost herself. Got outside herself, ran away. Some part of her washed up and dismembered from the rest. An abandonment of self by self. But now, it is utterly absent. Five days late and gone. Could this mean she is right? That she is capable of having a child?

Constance places her hands over her abdomen, her fingers resting on small rolls that make a tiered passage between her pelvis and her breasts. Steppes of flesh, though delicate, small. She cannot understand her own surprise. This is what she wanted. For months. Every time Ank touched her, this is what she saw. The touch of fingers, so awkward at first, finding their voices, singing aloud. Stroking hands at last. Flowing bodies.

This is her revenge. On Doctor Watts, Shoemaker. But something more as well. Proving to herself that she is capable, not an aberration. That she isn't the exception, the one who can't. She is like other women, she is a woman.

Then why is she stunned? The thought of a life, a light buried under her flesh in her own crushed body. How could something so deliberate, so anticipated, come as such a shock?

Constance examines herself in the mirror. She wants to investigate what is different about her face now. What about her has changed; suddenly, irrevocably. What new lines stare back at her. She hunts for difference, but she is utterly the same. Except now she is going to be someone's mother.

～

Ceylon is galloping, but his feet don't touch the ground. Constance looks for wings, but he doesn't seem to have any. His legs glide through the air, his long neck steering him through the clouds.

"Ceylon, Ceylon, over here."

He turns his head, flies to her. His teeth are white, so white, and his smile seems to take up the whole of his mouth.

What a smile!

He is almost on top of her, floating in the air. His legs dangle in her face. But she isn't scared. His feet are newly shod, and they dabble above her, dancing. She wants to dance with him.

Up above, his face, looking down at her with glimmering eyes. Shades of wisdom that she wants to shine all over her.

And horse breath. Warm. Sweet. Like grass. He'd like to kiss her, she knows this. She wonders what that might be like, to kiss the wide mouth of Ceylon.

The skin on his nose twitches, little hairs stand proud around his nostrils. He coos for her, content to once again be in her presence. Constance pats his long curved nose, slides her hand over the soft bumps and little furrows of hair.

Hello Sweetheart. I missed you.

Now she sees there are gloves on her hands. Where did they come from? A moment ago, her hands were bare. But now she is wearing little white gloves, exactly like the ones she wore the day of the accident.

Ceylon, I know you didn't mean to hurt me.

Ceylon nods at her, opens his mouth to speak. She waits on his words, knows that he wants to say something to her.

What is it, Ceylon? You can tell me.

Her hand still roving down his nose. Then, from above, her hand is caught. Fingers squeezed roughly. An arm descending from Ceylon's back, grabbing her.

Who has caught her arm? Who wants to roughhouse her this way? She looks up to the horses back, sees a shape sitting atop him. Who is up there? Who is it that is pulling her arm so strongly?

Constance looks at the hand tightening around her arm. White and wide, with hairs on the knuckles. Father. Father's hand. He leans over Ceylon, his eyes black.

Don't touch. Don't touch the horse.

Constance tries to pull back from Father, but he holds her too tightly. His fingers dig into her, break into her skin.

Let go. Let go of me.

There is something happening to his hand, to his arm. His fingers disappear and the shape of his palm begins to dull. His arm becomes one long rounded muscle. Pale skin transforms itself into green. White flesh melts into scales. Father's arm mutates into the thick rounded face of a boa constrictor, latched around her arm. It begins to squeeze her, sucking the life out of her.

Seven

Constance
India
1898

CLASSICAL MUSIC, SHE SAYS, AS SHE leads me into a bare room next to the temple. A young boy, his rascal smile in my face, holds his hand out and waits for the anna. I look to Ayah, who tilts her head from side to side in affirmation. I must pay him. Give him money for this free concert.

When the performers enter, I see they have mats. I wish I had a mat. Ayah and I sit on the dirt floor while the musicians fuss with the arrangement of their small coloured pillows. I worry there are spiders here that might crawl up my leg. Little worms that might burrow in my feet. Fleas and mosquitoes that will bit my ankles.

The musician's instruments squawk and squeal as Ayah puts her hand on my knee to stop me from fidgeting.

Ayah whispers to me, tries to tell me the history of the music, but I can't listen. I'm staring at the man behind the harmonium. He has eyes that bulge out like they are wooden balls tied to the outside of his face. And his lips — oh, his lips! I wonder if this is a pantomime the way he purses and gapes and blows so, even though the concert has not yet begun.

When he begins to sing — in utter seriousness I think — his words are so sharply delivered that it feels like my face is being slapped. His hand waves about like a fish dancing in air, while his face moons and twists.

I can't help it; I can't help the laughter splashing at the back of my mouth. All the while the tabula player, a thin jaw-set man, sits with his eyes closed, his head shaking from side to side in studied passion until he lets forth a periodic cry of "Baba!" and I think I am going to die.

I am shaking with held laughter. I clench my lips and try to shut my eyes, desperate to hold it all in. But the sounds, the hideous sounds coming out the man with the ape face who squeezes his harmonium in infrequent bouts of remembering. All the while the giggling prickling me from inside, burning its way to the surface. Fattening my skin like a bug burrowing, bloating in the heat.

I am dangerously close to wetting myself. Constance, *grow up, this is rather unacceptable behaviour!* But it doesn't help. It doesn't stop my shoulders from shaking or my face from going red. So I try harder. Think of something terrible, Constance, think of death. Think of the body you saw on the side of the road last month.

But none of it works. After several deep breaths of air, I think I am back in control until the sarangi starts. Oh heavens, a sound like a violin string rubbed fiercely over a skinned cat, feline howling. And then the sitar, like a ball that bounces crazily in my head.

That's when I make my break, Ayah blistering behind. I make it out to the laneway, and then let it out. The release of laughter! Not even her snappish voice, the pulling on my jumper.

Despite the fact that nothing is funny, I cannot stop my laughter.

 ~

Father and I in the tonga. Two men emerge from nowhere, asking questions. Neither Father nor I understand, we turn away. That is when they set on our bearers. Threatening them I know, though the words are lost in a rapid Marathi fog. Their hands on the bearers' shoulders, wrenching at them, bringing the tonga to an abrupt stop.

Father is up and begins to shout, and without knowing why, I join in. I can hear myself yell at the men to let go, even though what I say is useless.

Father is off the tonga with his hand on one of them. The man lashes out at Father, hauls him to the ground. Four men with a blur of arms and legs thrashing, and in a moment of frozen fear, I can only think: maybe I should run. That's when I see the mob of them, coming with sticks. Then I feel it: a stone hits my thigh, followed by a rock that thumps against my chest and fells me. And the music: a cacophony of shrill Indian wailing emphasized by the strident sound of several drums. For a ridiculous minute, I think that the classical musicians are seeking their revenge. I swear never to be so rude again.

Another rock hits my forehead. I feel the drop of blood linger over my eye, then slowly creep in. I need to get up because they are close now, close with their sticks and rocks and loud, angry voices.

Hands now under my arms and I am being dragged away. I look up, into the black tent of a woman — is it a woman behind that mesh? I see kohl black eyes, long lashes, and strength from

behind the black, pulling me away. I am off to the side when I
see the boots, the anger, the stomping. Father beneath them.

"What do they want?" I ask.

She answers me with perfect English. So soft, a woman's
soft midnight whisper.

"They don't want you."

I watch the heavy club come down on his head. This is the
first time I know that I love Father.

⁓

I bring him a statue of Shiva and Parvati dancing. I know he
will be angry at this, but I don't care. It is what I want to say.

As I predicted, he pushes it away. His lip fat and blue like
blood dried on spotted cotton. His head wrapped like a coolie,
though I don't dare say this to him, of course.

"You are looking better today, Father."

A grunt.

"I hear it's only a matter of days."

A sigh.

"The nurse says you are doing well."

Nothing. Then he picks up the statue.

"Why did you bring me this?" At last, language.

"Because it represents the creation of the world."

"Indian creation."

"Yes, Father."

The nurse lifts the bandage on his forehead, peeks
underneath.

"Why did they attack us, Father?"

"Some blasted thing."

"Someone told me they don't like us here. They want us to
go home."

Father pauses, licks the blubber of his protruding lip.

"Ah, is that so? Well, then, let us allow the whole damn country to fall apart, shall we? Any other ridiculous ideas?"

"I'm just wondering."

"About what?"

"About home."

He slides down in the bed and flicks me off with a rustle of his wrist. The English nurse, assuming she is not included in this dismissal lingers, only to be met by Father covering his eyes with his hands. *I'm not here, go away.* Her body pricks slightly, and she raises her eyebrows in a half moon, but scuffs away.

I leave the medicinal smell of the hospital and walk out into the punching heat of day. The wind is up, and the turquoise sky is on its descent to grey. I turn my body into the warm wind and let it dance around me. Shiva and Parvati dancing. Dancing in eternal bliss. Black hair sinuous, bodies entwined.

The mali is in front of me. He looks sheepish, *obsequious* Father would say in a condescending voice, even though this is what he demands of them.

"Miss, hello hello."

He holds a mango.

"I am told your Father very ill. Mango for him."

"Thank you, that is very kind."

"Father and Miss caught in uprising. Not for you, not for you. Tonga in way, must go down too."

"What were they fighting about?"

"They fight for things to be not as they are now."

"What do you mean?" I ask.

"For place to belong to them once more."

"You mean without us? The English I mean?"

"English only part of very large problem. Religion big problem too. Many problem. You walk with me?"

"Yes."

I want to hear more about Shiva and Parvati but he does not seem to want to discuss this today. Instead, he looks around the hospital grounds, at the sweep of trees and the ebbing hill.

"Beautiful, no?" He asks.

"Yes."

"My family not from here. We come from far away."

"Me too."

"You come and you go. But not me."

"What do you mean?"

"English people go back. My family not go back, land is gone. Ruin of war, yes? All the life of my family. And my great, great parents as you say."

"Grandparents? Ancestors?"

"Yes, many fights of ancestors."

We are at the place where I am to meet Ayah. I am surprised she isn't here already, waiting for me. I sit on the wooden bench beneath my parasol.

"Will you sit?" I offer him the place beside me.

"Not Indian chair."

"I know. But to keep me company. Until Ayah arrives."

The mali looks at the bench but will not sit.

"Please?"

He looks around for witnesses, then reluctantly hunkers on the bench.

"I'd like to hear more stories today."

"No more story."

"But I like them."

"Father not like them, miss."

"He's in there."

I point up the hill and the mali's dark eyes shadow the sweep of my arm.

"Please? Pretty please?" The pleading voice I am not allowed to use with Father.

His eyes flicker. "Alright, Miss."

He pulls out a leather-bound book from his dhoti, a text I have not seen before. The front cover is ripped, as if it was torn a hundred reads ago. The pages are curled up at the bottom, and it looks as though he has spilt chai over the entire thing. Despite this, I know it is a special book to him. I can tell the way he holds onto it for a moment, cradled between two palms. I want to grab the book from him, have a joke, be playful, but when I do, I take it so quickly that he is dazed for a moment. I hurriedly flip open to a page and see something I am sure he didn't want me to see. A black haired man overtop a woman who is on her hands and knees, her buttocks facing him. Both of them are naked. His large private part, entering her.

It is just an instant, but I take in with a greedy glance before the mali seizes his book back. But the picture is seared into my mind. A woman on her knees, the man behind her.

"Sacred book," He says.

I laugh. "Yes, I can see that it is sacred."

The mali looks at me in a way that makes me feel young, like a ridiculous, ignorant girl. I am instantly ashamed for laughing.

"Some day you know."

I can only imagine what Father would say if he were here. I can imagine the strike the mali would have against his cheek, red welt rising.

"Is that the story you're going to tell me?" I ask.

"No. That story for me. Cannot sit with book in dhoti, must take out. Story for you is Patanjali."

"I'd rather the book with the interesting pictures."

"Miss wants to know what she cannot understand."

He glances up the hill as if he thinks that Father might skulk out of bed and prey on us. I need this minute, this moment of silence to let go of the picture that still fills my head. I want to see more of the book, but it is clear that the mali has no intention of allowing me to see it.

"Now listen to story. Story of Lord Patanjali."

"Who's he?"

"Father of dance. Of yoga. Of medicine."

"My Father would call him an idol."

"Father not understand. Now listen. Woman named Gonika, kneeling beside a pond, praying for worthy son. Gonika old, and lonely, no son to pass on many lessons and knowledge. She pray to Sun god, please give me son.

"She close her eyes and meditate for long time. When she open them, scooping water in her palm, offer it as oblation to Sun God. When she look at her hands, she see in palm tiny snake moving. Little snake born from palm. Snake growing and growing and soon become a man. He pray to Gonika, please take me for your son. Of course, she took him for son. Gave him his name. Patanjali."

"The snake God?"

"No, no, Patanjali not snake god."

Like Gonika and Adisesa, we are silent for a long time. I keep looking at my palms. Then the mali is up, tucking his book back in his dhoti, his eyes focussed on Ayah, who is walking up the dirt road towards us, head down.

"You still worry about snakes, miss?"

"I don't know."

"They have kindness for you."

"I don't understand."

"Rising snakes tell you when dreams come true."

Ayah is bustling her way up the hill. She is angry that she is late. I can see it in the way her fingers are splayed apart, as if too hot to hold together.

"Tell me more, quickly."

"Strange dream girl, you already know."

The mali runs off, unseen by Ayah. When she approaches, she looks at the mango in my hand.

"Where did you get that?" She asks.

"From my friend. He gave me a mango to give to Father."

"What friend?"

I know I can't tell her of the mali.

"Whoever it is, no good friend. Mango not good. Every Indian know this. Why he give you mango? After monsoon, mango rotten. Small worms inside, no good to eat."

"It was a gift."

"What did he say to you?"

"He told me of a snake born from a woman's palm." I think about the worms inside the mango. Could they become wiggling snakes?

Ayah holds out her hand for the mango. I don't want to give it to her, so I hide my hand behind my back.

"Do you know that story? I want to hear more, Ayah, please?"

"I know nothing. Nothing but your Father."

She takes my hand in hers, walks me down the hill. I see her lips twitching and know that she does know the story, but steels herself against its telling.

I still have the mango. As soon as I'm alone, I'm going to open it. Look for worms.

I'm at this cliff and I know I've been here before. Ayah says no, I have never been here, but I know that's a lie. A long time ago, climbing this hill, hoping to see someone at the top. Rain clouds whispering, the shriek of grass, the smell of peanuts cracked freshly from the shell.

But this makes Ayah cross.

"Get such nonsense out of your head."

She wants me to stop talking now. Stop the gibberish foolery she was told by Father to interrupt. But a part of her, some small morsel of her, is dead curious. This I know by the way she hesitates just a second before telling me to quiet.

She hands me a chapatti. Then she tells me. What I have already guessed, what I have already felt quivering across my skin.

"You go home soon."

"England?"

"Yes, your Father too."

"When?"

"When he is well enough to travel."

"And you are coming with us?"

"No, I stay."

"But I love you, Ayah! I'll miss you."

And in Ayah's eyes, a pleading with me to know what she cannot say, because it has been forbidden by Father.

"Say it, Ayah."

"Say what?"

"You know. Say it."

"I love miss as well."

Then she holds me in her large arms, crunched against her moist bosom. I slacken against her, let her take my weight, let her absorb me. But even with the words that slide down from her lips into my ears, I still am not full. My breath sticks in my chest, egg yolks on raw bone. I cannot imagine home right now, cannot imagine anywhere but here. Here in the heat and the warm rain. Here with the mali and Ayah. Here with the coloured saris and the hair that feels like silk and a horse's mane all at once. Here where everything is so foreign and so familiar.

"Sweet miss. You go and I am sad." Then she lifts my face to her lips and a soft kiss lands on me, a cloud on my skin.

Home, home. I cannot imagine home. Cold grey island, so far away from teeming green land. So far from green. So far.

Eight

⌒

Ank
Victoria, British Columbia
1890

HE'S ENGLISH AND HE SMELLS LIKE dog's breath. But Bree insists, so I sit on the wooden chair and listen to him.

Mr. Harrow's got a stutter that makes me think of Eoin's lisp, though you couldn't ever confuse the two. You know how Eoin's speech was sneaky, like it was snatching you beneath the bushes during a game of tag? Well, Master Harrow's is nothing of the kind. His is like getting your fingers caught by the knife, all blunt and jagged and hurting like hell. But he has a black bag down near his feet and it's full of all sorts of brilliant things, like bandages, so I listen.

He wants to see if I know my maths. Like Da showed me, I can add up the sums, I can take away the numbers, I can multiply, but I'm shamed to tell ya, Ma, I still fumble when needing to divide. I know such a failing won't get me into the bag, so I decide to make some answers up. His jaw is tight, so I know I haven't guessed well a'tall. A'tall.

"Are you a doctor?"

"No, Mr. Maguire, I am a teacher. "

"Then why do you have a doctor's bag?"

"This is what is known as a s-s-safety bag. I go inland and, from time to time, my duties inform me that I need to at-attend to people's health."

"Why?"

"Because there are very few doctors there."

This clear doesn't make sense, a teacher acting like a doctor cause no doctor wants to go inland. But I better leave off with the cheek.

"Who lives up there?" I ask.

"Indians."

I think of Bellicose. "Are they savages?"

"One of them is my wife."

I might never see into that bag.

"So, your numbers need work, this is clear. What about writing? I trust that even in Ireland, not everyone is illiterate."

"I know my letters."

"Write them for me."

I write out the entire alphabet as fast as I can. His eyebrows go up so I know my speed has surprised him.

"I see. Can you put them together and make a sentence?"

I write: *This is boring.*

"I see. Can you write anything worthy of my attention, or just field rubbish?"

I write: *I want to see into your bag.*

"Hmm. Perhaps after our lesson. I need to assess you."

My scribbling interrupts him. I write: *Now!*

"Did you attend school in Ireland, Mr. Maguire?"

I write: *From time to time.*

"I see." He hums.

I write: *The bag?*

The question mark is rather big and Mr. Harrow looks over his spectacles and stares at me as if deciding whether or not to be angry.

So I write, *Please?*

He softens. "Ah, very well then."

That's when he lifts up the black bag and slowly opens it. It's almost like I'm about to eat one of your mutton pies, Ma. He lifts the items sweetly from the dark of the bag.

First, he pulls out pointy scissors. Then, some clear liquid in a small bottle that smells like cedar. Next, what I've been waiting for. A roll of cotton bandages.

I hold the bandage up next to my arm, let the bottom of the roll drop. It uncurls down onto the floor.

"N-n-no, like this."

Mr. Harrow leans over and takes a long time to pick up the bandage. When he comes back up, he holds the bandage away from me, like it's a honeycomb he doesn't want me to lick. Then he makes a grand show of rolling it up into a ball again.

I'm fed up with the time of it all. I just want to feel it on my arm. Nice and tight. Finally, Mr. Harrow holds the bandage against my arm.

"I shall roll it here."

"Please."

He lets just the tail of it rest on my skin, then he lengthens and pulls it all at once, unrolls the ball, crossing and criss-crossing it around my arm, keeping it snug. I love the sweet, stinging feeling it gives. The tautness as Da would say. The way Da would tie up a fence post that needs to make it through a storm.

"Is there another, sir?"

Again, the eyes over the spectacles and a look to the door to see if Bree is about. He reaches back into the bag. Another bandage roll.

This one he lets me do myself. I copy him, unroll, pull, lengthen, wrap. Unroll, pull, lengthen, wrap. 'Tis the smartness I feel on my arm hairs, how the skin on me sucks down to the bone.

"Another?"

"L-l-last one lad."

I want to put this one on my head. Of course, he has to help me with it. His eyes keep looking to the door, then down to me with one side of his mouth in a leer. He wraps it around my head, just atop of my eyes. I want a mirror, first off, see how I come out. Want to know if it looks as tight and snug and warm as it feels.

A knock on the front door and I beg him to let me answer it.

I can see he is about to say no, but Bree enters the room. She doesn't even look at me, even though I must appear like there's been a grave happening down at the mine. She climbs on the sofa and throws her shoes off. Mr. Harrow leans back in his chair, rolls his chest out. That's when I make for the door. I make sure I lumber, my arms outstretched. I even grunt when I open the door.

'Tis Bellicose, smoking a big cigar and smelling of the drink. I'm waiting for him to notice the bandages, ask me about them, but he doesn't. I go ahead and say it.

"Big problem here, been bleeding the bandage right through." I'm chiding him, I am.

Bree and Mr. Harrow snicker from behind me, but Bellicose just wipes at his ear with the back of his hand, like there is too many bugs about.

"Been to the wilderness lad. There's money to be had in falling trees and clearing ground. That's where the money is."

"I'm taking the lessons." I say.

Bellicose looks past me and I turn to see Mr. Harrow slipping over to the sofa where Bree sits.

"What are you doing that for? 'Tis a waste."

"I'm to learn like the English boys," I say it proud.

"So you can be a goddamned petty politician of some god forsaken neck of the woods where all your friends are really enemies and all the women whores?"

That word again, whores. And the rough taste of liquor on my tongue.

"I want to go to school like the English boys."

"Bunch of fecking slave owners, they'll grow up to be."

I look back at Bree and Mr. Harrow, but they're gone now. I want Bellicose to go, too.

"For god sake's lad, there's trees up there. You know what that means? Money. Back some there was gold too, and there may be more. What you want to learn to be a gentleman for? Don't you know they can't even piss by themselves. Need a whore to hold it for 'em."

I start to see this in my head, but I don't think I should finish the thought. I'm right, aren't I, Ma?

"Ah, God, a disappointed man am I. By the way and way, how's the Aunt you got looking after you. She treating you right?"

I pull the bandage on my arm again, it doesn't seem tight enough.

"Indeed."

"Let you have a drink from time to time?" Bellicose has a bottle out, and takes a swig.

"Indeed," I lie.

"I'm off then. Be looking for a different little camp boy."
When he leaves, I feel proud. Tight and proud.

⌒

She's got on the dreary black again.

See her all the way from here, even. Behind this column.
Thought of it this morning, as I was brushing the horses at
Bowman's. That I'd see Mrs. Maynard from outside the saloon
here and she wouldn't see me. And there she is, still in the
funeral dress. With her family.

They know where they're going, that much is clear. No
discussion going on, got the rhythm of a dance, they do. Pack
up the carriage with baskets like it's the setting of tea.

Though it's odd that a woman who makes photographs like
those has a family. Children even. Can't think of what it must
be like to have a Ma who has portraitures that can grab you
around the neck, sneak in your ears. Could probably taste that
in her cooking.

But the Mister, he doesn't seem to mind. Not now, not in
that deerstalker hat with his wild beard. Makes him look fierce
twice. He's thin though. Agile, Da would say, and I can't say as
I seen a thin man be brutal.

They're loading into the carriage. Her, the Mister, four
children. Going to wherever it is you go when you bring that
many baskets. She slips out of my view, beneath the black
canopy, and I guess it's the horses being flicked by the whip,
that's the sound that carries me. Cause I'm off, running after
the carriage. And don't I leap and grasp that back beam before
I can think that this is a right daft thing to do. There's a board
beneath me I use as a seat. Sit facing backwards on the hard
plank, the road a stream rushing beneath my feet. Them inside
the carriage and not one of them know I'm catching a ride.

So I have to be quiet, I do. Have to sit here hushed now, though I haven't an idea where we're going, never been out this way. The trail beneath us a dried mud bath, and I'm watching the thin wheels dip and shudder themselves stupid. I have to catch my mouth when the carriage tilts into a rut, shaking itself like a dog flicking off water. I hold my tongue but the children don't, can hear some squeals leaking out from beneath the canopy. I'd like nothing more than to poke my head around and tell them that I'm in trouble with the road, too.

Garry Oaks and a house with a turret, no less. 'Tis a wonder to think that people live out here, in such grand homes. Riding high over the farms, these homes are. If you'd call them farms. Not like the ones at home. These ones sport clean fence lines and fancy foreign neatness. Not like Ireland, where the farms have the good sense to be held in by the ocean or a stone fence or a road. Here, they sprawl out, almost loafing on the land with their fat hips.

And doesn't the sun hurt my eyes. No wind, either, to move the thoughts about. Time badgers me, like a long dream I never wake up from. Time like a song that won't end, a story that's left hanging without a hook to tie it up neat and right. I'm needing some water to wet my tongue and a friend to say hello to. But it isn't to be, just me and the massive trees and the long milky grass that tempts my parched mouth. Would be nice to snap off a bit, suck on it, let the savour in, as Da used to say after dinner. But I can't think of the dinner nor the milk, cause there's an emptiness inside me and no food to fill it.

Can smell the ocean again, 'tis off somewhere, over to the left I think. I'm craning my neck around and see we're coming up to a mountain of sorts, far grander than Emma's Indian hill. Now what's a mountain doing out here? Was it a fib she got into me?

The carriage comes to a stop. I remember that I'm a lad who shouldn't be here and I've got to decide quick what it is I should do.

So I seize the opportunity and leap. And of course I run straight for the trees, imagining that as the Maynard's climb out of the carriage, they'll see me, point my way, startled voices demanding to know how I got to be where I am. But with the Douglas Fir in front of me now, I look back, and disappointed am I. Not a soul looking, no one beckoning. They haven't seen me a'tall.

So I'm back to spying again. Other carriages arrive, more folks with baskets. Lots of children, too. Some my age, who know what to do with the hand-shaking men and the women who tell them where to put down a blanket, what food to unpack. That's what spits on my soul. The food. Biscuits, cakes, loaves of bread, roasted chicken, meat pies.

Nothing left for me but the forest. So in I go.

'Tis quiet. All moss-covered trees and splashes of light. A freshness too, like a good ocean breeze coming off the cliffs at home. I'm liking the green and brown and tan as I hide from the people and their picnic. You got to understand, Ma, these trees, they're not like the ones at home. They're grand, they are. Can feel their strength in the way their branches move. Can sense they got eyes on their bark. And I'm wondering if they got their own guardian angel, these trees. Or is it a huge giant inside, gone fickle because of the hunger? Perhaps he's rough, Ma, vicious. Might throw me out in a mere breath's beat. So I talk to the trees, promise not to harm. I'm begging not to be harmed.

Then a rustle that snaps me into the freeze. Is it a bear in the bushes? They have the bears here. And cougars too. Some of them come into the town so I'm sure as salt they're out here too.

I listen good but I can't hear anything but the squeaky-wheel call of the birds, far above.

'Tis enchanted, this place. Green dust on the trees and wood that feels like small waves under my fingers. Bushes with leaves like big teeth, others like wide open palms. And hideous slugs, uglier than even a madman would draw, with splashes of black on their slimy green backs. Making their way across the path.

Then a clearing. Green leaves that soften my steps, a space where the tangled arms of the branches don't reach. Lean against a cedar, the whole of me in shadow beneath its umbrella hut.

A terrible squealing above, sharp, over and over again. Sounds like it comes from some high pitched machine. But there's a sweetness in the sound. Some kind of hope it has, like prayers in church spiralling up and up until they disappear into the heavens.

That's when I see it, the eagle. He's got a crooked beak like an open smile, a clean curved line to his head. But it's the eyes, that's what's special. Eyes like a master painter, looking in while seeming to peer out.

He sees me but doesn't care. Both of us silent now in the hum of the forest at mid day. Him my watch, knowing he could spot an animal, warn me of its approach, protect me even. Thinking this, I get rid of some of the cloud in my head, let the knot unravel some.

Which makes me think of Bree with the echo all around her. How I'd love to bring her to this clearing, let her be still. And you, Ma. You're like the cedar that hugs me now. Thinking that if I keep on talking, your voice will come back. You'll return. And Mrs. Maynard, with her secretive smile and heart filled with ghosts. What would she say now?

A sound. Not the eagle. Not the trees. Not a bear, or a cougar. A crack of twig on the ground. I flatten myself on the ground in case it's a bear.

"You were much better before."

Mrs. Maynard!

"Clever boy! Adventuresome boy! Wonderful boy! I am so pleased to find you here. Just sit back and think about whatever you were thinking about. It was a brilliant image, but remember, you mustn't move."

She has her camera on a tripod and she dips behind it to fix me in the lens. She must have been here for a few minutes. Her equipment is ready and her eye is trained. On me.

"No chicken for you until I make this one."

So I smile.

"No, like you were before you knew I was here. What were you thinking about?"

Twas her. And you. And Bree.

"Beautiful light! And what else were you thinking?"

I was thinking of Bellicose and the bottle that took your voice away, Ma.

A clang from the camera. A hum from Mrs. Maynard.

"Brilliant. What else?"

The eagle, Ma. The peace sitting here. And the forest's breath. That's what I was thinking.

"Yes."

The last burp from her camera. She comes and takes my arm. Leads me through the trees towards the picnic. When we arrive, the whole lot of them fall into a stare. I know I should say hello, explain my being here. But there's only one thought in my mind. I'm saying it over and over again, like the lines at school. *I don't belong here.*

The children glare at me like I'm a reptile Mrs. Maynard has dragged from the bush. When I come near, they scamper up to give me room on the blanket. Back away. But Mrs. Maynard is up, ordering folks about for a group portrait. Directing everyone here and there. She tells the children to sit near me, but they take their places far away.

Then she nods at her husband to operate the camera while she slides into the group herself. Tells us to look straight ahead, be still. Everyone looks to the camera except her and me. She faces sideways. I look at her.

All up now, she orders, form a circle, hold each other's hands. The children are at one end, flickering eyes all, their faces saying they hope I don't come too close. Mrs. Maynard tugs me to her side, squeezes my hand. A snake-thin man with cold hands clutches at my other hand.

All quiet and eye lids closed. Some looking like the saints in your paintings, others like they're in line for confession and scared because they're gonna get it from the priest.

Then a man with greasy hair clears his voice from the other side of the circle. I see him but the others don't because I haven't yet closed my eyes. He's got four huge rolls of fat that pour over his trousers, makes me need to snicker, bad. So I close my eyes and let his voice fill my head like pouring rain. And isn't it a slap to hear what he says.

"The dead are with us, among us, and around us. They are but the spirits we hope to be."

Sounds like they say, "Amen" but they don't.

They're singing and clapping their hands and I want to join in, I need to join in. So I sing though I don't know the words. I just want to be loud. Rid myself of the quivering inside. The quivering that came when he mentioned the dead.

~

My mind is too full and I need to spill some of it out. I think of Emma, knowing that she's the one to tell. Tell her about the picnic, about the dead children in Mrs. Maynard's house. So I set to work on getting permission from Bree. I offer to help her with the washing up after tea, not one of my usual chores, mind.

"And to what do I owe this pleasure?"

"Thought it might be nice to chat some."

So on I talk. Telling her about my village at home where she's never lived and the stories I think she'll want to hear.

"There's a crazy man in our town, he's broken right and square. Lives out past Flaherty's road, no one even knows where. And he comes around, looking for silver, but each time a lad such as me walks by, why doesn't he break into song. Knows hundreds of them, songs like you never heard in your life. One of them starts, 'Tis a long road that goes nowhere, but no one's counting 'cause they're drunk.'"

She goes on with the washing and passes me a fork as if she didn't care for the song at all. I'm all warm with the embarrassment of it, remembering how Da used to sing like the crazy man and we'd all join in. Getting the family laugh. But Bree's not having any of it.

"Bree, can I go out tonight with Emma? Think her cat's coming on tonight with the kittens."

"That English girl?"

"Aye, she's a friend."

"Watch out for her mother."

"Indeed, I will."

"Go on then."

～

Emma's in the kitchen, working alongside her mother, cutting, steaming, canning. Four hands at task through the window.

So I run to the Garry Oak and climb it, rattle a branch and a cascade of acorns fall. The shower brings both of them to the door while I hide best as I can behind the tree.

Emma's mother rubs one hand over the top of her head, slow, like there's something inside she's trying to soothe. Her hair in a bun, bouncing brown at the back of her, but she doesn't see me. Emma does, though.

So I wait. Know that Emma, being Emma, will find a way out.

I go around the back, catch a scent of the outhouse, know that someone has been lax with the ashes. 'Tis a scramble of chicken and chicken droppings everywhere. Hone in on their beady eyes, when Emma appears.

"You dog, Ank. You know my mother hates boys."

"I know. I just — "

"You want something. I always know when boys want something."

"How?"

"They come around."

I scratch my ears, try to bide the time because I don't know what to say next.

"Emma. I come here — "

"For what?"

I'm half way to telling her about Bree and the picnic, but her breath is in my face and she's talking to me.

"Have you ever kissed before?"

A messy cloud moves through my head. I think of you, Ma, think how you might not like it at all.

"Well, I kissed my Ma."

Emma laughs a little too loudly and we're both dead sure that her Ma is going to find us.

"I mean a girl, silly one."

"No, but I'm ready for it."

I say this and wait for your voice in my head, Ma, scolding me, but it doesn't come. The night around us is quiet, just a thin slice of the moon in the sky. The trees above wave their arms in the air and a wind slides along the ground and crawls up my trouser legs. I hear Emma's breath, soft and regular.

"Emma?"

"I'm waiting Ank."

Oh wouldn't you know it, she's waiting for me! I'm stone glad she can't see my face well, it's red and hot and don't I feel like a daft lad. Here all this time I've been waiting for her to kiss me and all the same time she's been waiting for me.

So I move closer to her face, but it isn't right. What I see. In my head, it's a picture, but not of her. 'Tis a bad picture, I tell you, and it's only with the darkest shame that I'll pass it on to you.

'Tis Bree. Her eyelashes fluttering over those grey-blue eyes.

I want to kiss Bree, slide my hands up her skirts and find out what causes the swishing noise when she walks. I want to see what her belly looks like, if there is a dip at her waist.

But I know it's not right. So I put my lips out and try to kiss Emma, hope it'll get the picture of Bree out of my head. But it's loud and wet and I think I caught her ear.

"Yuck. That wasn't like I wanted."

Now I got the coldness in my legs. Coldness all 'round my privates. I was supposed to kiss Emma and all I wanted was to kiss Bree. My stomach's ready to heave.

Emma is already up and marching away. And I'm thinking that for her, this was a right failure. For me, it was a right sin.

~

Johnson street. I'm wandering about after working in the livery, knowing I should turn left to go home, but all I want to do is turn right. Don't feel ready for Bree now, need to have my thoughts about Emma, and Mrs. Maynard, and being in a strange country when all I want to do is go back home.

Two Chinamen are ahead of me. They're talking, loud it seems to my ears, as they pick their way along the street like they have all day long. On their heads are egg shaped caps and on their bodies long robes that look to me like a woman's night dress. And course it makes me think of San Francisco, and the plait, full of dirt and lying on the ground, until I picked it up and got the knee in my back.

I know you told me not to be rude, Ma, but it's stone fun to walk like them. They're all agile and I like their hand movements, arms speaking words they don't have to, the bobbing here and there of their heads. So I make believe I'm Chinese and follow them.

They turn onto Cormorant Street and just as they do, one of them spins about and doesn't he see me. I'm behind the store front pole before I can say how I got here, but it's too thin and I know they can see me right and fair. They laugh, both of them with big rotten teeth smiles, so I guess they don't mind.

Got to follow them. Got to do an investigation. Got to look into where plaits go when they are still on some Chinaman's head. So, I tag along behind the men and isn't it a game we're playing now.

They stop in front of a shop that has a sign that says, "Sugar, Rice, Tea . . . " but I don't get all the way to the end of it when they dip into an alley instead.

It was done so fast I'm thinking that maybe they don't want me following anymore, but I go into the laneway all the same. 'Tis narrow, it is, I can hold my arms out and run my hands along both sides of the red bricked walls. 'Tis darker in here too, and cooler, and I like the way it feels, like a secret alley where a lad like me has no business to be.

I wonder what's down here but all the signs, they're in Chinese, and I can't say as I can see a thing through the dark windows they got. I smell tobacco and cooked rice and something sour I've never smelled before. Then wind chimes jingle on a door, telling me where they've gone. So, in the interest of the case of the plait, I slip in.

'Tis a dim shop, piles of turnips ahead of me and cans all around. I sneak now, duck behind the rows, and I'm sure the men have forgotten about me because they head for the back of the shop. I go too, slink past a young man who is packing fuzzy vegetables. Past the ancient Chinese woman with a small baby strapped on her back. Behind a table with packages of orange shrivelled candy and hard brown balls with hairy vines.

I follow them through a door that squeaks but no one comes to catch me now. It's dark in here, and I'm quiet because there's a thick mat under my feet. Takes my eyes a few minutes to get a hold of the little bit of light, but I can smell alright. 'Tis a sweet, smoky smell. Not like a fire and not like a cigarette and not like cooking, but foul and honeyed all at once.

And I'm startled near death by something furry that runs past my legs. Maybe I need to stop the game of the plait, because this is nowhere I've ever been and it doesn't seem like somewhere I ought to be. I so hope it isn't a rat and just as I plan the retreat of me, I see something that doesn't feel like it should be in the back of a shop. A row of beds. Not one bed, no, but a whole lot of them, each with a pretty mesh-like canopy like they have in those stories of Arabia. And all over them are fluffy pillows and pretty blankets, and people, too, dare I say. Chinese men, lying on their sides, curled up, sucking the end of long thin pipes. And not a one has seen me, not a soul is looking about for a lad like me. So down I go on all fours and wait till my eyes take in more.

There are small trays with coned lamps, fat sponges lying in oyster shells, long needles propped on small blocks of woods, curved knives, scissors, and boxes everywhere. They got it over Mr. Harrow's safety bag, this much is clear.

I scoot further down, and I see some boots off and all await on the floor. They're white men's boots, these are, and just as I think it, I see them. White men, down on the beds, taking in the sucking and the sighing.

I'm thinking that this is too mad to believe when I hear a sigh that I know doesn't come from a man. 'Tis a women's sigh. A woman lashed out in oriental silks and dark rich hair.

I'm not understanding a woman being here. But I see more now, Chinese women on their sides with their mouths on long pipes, and their eyes, half closed eyes, sleepy eyes.

And I'm looking at the toes on one of them, but see they are white toes, white toes peeking their way out of an Oriental dress. That's when the breath in me goes. It goes and doesn't come back for a time because I see the toes and they're talking to me, those toes are telling me a story. My eyes rove up, away from the toes, wondering if it be true. And don't I see that long body, the longer neck, the soft cheeks, the half opened grey eyes.

Bree!

I scamper, I'm up and on my way to the door and I swear never to follow a plait again. But she sees me.

"My dear Ank. Come, give me a kiss."

The fumes get thick, too thick, like smoke, like the cabin on fire.

Bree with her mouth on that pipe, her fingers calling me near. I feel a burn move down my throat. Smell the mud flats in their stink. I'm like the eagle in the forest, staring.

Everything close. Too close. I need air.

❧

She's got my arms out and is holding onto my hands, trying to teach me the steps. I can't do it like she says, not without scrunching up my shoulders and that hurts. Besides, I'm falling all over her feet and when she moves too quick, I get the dizzies.

The fringe on Mrs. Maynard's dress bounces up and down like one hand clapping and her long black dress slips over the floor, making a *shhh shhh* sound. Like someone telling me to be quiet. But she's not trying to silence me, I know so. I think she's trying to have me talk.

"Been thinking of telling you something," I say.

"Yes. Go on."

"About your photographic arts."

"Hmm, I'm very interested." But she doesn't sound so.

"It isn't proper — what I'm going to say."

"I'm not interested in you because you're proper, Ank."

"You're going to be angry some."

"Nonsense.

"I'm right when I say you're going to be cross."

"Oh Ank, just say it. You don't like my portraitures, do you?"

"No." I say.

Then she laughs, that merry laugh she has, when you realize that she doesn't give a blast whether you like her portraitures or not.

"They're mean, they are. Wicked." I tell her.

"Ah, wicked. Well, yes, some of them are wicked. They truly are."

"But I don't like them. They scare me."

"Yes, I know. That's why I'm teaching you to dance."

But I know it isn't true. The dancing bit. She isn't teaching me because I don't like the portraitures, she's teaching me because I need the other thing from her. The favour. I know she's going to give it to me, but first, she's dead set on this.

She glides me forward. *Whoosh!* Spins me around. *Whaah!* Even dips me. And then with a laugh, lets me go.

I'm standing clear in the middle of her parlour, but I'm back at sea. The room is hiding from me, because just as I look at a wall, it jumps away. I think I better sit down.

"Tea?" She asks, seeing the whiteness on my face, I'm sure.

"Please ma'am."

"Milk and sugar?"

Don't know why she asks this, she knows how I like my tea.

"Please, the two of them both."

Mrs. Maynard fixes my tea exactly how I like it. She lifts her cup, waits for me to lift mine.

"To the two of us."

"Cheers," I say

A moment of tea: her sips, my slurps. It's no trouble to drink tea with Mrs. Maynard. None of the jeering of the kettle like with Bree, so my tea is gone in a few hasty, hot gulps. Mrs. Maynard, on the other hand, she savours hers, drinks with the slow poise and all. When I look at her face, I can tell she doesn't want the conversation right now, can tell by the way her eyes look down into her cup, lost in a thought that makes her face go dark. So I look about me at the parlour and feel grand that she doesn't have me in the studio where the strangling children are.

There's portraits here too, but none of the wretched ones. Just the same little girl's face everywhere you look. Painted on two little vases, on a plate. And a photograph of her in a frame on the table. I wonder who she might be.

Mrs. Maynard puts her cup down. Think I might be able to say to her now.

"Who's the girl?"

"My daughter, Lillie."

"The one at the picnic?"

"No, the dead one."

Mrs. Maynard's lips on her cup, pursed as they are.

"Didn't know you had a dead one too."

"Yes."

"My Ma's dead. And Da. And Eoin. I know what it's like. To have them dead, that is."

"I know you do Ank. It's what makes us friends."

"What makes us friends?"

"Listening. For them." She says this so softly.

"My Ma used to talk to me, but she doesn't make a sound anymore."

"What did she say?"

"She told me about her wee baby sister dying. Rosa."

"My darling Lillie doesn't talk. She whispers." Mrs. Maynard whispers too.

"What does she say?"

"She has words only for her Momma. Besides Ank, I'd never tell."

"But you asked me! And now you won't tell me what Lillie says? 'Tisn't fair, 'tisn't."

"I was testing you. Because, it's a secret, Ank. What the dead say."

"Why?"

She takes an extra long time sip of her tea.

"It's a hidden grace." She says.

"I don't understand."

"You will, someday."

I lift my cup up to my mouth and wish it wasn't empty.

"Doesn't matter now. Ma won't talk."

"When did she stop?"

"On the ship. Because I took some of the drink from the Bellicose."

Mrs. Maynard gets up and with her sleeve wipes the dust off a vase that has Lillie's photograph on it.

"You can resume if you want."

"Resume what?"

"The conversation with your mother."

"How?"

"The same way I talk to Lillie."

I look to Lillie to see if it's true. Her mouth moves, she wants to tell me something, but of course I can't hear.

"My friends and I can help," She says.

"Like at the picnic?"

I'm recalling the circle of hand-holding people, the children afraid they would have to stand next to me, the strange outsider. Can feel that day still on my skin, a rippling, a sting. All of those folks giving name to the secret inside me. Like letting my fire out one puff at a time.

"Yes. At our next meeting. First of the month."

Lillie nods her head. She wants me to say yes.

"Can you get me into the boys school, Mrs. Maynard?"

"You're already in."

181

~

In the tub, warm water all over. Enveloped, Da might say, enveloping me. And with my head under the water, I puff up my cheeks, pop the bubbles out.

The creak in the door and it bolts me up. There she is, Bree, slinking in, and in her hand is a glass of water. I press my seat to the bottom of the tub, try to hide my privates beneath the greyish fluid.

"Need a splash on your tongue? If you're anything like me, you'll need a drink, you will. Don't you just get thirsty in the tub?"

I nod while she places the glass on the stool. And of course I wait for her to leave, but on she stays.

"No tubs in your cottage?"

"Right."

"Sponge & splash was it?"

"Except when we went to town."

She's on the floor, squatting, like the Chinese do.

"I had a bath the night I arrived. Desmond was talking outside, and the Indians offered him a baby of all the god forsaken things. Can you imagine how he would have made out with a baby?"

"Can't ma'am."

Of course I heard this one hundred times before, except sometimes the baby is for her, sometimes for Desmond.

"A brown one at that. Me, having never seen the likes of it and making my way in town with some Indian baby."

"Mmm." My knees peeking out.

"Life is hard enough. What's an Irish widow to do with a baby?"

I'm dead tired of this, I am.

"Ma'am. I don't mean to be cheeky ma'am, but I need to have the privacy, see. Because I'm a lad."

When she laughs I can see the funny hanging skin sack at the back of her mouth.

"You fancy this the Park Hotel?"

"No, but my Ma — "

"You're Ma's dead."

That's when I take a big gulp of air and lean back beneath the water. I won't come up, I'll never come up. How could she talk about you like that, with that coldness in her mouth, no less? But her fingers plunge beneath the surface, tunnel about for my arm. I punch out, I splash. I will not come up, I will stay here until —

Her arms wrenches me up.

"What did you go and say that for?" I've never made my voice so loud before.

"Ah, God love us both. We're a sorry pair."

"I know my Ma is dead. Do you think I don't know my Ma is dead?"

"Ank, don't be cross, was a mistake."

"You're full of the mistakes!"

My arm crashes into water. A splash on Bree's dress.

"Now you mind your tongue young man."

"I won't. I will not mind my tongue nor myself. Now I'm a growing lad and I need my Ma left out of my baths."

She gets up and I can see she's shocked for all the shouting coming out of me. Can see her body half twisted. One part looks like it would smack me but good, the other part wants to flee.

"Mrs. Brennan, I'll need you to leave now."

A lost look crosses her eyes, but she goes. So I lean back a third time and blow twenty seven bubbles beneath the surface of the water.

~

Emma rubs my right shoulder. She has a grand way of doing it, her fingers like small eyes that see which way to go. I groan, hope to let her know that I like it.

Emma should be in school. That place where they teach her how not to be a child anymore and prepare her to be someone's wife.

"But I shall never be someone's wife." She says this strong, like most things she says.

"Why not?"

"Because then I'll be cross all the time like my Mother."

And of course I think of you, Ma, who wasn't cross at all, and Bree, who's mostly too sleepy to be cross.

"Maybe she's cross because she's here. In the new country."

"No, silly Ank. It's because she got married."

Now she has her fingers on my neck and digs in.

"Where did you learn how to do this?" I ask.

"I made it up."

A sprinkle from a big wave comes through the logs of Emma's hut.

"If you're never going to get married, what are you going to do?"

"Have oodles of gentlemen friends and have secret hiding places and do everything that I'm not supposed to."

"Like what?"

"Like never wear the proper clothes, and always sit with my legs apart, and interrupt as many people as I care to, and chew loudly, and never make the tea and wait until someone comes and serves me."

"You're going to have to be pretty flush then."

"Then I shall."

Now her fingers are in my hair.

"And what are you going to do when you're grown up, Ank?"

"Go home."

"When?"

"As soon as I find a way."

"And then what?"

"I'll work the fields like my Da."

But in my mind, the fields are on fire. Can see it clear now, flames up and licking the sky black. Don't know why I think these things, I don't. But I sure won't be telling Emma.

"Or maybe write stories," I say, to cover up the fire.

"Irish people don't write stories do they?"

"But they do."

"Well I've never heard of any."

Now this makes me angry, her thinking we don't write the stories. Like the rest of them from England, they think they do everything there is to be done.

"If I go to Ireland, will you come and visit me?"

"No. Ireland's dirty."

"That's a fib!"

"That's what my mother told me."

"Has she been there?"

"No, but everyone knows. Ireland's dirty." She pouts some when she says this.

"'Tisn't."

"I heard."

"You heard wrong."

"But my mother — "

"Your mother is cross!"

"She is not!"

"You said as much just a minute ago."

"Ank, it's because you're Irish, you don't understand."

"I understand when someone is fibbing!"

I crawl through the opening, cross as bees, but Emma grabs my jacket and pulls me back.

"You can't go anywhere, you're my mate!"

"What's the point of having a mate if you'll never be married?"

Emma lets go. By the look on her face, I can tell that she has never thought of this before.

"You mean you can only have a mate if you're going to be married?" She asks.

"Don't they tell you anything in that school you go to?"

"Yes, but I don't listen."

"And what will happen when you aren't there today?"

"I'll tell them I am ill."

"And your mother? What will she say?"

"She's at the women's league."

And where might Bree be? Probably lying down on the bed of silk, with the sweet smoke leaking from her mouth.

"You're a very naughty girl."

"And you are a ruffian."

"You are a cur, a dog!"

"But you only call men that."

"Then what do you call girls?" And don't you just know it, I'm having to push the whore word out of my head.

"You call us 'Lady'."

"But you don't want to be a lady."

"I just don't want to be cross!"

"Take back the dirty Irish."

"I take it back."

"Swear on your life."

"I swear. Now kiss me."

So I lean forward and kiss her quick.

"Am I to feel thunderbolts?"

"Be serious, Emma."

"Am I to swagger? To swoon? Oh my dear Ank, you've come for me at last!"

She is laughing, making fun of me. So I grab her waist and pull her to me like I seen a man do with a woman outside a pub. I even open my mouth, slight like I seen. But her eyes aren't closed and neither are mine. She looks like a one-eyed monster at this close range. But I kiss her all the same. I kiss her despite Bree, who comes into my mind, wafting up my head like the suck and the sigh of a long pipe in a dark Chinese shop.

"Again," Emma says.

So I kiss her again. See Bree's toes. Her smoky eyes. Her long fingers.

"Do it again."

I kiss Emma hard. I take hold of her chin with one hand and the back of her head with the other. I kiss her lips and I kiss her cheeks, over and over again. I kiss her until I don't see Bree no more. I kiss her until I see Emma, even with my eyes closed.

<hr />

Her skin glows dark. It's shiny and smooth, like she's wearing a secret. She has the darkest eyebrows I've ever seen and her eyes, I can't right see her eyes, but I'm guessing they're black.

She has on Mrs. Maynard's old dress and she's allowed a seat in the parlour. Right beside the picture of Lillie. When I first came in, she smiled at me the way any of Mrs. Maynard's friends would, but then she opened her mouth. That's when

I seen the difference. Her teeth, rotted and knotted, give her away.

"You're da boy," She says.

Mrs. Maynard hands me a plate of cut sandwiches. I'm looking at the cucumber one and go for the jelly instead. No crusts, of course. Bree never takes off the crust, but Mrs. Maynard always does.

"Mrs. Blackman, Ank Maguire. Ank Maguire, Mrs. Blackman."

She nods without looking at me, keeps her eyes to the floor. Her body rocks in a childlike manner, but inside the folds of Mrs. Maynard's black dress, I can see she's strong as a mule, she is.

"You're da boy," she repeats.

"Yes, the Irish boy whom I spoke about. Isn't he brilliant? Look at those eyes."

I sputter because I think I need to say something and there's nothing in my head to say. But still, Mrs. Blackman doesn't take her eyes off the floor.

"He's charmed." Mrs. Maynard says.

Mrs. Maynard offers a side plate to Mrs. Blackman and I can see it is the blue and gold one that she normally keeps for herself. All over Mrs. Blackman's hands are cuts and sores and don't they look like they hurt some. I want to ask about them, and about her teeth gone black and missing, but it's in me to know not to be rude. She eats funny, too. Takes just one meat sandwich from the tray then holds her plate next to her belly, cradling it with her left hand, like she's holding a baby.

"Mrs. Blackman has a charmed tradition all her own." Mrs. Maynard says.

But Mrs. Blackman shakes her head and lifts her right hand up to indicate that Mrs. Maynard shouldn't say more.

"Ah, yes. You see Ank, Mrs. Blackman's people don't chat about such things over tea."

I don't know what the charmed tradition is, but I surely want to rock like Mrs. Blackman. I like it, the tilting to and fro, and I hope now that someone will ask me a question because I'm dying to stare at the floor and sway the way Mrs. Blackman does.

But of course no one says a word. All I can hear is tiny swallows and the tinkling of china. 'Tis a waste, 'tis. Here I am, sitting in Mrs. Maynard's parlour with a real live Red Indian and no one says a word.

Then the Bellicose comes into my head as do the Natives in Panama. And the boy who was tied to a tree and the Indian folks offering Bree a baby after she was in the baths. I'm tasting the mango again and can smell the sweating train and I'm right dying to tell it all to Mrs. Blackman, see what she thinks.

"Do you know Mr. Harrow?" I ask.

"Harrow?"

"Yes, he's married to — " I want to say 'one of you', but this is what the English say to me and I don't like it much at all.

"Mrs. Blackman is Songhees. From the village." Mrs. Maynard says.

Ah, the village across the bay with the long wooden buildings that are falling apart. Open fires near the shore. I've heard the men at the livery talk about the village and I seen the signs asking for money. For the improvement of the Indian's social and moral condition, the signs say, but somehow, no matter what, the village still doesn't change. Bree says the money goes to the government balls and the Indians see none of it, but she's an Irish widow and isn't invited to any of the balls, so how is she to know?

"What's it like there?" It's the only way in I know.

Mrs. Blackman shakes her head, but this time looks at Mrs. Maynard.

"Is it like Chinatown?" I ask.

She looks down at her half-eaten sandwich and continues to rock herself. I must be wrong, rude wrong. I must be.

"No Ank. I do believe it is quite distinct." Mrs. Maynard says.

"Are there ghosts there?"

Now Mrs. Blackman looks up at me, and for the first time, I see her eyes. They are black, blacker than I ever seen before.

"Never be afraid of ghosts. They're your ancestors."

A cold finger slides its way down my back.

Mrs. Maynard takes a large bite of her sandwich, leaking a glob of jelly at the corner of her mouth. Mrs. Blackman rocks herself again and puts her plate down on the table.

"Washing to do." And she is gone.

Mrs. Maynard picks up the serving plate and offers me another sandwich which I take, not caring what is inside.

Then there's the silence. The kind I've heard before. The kind that comes when you are thinking things too heavy for your tongue.

~

"Aren't I knackered."

She unlaces her boots and swings her legs up on the sofa.

"Ank, the fire."

I'm already at it and don't see the need for her to tell me the fire needs tending. I'm the one who keeps my eyes on it all the day, anyway. Could do without her fussing.

God help me she's got her fingers on the buttons of her dress, again, loosening them one by one. She opens her neck to the air, the cotton on her sputtering. And of course her hand reaches down and tugs at something that lies under her dress that I plain can't see.

"Could you fix me a cup of tea?"

I'm up and on my way to the cook stove, grateful to have my eyes on something but the open buttons on her dress.

"Ah Ank, you know it. I love to dream."

In the tea pot there's a heap of leaves like you'd never have left in your life, Ma. Can't imagine you abandoning them so. You'd have spread them over top of the garden, or plunked them down the lavatory, or dried them and added them to the animal's food, depending on what kind they were. You wouldn't have left them awash on the bottom of a black chipped pot that sits about with a dozen dirty plates and crumpled tea towels and bits of dried bread that have fallen to the floor and never been swept up.

But Bree doesn't care about the leaves as I do, her dress half open, hair unhooked, fingers sighing through it.

"What do you dream about Ank?"

And of course I know that she's not really wanting the answers.

"I dream about Ireland sometimes. Remember what it felt like in the early spring when the sun finally shone? Like you've been let out of a cage."

"Same thing here," I say.

"Not the same thing, not at'all. Here, it's always a cage."

"'Tis nice when it's not raining."

"'Tis never nice."

I dump the tea leaves into the bucket. I'll use them for good later, I will.

"Is Mr. Harrow coming today?" she asks.

"Indeed. 'Tis Monday."

"Ah good, perhaps Mr. Harrow and I can play cards."

She lifts the bottom of her dress up to her knees and rolls her stockings down one at a time. I'm looking at the tea still, trying to keep my eyes on the tea.

"Be a love and roll these up for me."

She holds the stockings up, lets them sway some, and I can see where her foot shape is. The scent of her free to mushroom in the air.

"I don't see it's a boy's job."

All she does is rub her eyes.

"Together, not separate please. And Ank, make sure your fingernails don't catch."

And aren't I rolling the stockings up into a neat ball, though this is no work for a lad, it isn't.

"Mr. Harrow is grand, don't you think Ank?"

"He's grand."

"I like him despite the fact he's English."

"Indeed."

"And despite the fact he's thin and gangly."

"Indeed."

"And despite that perfectly miserable stutter."

"Indeed."

"And despite the fact he's English."

"You've noted that one already."

"Ah, yes. So I have, so I have."

She closes her eyes and rubs her bare legs together.

"I so love to dream."

She dozes off, without so much as a mere sip of her tea, so I take the cup myself and drink it down, make sure it doesn't go to waste and all. And I'm sleepy just for looking at her, and for the fact that only babies and Bree sleep during the day. Can't imagine sleeping during the day when there's good work to be done. I couldn't even close my eyes with the mess staring me down the way it is, the books piled atop each other near the end of the sofa, the jumble of dirty clothes waiting to be washed on the morning table, the open container of ivory gloss starch on the counter, with splashes of it ebbing, and —

And it's almost like I heard you there. *Quit the cheek and get up and do the chores.*

Takes me an hour it does, doing the chores of a woman who's set on sleep. But it keeps me right busy until Mr. Harrow knocks on the door. I answer it with a finger to my lips, warning him not to wake Bree. Almost like she hears me, she moans, rubs her legs some more and turns to the other side.

'Tis Roman history today, preparing me for the school. Mr. Harrow says I have some catching up to do so they don't think me an Irish fool, and I'm right pressed on making it so. I study the centurions and testudos and javelins weighted with lead, while Bree shifts and softly smacks her lips together.

I'm with the Emperors and all those Caesar's that get me mixed up and Bree is here from nowhere with her arms wound around Mr. Harrow's neck. He blushes right pink, of course, but doesn't push her away as she puts her lips on his neck and kisses him, the gape of her dress flung open wide, her bare skin rubbing on his wool jumper.

So I make to leave, but she grabs me, she does. Plants a wide, wet kiss on my lips and lingers there, opening her mouth to let out my name.

"Ank."

Her eyes, wet with sleep, so near me.

"Mrs. Brennan!"

'Tis Mr. Harrow now, who didn't complain till she lit on me. He pulls her off, yanks her down to the chair. She just holds her head in her hands, and laughs and laughs and laughs.

She's severed off my head. It sits on a white marble block now.

Then there's my eyes, tripled. Gleaming from a plant, peering up from the floor, glimpsing out of a teapot. She calls it, "Ank, searching." It's her current favourite and it's surely the most haunting thing I've ever seen.

"It is a perfect photosculpture. I shall display it proudly."

I just nod. When she's fed like this, there's nothing that can take away her appetite, not that I'd even try. But I feel mean guilty for bringing Emma here. She's off in the studio, where the laughing pictures are, probably not even scared. I still won't go in there, but Mrs. Maynard doesn't seem to mind. She set me up in the parlour, near the table in the corner, where Lillie is.

"Ready to help me?" She asks.

I call for Emma, and in she comes, a regal lift to her head.

Mrs. Maynard first twirls her fingers through Emma's blonde hair, looping the rings around and around, reinforcing them the way she does. Then she positions Emma's hand above her eyes as if she is peering out, far across the horizon.

"Good. Now, with your other arm, hold the flowers, but let them droop ever so slightly."

I help Mrs. Maynard with the painted backdrop — the flat house front with the window looking right real — and we place it in front of Emma. Now she really looks like she's watching and waiting, lonely like, as Mrs. Maynard wants her.

"Round the back, make sure those legs are all the way out, Ank."

'Tis my job to make sure the back supports are resting on the floor, square and proper. Mrs. Maynard reaches through the cut out window to Emma. She hauls Emma closer to the window, tilts her body slightly, adjusts the flowers some, cocks her head.

"So you're Ank's friend."

"Yes."

"And in what kind of folly and mischief do the two of you engage?"

"I like boys."

"Yes," Mrs Maynard says, and she cranes her head to see me, "And little Irish Ank rather seems to like girls."

Emma giggles. Me, I'm glad I'm behind the backdrop caring for the back supports, that's what I'm glad of.

"Now Ank, as soon as those legs are steady, come here. When I am ready, I want you to do as I say. Yes, my little leprechaun friend?"

She dips beneath the black cape of the camera, then pops up, holding a cord.

"Now, pinch Emma's cheeks."

"Pardon, ma'am?"

"Go on, for the look. Emma, keep your hand above your eyes. Remember, you are waiting, forlorn, your heart is heavy. Pinch Ank!"

I'm waiting to do the pinch but my hand is frozen for the likes of Emma.

"Now Ank!"

I feel a hot river down my front, but I do what Mrs. Maynard says.

"The other cheek now, go on. Quite hard."

I clear don't want to, but I go on, and doesn't it bring a sting to Emma's eyes. It's when they're glistening with the tears, that's when Mrs. Maynard lets the camera go off.

But Mrs. Maynard isn't satisfied with just the one. She wants me to pinch her again. Again and again, until Emma begins to cry. That's when she asks me to lie down in front of the set, with Emma crying and me reaching up to her. It isn't right, to make a girl cry just for a picture, so I pop up to give Emma a wee peck on the cheek and I can't help it, I see it in her eyes. All wet and searching, like your eyes. Your eyes after you were dead.

~

I've been worried about this.

Bree dazed by Christ Church Cathedral, all that mammoth grey stone that sprouts up to the sky. And doesn't she love that cloister balcony. Which she reaches for, trying to swing her legs up, climb in.

"Rakes of 'em nuns must have come out here to get some air."

Mrs. Maynard is walking towards us, her head at a slight tilt. Her cheeks look puffy from this distance and the heavy lines of her eyebrows look like they're joined. But there's nothing I can do. She's seen us.

"Downright hooley they must have had out here, those nuns."

I just know that Bree is fancying herself one of the nuns, pretending she slipped out into the stone alcove for a breath of fresh air after too much dust and God. She's failing something miserable at her attempts to climb up the stone wall, though. She has her arms through the slates and is on her tip toes, when Mrs. Maynard arrives.

"You must be Mrs. Brennan."

When Bree turns, her cheek bears a crease of brown dirt from the wet stone. She deadens, looks Mrs. Maynard's burly frame up and down.

"I'm Mrs. Maynard." She bows her head a bit, in greeting.

I squeeze my eyes shut. I don't want to be here, don't want Mrs. Maynard to meet Bree, or Bree to meet Mrs. Maynard for that matter. I'm dead embarrassed of Bree, Ma. Maybe, just maybe, if I can hold my eyes tight enough, they might both just go away.

"You are who?" Bree says this, so rude, Ma. I guess I have to open my eyes.

"I've met your little Ank."

"Then you must know he isn't *my* little Ank."

"Ah, so you wish it to be clear."

Bree still has her arm extended into the stone cranny. Mrs. Maynard looks over to it, then her eyes wander up the face of the church.

"It's beautiful inside. Have you ever been?"

"I'm not of the faith."

"Regardless, it's most impressive."

"It's grand I'm sure, but the answer is no." Bree still has the rough voice.

"Very well then. I am less interested in the religion than in the architecture myself."

"I am interested in neither."

I'm crazy ashamed of her, of Bree, I am. What if Mrs. Maynard knew that Bree spent her days in Chinatown, lying about, inhaling those fumes? In front of Mrs. Maynard, Bree seems like a dress half made.

"Where did you meet Ank?" The question I was hoping no one would ask. And don't Mrs. Maynard just lie for me.

"At the livery. We keep our carriage there."

"I'm sure."

"And Ank has been good enough to take care of the horses in a most expert manner."

"I'm sure."

"He's a wonderful young man."

"Mmm."

Bree has finally let go of the wall and now grasps the front of her brown dress.

"Mrs. Brennan, would you like a portraiture?" Mrs. Maynard inquires.

I blurt it out. "No!" A secretive smirk moves across Mrs. Maynard's face.

"I am referring, of course, to a proper parlour portraiture as I have done with many of this city's fine folks."

"No." Bree tells her.

"Why not, may I ask?"

"I'm not interested, at'all. At'all."

"But it would be a gesture of our appreciation for how well Ank has taken care of our horses."

I need to stop this. I can just see Bree sitting atop a grave with another image of her spirit hovering like an angel overhead.

"No!" I say.

"Why Ank?" Mrs. Maynard is chaffing me with her eyes.

"Because we believe in the bad luck."

"Ah, the Irish believe this, do they? Have you been talking to the Indians?" Mrs. Maynard is looking at me and reminding me with her eyes that I've met Mrs. Blackman.

"'Tis true. The village priest back home said so."

"Ank, stop this nonsense about the bad luck." Bree's cross.

"The bad luck. Like knowing the weather will be bad when a cat sits with her tail to the fire. Or dropping an umbrella on the floor means a murder will happen. Or meeting a nun or a monk on your wedding day means you'll be barren. Or if a dead person's eyes are left open, they'll find someone to take with them. Or the spouse who goes to sleep first on the wedding night will die first."

I've said the wedding night thing before I had my thoughts right and Bree's eyes are already narrow.

"Well, I am quite amused by this. I have certainly learned something of the Irish today."

Mrs. Maynard is trying not to laugh, I can just see it. Then she says, "I shall leave now. Thank you so much for your edification of all things Irish," and I'm wanting to howl with the shame in me.

Just when I'm all glad to see her go, don't Bree stop her.

"Mrs. Maynard?"

"Yes?"

"Do you keep a rifle in your home?"

This is something I haven't seen before, Mrs. Maynard surprised.

"Yes, yes we do. My husband — "

"I just wanted to know."

Mrs. Maynard is pausing, trying to make Bree out.

"Ank has never used a rifle," Bree says.

"I suppose there hasn't been an opportunity."

"Will your husband teach him?"

Mrs. Maynard nods.

"In lieu of the portraiture?"

She nods again.

"Then, I thank you. Ta."

For the first time Bree looks polite at Mrs. Maynard.

"I understand. No Father — "

"Yes, Ank's Da is dead. No Father, as you say. And here, on the edge of this forest, it seems so wise for a young boy to know how to manage a rifle, don't you think?"

"Yes."

"After all, some day, he just might have to help put me out of my misery."

But as Bree says this, she is smiling. Smiling in that sleepy, undressed way that she has. "It was a privilege to meet you." And she turns and walks away.

Mrs. Maynard nods at me and walks in the other direction. For a moment, I don't know which one I should follow. I want to call out to both of them. Both of them. Shout: didn't you hear what I said. That if a dead person's eyes are left open, they'll find someone to take with them!

Your eyes, Ma. Your eyes open and wanting someone to take away.

～

'Tis the parlour, lit by a clan of candles, placed in a circle on the floor. Chairs pushed into a tight loop, all curtains drawn. Not enough light to see my way good, so I bump into a stool as I bumble my way to the chair Mrs. Maynard has for me.

Then a hand on my ankle scaring me near blind.

Takes a moment for me to see her, but it's Mrs. Blackman, down on the floor on her hands and knees. Hunkering in the darkness. Waiting. I don't think anyone else knows she's here. She's hiding, she is, scurrying about underfoot. Like a rat near my leg in a Chinese shop where long smoking pipes make the likes of Bree lazy.

It isn't until we're all seated that she rises. Makes the others shudder, makes them gasp. No one but me knowing she was here.

She has a small drum, held in her china cup hand, the other palm open and beating. 'Tis a haunting sound. Ba-bum. Ba-bum. Ba-bum. The sound that comes across the water from the Indian village when their fires burn high.

Mrs. Blackman walks around the circle, and it isn't till she's in the light of the candles that people can see who she is. A woman near me huffs, stands up and leaves. I know why it is, there's an Indian in the parlour room and some of them don't like it at all. But Mrs. Blackman continues to beat her drum.

A gentleman clears his throat. Someone rustles their shoes. Ba-bum, Ba-bum, Ba-bum, and I can feel that they're waiting for Mrs. Maynard and have had enough of the beating of the drum.

Mrs. Blackman begins to moan. Rhythmic it is, low, heavy, like an animal defending its lair. She circles the group again, the sound of her voice rising up, growling louder, higher.

No one dares to speak. Then some whispering and a man and his wife that I've seen in one of the portraits stand up brashly and take their leave. Mrs. Maynard appears once they've gone and moves the chairs out of the way, as if she had been waiting for them to go. Mrs. Blackman's voice high and screeching, a wail, almost a keening.

Mrs. Maynard sits in the chair beside me, takes hold of my hand, grabs too tight like the day at the picnic. On my other side is a woman who smells loudly of lilac, she takes my hand too, but her touch is soft, unsure. All around the circle, hands together, the whole lot of us silent, ears keen to the drum.

Then Mrs. Blackman speaks in a language that sounds like clicks to me. I can see only the whites of her eyes in the darkness while she goes on and on with a chant in her alien tongue. She puts her drum down, lifts her hands to the ceiling. A howl, a long high plea that makes my feet go cold.

Mrs. Maynard breaks the hand holding, goes down on her knees. Speaks so soft I cannot hear. A man with a too-thick moustache joins her, he too on his knees, his hands in prayer, mouth moving.

Mrs. Blackman takes up the drum again, beats it. Rain at the window. People begin to wail.

"Lillie!"

"Peter!"

"Heather and John!"

Everyone calling out names, dead people's names. Some bellow them out, some whisper them, then drop to their knees. The drum beat goes on, and an old woman begins to cry. Mrs. Maynard pounds the floor with her hands in time to the drum.

Then a call, rising above the rest, Mrs. Blackman's open mouth, silencing us. Everyone quiet, obedient, taking hold of the hands again.

"Show us." Mrs. Maynard's voice low, so low.

All the candles go out at once, and not a soul is near them.

"They are here."

But I can't see a thing. The room is too quiet, all these bodies in a circle and just barely breathing. And the rain. The rain outside. And then the cries and the mumbles and the whispers to people who are invisible to me. Long minutes like a night on a ship at sea.

"They are gone," Mrs. Maynard says.

Everyone a 'flutter, talking about the visits. Who came. Who didn't. Everyone talking about the words of the dead, whispered in their ear. Everyone but me.

⁓

They're wearing identical white frocks. Hideous, the whole lot of them. But there they sit, each of them at a wooden table, books open.

I need to smudge the window to see. The matron is moving about the classroom, peering over the shoulders of the girls, her large bosom swaying like an old dogs head. Shuffle shuffle, sway sway. It makes me want to howl.

I can't see Emma and I'm worried that if I don't spot her soon, I'm going to get caught. So I rub at the murky window some more, breathe a small circle of the glass to life and look again. Still no Emma. And it's cold out here.

I step off the wedge of wood that I was using as a foothold and pull my cap further down my head. I'll lurk about the Academy grounds, I will. Wait for her beneath the trees.

It's me and a large pine and the book Mr. Harrow gave me. Written by an Irish man no less and aren't I dying to show it to Emma who still thinks that everything that was written came from England. I'm trying to memorize the words so I can repeat them to her but get distracted by a cat that is trying to butt its head against my leg. I decide it's a girl cat, as this is the Academy grounds and all. She has two half ears, both of them jagged and rough. I rub the ends of them and wonder how they got torn off and doesn't she just roll over on her belly, demanding more.

A spit or two of rain. Then a bucket full, a tub full, the sky dousing. I'm glad for the tree and though it's cold, I'll keep up the wait. Believing, the way I do, that Emma will appear.

But she doesn't. As I take my leave doesn't that cat purr and meow and go beneath a nearby tree and yowl the louder.

"Go home. Go home kitty." I'm scared to leave her here, not knowing where she lives and all.

The cat sniffs beneath a bush, meows with news, back arched. I bend down to shoo it away and meet Emma's eyes. She is huddled, knees to her chin, eyes dark.

"Emma!"

"Go away Ank."

"What's you doing? Come out of there."

"Go home Ank."

"Why weren't you in school today?"

"You need to leave Ank."

"C'mon Emma, you promised the friends for life."

Nothing but the silence again.

There is something about Emma under the tree that makes me have wobbly knees. Like the goat I found in Galway, hoofs cut by sharp wire. I got the bad feeling in me again and I'm not liking the sound of my gut.

I reach for her, trying with all my might to pull her out, but she flails at me, tries to ward me off with swats and punches. Finally, she bites me, but doesn't break my skin. I pull my arm out, see her blood on me. Some of it fresh red, some of it dry, crusty.

I'm down on all fours, grabbing for her, demanding she come out. She's stopped the protesting and now she doesn't say a thing, just lets out some soft cries and moans. Finally lets me pull her out.

The rain beats down on both of us and I can clear see why she was hiding. Her eyes are purple and red, a blood stain jaunts down her cheek. An open cut, thick and even, scores her chin.

I try to hold her, to hug her, but she won't let in my touch.

"Who did it to you?"

She shakes her head.

"Tell me! Was it your Ma?"

Emma turns her head away.

"Why here? Why not at your hideout down at the beach?"

Finally Emma speaks. "You'd find me there."

"Well I found you here, so let me help you. I got things at home. From Mr. Harrow's kit. Let me."

Emma is standing, unsteady.

"You need to clean that." I point at her chin.

But Emma is up and running half-sideways, half-forward away. I make after her but the shadow comes back, the shadow near my ribs. It staggers me, and I lose my balance. The cloud in my head gets altogether too thick while Emma gets away.

~

Early morning light stings through the window, wakes me. I roll over, pull the wool blanket up, tuck it beneath my chin. Pretend I'm asleep in case Bree enters.

And she does, with a soft push on the door. Pads over to me with the gingered steps, surveying. She pauses for a full minute or two, stares. Then she puts her cold, early-morning hand on me. And says it.

"Ank, my little man, rise and shine."

It's always 'my little man', which I sorely don't like. Sounds like a kind of needing to me, an expectation.

She sits on the edge of the bed. I still pretend to be asleep, but she puts her hand on my feet and cups my toes all the same. Just cups them, nothing else, but there she sits, in what I imagine is a slice of morning light. Can't be sure, of course, because my eyes are still squeezed shut and I'm still pretending to be asleep.

"Rise up my little man."

There it is again. So I open my eyes, feign a yawn, stretch.

"Are you awake? I was just thinking," She says.

"About what?"

"About what on earth I'm going to do with you."

This doesn't sound good to me, it doesn't. Sounds like I'm a fence she's meaning to tear down because it's too far gone for mending.

"Nothing to do, it's all been done."

She tilts her head to the side, licks a hair that creeps at the side of her mouth.

"'Tisn't enough."

I don't understand that. What about home, if she can remember the life before this. There it was enough for a boy to learn some school, do the chores, be a companion to others, have a bite of free time on the side. She wants me gone, she does. So she can lie about in Chinatown.

I pull myself up in the bed to say as much but she slides her arm up the bed along with me, still cupping my toes. Her hand on me takes my tongue away.

"What about up North a' ways?"

"Where might you be meaning?"

"The bush. Blasting trees and the like."

Bellicose and the sting of the drink and the talk of whores. I shake my head no.

"I want to learn."

"Yes, Ank Maguire, but sometimes you must do what it is you must do."

"I'll not go. I'm starting the school soon, the one the proper boys go to."

"Yes, Mr. Harrow has been promising."

"Please then, Auntie Bree, you'll let me stay?"

"Don't you know that we all want something we can't have? That is what being alive is all about."

"But we need to chase them. The dreams, I mean."

"Ah, we chase them, we fail. We chase them, they run away. We chase them, they turn around and beats us good about the face."

I can only think to swallow because there's a pain in my throat.

"You want this and that, all of us do. But that's not the way we know. 'Tisn't the Irish way, is it?" She asked the question, but her gaze is out the window, not at me.

"There, it's all misery and sweat and Jesus. Do you remember, Ank? There's no catching the dream there, and there isn't here either, if the truth be known."

My chest is all hot and tight.

"Have I made you go to the masses here? I haven't. And God knows, your mother is cursing me from Jesus' right hand side, she is. But still I didn't make you go. Though the religion would do you good."

"Why haven't you made me go?"

"Cause it's in me to think, religion, it's not for the wee ones. Not for children."

"But if we die — "

"I'm not talking the baptism, boy. No, all of you should be good and baptised, but the duties, say, the attendance, the Latin, it's not for the likes of small people. So I didn't make you go. But cursed with shame I am. My father would have had my eyes plucked. My brother would have said it was a feckin' sin."

"Is it a feckin' sin?"

"Mind your tongue!"

And we both laugh, Bree and I, laughing! For this sweet Jesus time, she's crawled out of her dark cave and she's laughing. I so want it to go on, to continue right along, so don't I try to keep up with her joke.

"And you mind your manners with your hand on my boyhood, whore!"

But now she's not laughing, and neither am I. I can't believe that word slipped from my mouth. The drinking man's word. Bellicose's word. I didn't even mean it. And now she's red and tight and standing up. Now she's picking up my shoe and coming for me, swatting at my head. I got my arms over me so I can't see her but I can hear her voice and it isn't right. I hear pants and chokes and it seems like her voice is caught way far down.

"I'm sorry, I was only keeping the laugh — "

And now her voice comes.

"Ah, a whore I am! Is that what your young maleness says! Oh, you grand, wise old man. You know right enough. Like my father and my brothers when I set sail on that goddamn slave boat for brides. Too much drink and too many grand hopes they had for me and when I didn't listen, out came the same old words. Did you know, Mr. Ank, that I gave them up for here. For you? You think I wanted to stay in this treed hell? This grand passion of nothingness? This bloody English purgatory of feigned pomp and circumstance? Do you know why all those people are here, Ank? Not because they were admired and respected at home, but because they weren't. Bloody England was glad to be rid of the whole lot of them. Outcasts, they are. And you know what they do here? Petty fecking pretending. Pretending they are important. They throw dancing balls where everyone is so bored their eyes bleed but no, oh no, they will tell you it was lovely, lovely. You want to be like that? Lose the Irish in you? Lose the strength that centuries have given you? You ungrateful lad!"

I have my arms over my head still, to ward off the blows the shoe is banging out.

"Bree! Please."

"Ah, Bree me, will you? Like the men, like the other men! I'll tell you right now Ank Maguire, men are nothing but stallions in fine dress. The lot of you wouldn't know a genuine thought from some crock that you all learned at school. Your Ma had the sight, you know that? How many men do you think have the sight, Ank? Feckin' none! And do you know why? Because you all figure you're too grand for it. The whole lot of you, thinking you're too grand to know the truth when the blasted truth is right before your eyes and you're blind to it. Ah Jesus, we know who the real men are. We know 'tis the women. And the problem is that most men know that too, but keep on with the feigning. The folly of it! We're all actors in a play we cannot stop, even though we no longer believe our lines. Bleeding stupid it is. And you're one of them."

The shoe is thrown against the wall. I'm deep under the bed clothes, arms still over my head. I wait in the silence, but I don't hear her leave. She's still out there, breathing into the room. I need to wait her out.

A minute. Two minutes. How I wish she had the sweet smoke in her now.

"I wanted to go back! To Ireland. But no, they wrote, stay and take the boy in. He's lost everyone. He needs the new start in the new country. So, I did. And this is where I am now. With you. A bastard boy with the mouth of a miner. I should have told them push you off the ship."

Heavy breathing. A kick against the wall.

"Do the world a goddamn favour and never become a man!"

The door slammed. Bree gone.

～

The fire crackles as do the pages of my book. The whole room trying to fill the silence of me and Bree. The two of us silent, days now.

I fancy the book, 'tis big and heavy and thick. Can use it against her. Not as a weapon, mind, but as distraction. From the quarrel without words we're in the middle of.

The book is filled with pictures. Diagrams, Mr. Harrow says, of all sorts of things medical that I mean to put into my brain. Splints, slings and best of all, scalpels. These are my favourites. I favour their sharp lines, their lean, straight cutting edges. I'd fancy to have a scalpel in my hand, I would. Hold it steady, cut long and deep and narrow. Like a doctor would, like a man would. A fecking good-for-nothing man.

And the bandages. Aren't no diagrams of those, but there's a description of how to bandage up a limb that's injured. I remember the feel of them on my arms and head the day Bellicose came. How when I pulled tight, the hairs on my arms sang. How inside it feels all warm and together.

Bree bangs a pot on the stove. It's my new call to tea, these strikes and thumps and thuds. Meals now a new war of slurps and crunches. Agony, it is, the great silence we have. What with all those words I can hear welling up in her head that she won't shout. 'Tis like reading a whole book you pretend you never heard of.

So it gets me wondering what she would do if I ignored her. Would it push her some, force her to speak? Would she untether her lips and once and for all let the rant go? I'd like that, like the clearing of it all. So I go on with the reading.

She hits a glass jar with a silver knife. I don't care a blast. I ignore her solid, concentrate on the bandages. What I'd do for a good thick one now. But there isn't no bandages around here, so I look for a stand in, a replacement, say.

Take up the newspaper, think maybe a strip of that would do me up right. Rip thin lines from the Colonist, following the instructions in the book. Says they need to be straight, they do, long and straight.

She clangs a wooden spoon on the counter but good.

The newspaper strip is on my arm. I tuck the end in, fold it under, but blast if it doesn't tear as soon as I move my arm. Need something else, something thick and pliable. My mind rests on the linen, the one from Ireland that was supposed to be the wedding present of Bree and Desmond. It's in the chest and aren't I sneaking to snatch it up. I wrap it about my leg, taking pains to twist and pull the way the book tells me, the way Mr. Harrow showed me.

She lifts a pot and crashes it against the cooker.

But the linen is bulky, I need something else. And don't I just think of the perfect thing.

I know she's watching me, but bolt for the door is what I do. She'll come, silent of course, pull me to tea. So around the house I go, cower behind the woodshed. And in just three breaths, she's on the path, all a' scour for me. I shrink back, watch her open the door of the outhouse, then I take my mark, and run to the house. Make for her bedroom, for what I need.

On the ledge, hanging limp over the edge of the bed frame, that's it. Her one pair of stockings.

I have them in my hand and rush back to my room. She comes into the house, on the search for me still. I don't know where to put the stockings so she doesn't take them back, so I stuff them down my trousers.

She sees.

I try to get out, slip on past her, but she nabs me, she does. Looks me hard in the eye, then opens her mouth and breathes in my face.

"You're a man, are you Ank?"

I dare say she's spoken. First words from her in three long days. I'm staring at the ruffled weave of dress that is pulled over her breasts. 'Tis all I can see as she faces me, as she pushes herself into me. Grabs me by the neck and with her other hand, undoes the top button of my trousers.

I know I should be pushing her back, turning away. But I stay. There's a man in me that's dying to know what a woman might do.

She slips her hands down and slowly, far too slowly, tugs on those stockings. All the while with her mouth close to mine, so I can feel her breath on me, the scent of green apples.

It's far too slow for me. I'd rather she make haste, tear the stockings out fast, but she draws them up with ever the slow hand, smiling all the while.

Can hear the fire crackle. Can smell the bread in the oven. Can see her mouth big and open. Can feel my privates tickle. Then the last of the slow pull is over.

"Ah," she purrs. "A man indeed."

And she leaves the house to chop more wood.

⁓

Emma gone, along with her mother. The two of them packed up and disappeared. My friend for life gone and not a word of goodbye nor a note to tell me where she might be.

The ocean doesn't know what to say, but I ask anyway. I stare hard at the jagged peaks across the water, mountains in another country. Inside Emma's hideout, without Emma, filled with as many pieces of dry wood as I can manage. Piled up, lots of space for oxygen. Multi-layered.

I wonder what Eoin would make of this place, this wooden hovel at the bottom of the hill. If he was here, we would have dashed across the cliff above, wavered at the edge of the bluff, pretend pushed each other off the way we did at home. Home, where the mud and sand give way to water. Just water. No mountains, no foreign country.

The water that Eoin said he wanted to die in, so that he would never have to leave home. But it wasn't to be. He didn't walk brave into the depths at the end of his life like he always said he would, all content and well. He was a lad, a mere lad, sliced out of life, all ablaze. His body broken by the weight of charred rafters.

I'm cold, Ma. The wind, it slips through the cracks in the hideout, clams onto my skin. But I won't move. I want to be here, close to Eoin, close to Da, close to you. In Emma's secret place.

So I bring out the safety matches. Stolen from Bree's shelf above the cook stove. I light a match, but the ocean air blows it out. Another swipe and the second match burns for a beat, then fizzles. You died warm, didn't you Ma, so warm? I strike the third match, bend my body over it, light the kindling. It fizzles, threatens to go out, but the wind shifts, inflames it.

In the orange glow, I feel Eoin. His slight lisp, running after me, calling out brother jeers. I feel Da, reading by the fire, spending his eyes on the books. I feel you. Calling to me. Calling me home.

The wood warms me all the way through. Warmth in my toes, blood rushing, neck heated, cheeks aglow. Finally, I'm warm and so close to the lot of you. This is what you felt like, isn't it? This is what happened? Asleep, the lot of you, rafters afire and smoke in your lungs?

Ma, I love you Ma. Bitten with the love as you'd say. Da, you're grand. Stone glad you were my Da. Eoin, you're cracked altogether. How I miss you.

And in the heat, you're here for me, you are. All of you, so near, warming me. A small shanty fire, bathing me in you. Burning me with Ma and Da and Eoin.

Nine

~

Constance and Ank
London, England
1899 -1900

ON DECEMBER 31, 1899, WITH ONLY four hours left before midnight, Constance begins a throbbing voyage through the flat. Unable to speak through her pain, her arms beckon Ank, her fingers demand his bent back. She slumps over him, riding out each contraction on his bumpy spine.

Her own lower back screams with a thousand demands. With nimble fingers, Bridget presses and strokes, streaming the pain out of its locked knots, begging it to break up and dispel.

Constance howls and even to her own ears, the sound is like a feral cat. She is exhausted, dangerously tired, lost in the ceaseless rise and fall of sizzling agony. Inside, she is bathed in a hot halo of fire. She knows she must push, but outside, on her skin, she is cold, so cold she fears that she will freeze up, crystallize.

Ank and Bridget are now just blurred movements, sweeps of light. Ank is speaking to her, giving measured instructions, but his voice is lost somewhere in her ear. A tunnel of stuffed cotton. The Mali's blue-tipped material stuffed inside. Sun blindness. Sun deafness.

She is worried she cannot complete this job, cannot do what women throughout all of time have done. Perhaps she should give up. Quit. Cease this pain and walk through life with a child half out of her, too tired to finish the job.

She knows they want her to push harder. But harder does not exist. There is no more strength in her. No vigour left. The teeth of birth bite with insatiable hunger.

This will all be over with soon, a song like a children's rhyme. She repeats it through the crowning, through the breakthrough of a head, the ceaseless rhythm not stopping even as Ank pulls the baby out and holds him in the air. At two minutes past midnight.

It is Elvin, a wet mass of red skin and tangled black hair who remains silent despite the encouraging pats that Ank gives him to start breathing. Elvin has plans of his own, his lungs filled with embryonic fluid, his eyes refusing to open wider than a slit. It is clear from the first moments of life that Elvin is not going to co-operate with any of them. He is obstinately holding on to the other side, not interested in this new adventure. He is angry to be born and isn't going to give up his rage easily.

Ank smacks his back and strokes his little chest to warm his lungs and dispel some of the fluid. Bridget shoves the suction bulb in his mouth, sopping up the pea green mucus that paves his tongue. It is chaos, but Constance, with yet another baby determined to emerge, is too busy to notice any of it.

Seconds roar past them and Elvin is still refusing to breath. Ank begins to panic, his hand on the baby's back a paddle on blue skin. Constance calls out, tries to draw their attention to the next baby that now juts out of her, but their panic deafens them. They are not aware of Samuel as he pushes his way into the world. Undeterred by the pandemonium, he forces his own head through the birth canal. Twisted to one side, Constance catches the gleam of a skull and a tiny, perfectly shaped ear.

It is only when Constance thrashes her arm and squeals does Ank and Bridget turn to her. They have to, for Constance's arm hits Ank's and Elvin is now on the floor. Dropped with a thud on the wood. Bang! And breathing begins.

Samuel, from his very first moments of life, is markedly more cooperative than his elder brother. He lets out a robust wail and with his hands in little fists, swings deftly at the air to prove he is master of his birth.

They are a study in contrasts, and Constance loves them both. She loves them for ten long minutes before she falls into a sudden sleep of exhaustion and relief.

~

Ceylon is riding away, down Snowsfields road, with Elvin on his back. Despite just being born, Elvin is sitting up on Ceylon, holding onto the reins. He waves to me.

I run after them. Wait! But I cannot run very quickly, because there is blood flowing down my legs and I am sore, more sore than I have ever been before. The blood is very dark, and is clotted, like a syrup that keeps me stuck. It is congealing down my leg, cloaking my bare feet. When I look, there are little hands and feet stuck out of it, babies' limbs. They are hanging onto the massed blood, sticking out like kippers in a fishing net.

I try to scream for my baby, but my voice is small. There is a hand over my mouth. Father is here. I try to push his hand away. I must call after Ceylon, the horse is taking Elvin away.

Father's hands take a firmer grip, pushing my cheeks into my teeth. Tear, rip. Tender skin splitting. But I cannot think of my mouth. I must think of Father, watch Father. His skin moulting, turning from an arm into the body of a snake. A serpent over my mouth.

Then it comes to me. I must wake up, I must wake up, that's it. This is a dream and I can get away from him if only I am able to wake up. But the mali stops me.

"One minute, one minute. Dream girl is hurry, same as before."

He smiles at me, and I want to scream, "I must get my son!", but he leans forward, so slowly, too slowly, and whispers in my ear. My ear that I know is so perfect, so tiny.

"Rising snakes tell you when dreams come true."

Constance opens her eyes. Bridget is standing before her, her cheeks bloated with anguish, holding Elvin.

He won. Elvin went back to where he came from, refusing to embrace his life. He won.

〰

Bubbles of spit blossom out the side of Samuel's mouth. Eyes are wide and watchful.

Constance has to vie with Bridget and Ank for turns to hold him, and between the three of them, Samuel is cradled nearly every minute of the day. Constance says this is important. He can't be alone. He can't think they've abandoned him. He's been alive three weeks now and he mustn't be given any indication that life here isn't good. Give him no reason to leave.

Outside on the streets the century has turned and Constance thinks that Sammy's birth is a harbinger of luck. His soft belly that she loves to rub with her lips tells her that things are different now. She has defied her physical ailments, refused to supplicate the doubting medical staff, broken loose of the curses that followed her from one, at least, disapproving nurse. And given birth. Despite 'the complications'.

Sammy has shown them. She has shown them. They are the winning team.

Having Sammy laugh and kick means that Constance doesn't have to think about Elvin. The dead one. The one that got away. He was just a tease, an appetizer, an enticement to stay for the feast.

"He wasn't meant for the earth," Bridget tells her. "Some babies just come to see what all the fuss is about. They really don't want to stay and grow up."

Constance acknowledges this with a smile, but doesn't believe her. She keeps thinking of the moment that Elvin began to breath. Didn't he look her in the eye, see who his mother was, flatly reject her?

When she thinks this, a stinging comes. A sting that creates the buzzing in her ear, the high pitched wail. Like the one she heard just before the horse let its leg plummet into her, crush her. Crush out Elvin, the future Elvin, knocking him through a hole in the sky. Back to the place babies go.

Her thoughts move to her own mother, already dead as Constance's tiny frame was pulled from a rapidly chilling womb. Like a kitten, wet and blood soaked, lifted up by a strong pair of hands from a sinking ship. Mother going down, baby floating to the surface. Head pitched above water to hear the words of Father for a lifetime. "It should have been you."

Ank is playing with Sammy, he rubs his lips across Samuel's forehead, kisses the end of his nose, whispers stories. Constance can guess they are stories that Ank heard from his own mother. Filled with magical this and that. Filled with promise. Filled with none of the rubbish that fills her head. Like where Elvin is, where dead babies go. She says this to Ank. He does not answer her. Instead, he leans over and whispers to Samuel.

"The children, after they die, they don't stay the same. What I mean is that they don't stay the age they died at, see? Everyone thinks that. That if they died at three, they'll always be three, but it don't work that way. See, they grow there. Dead children, they grow in Spirit."

~

Constance asleep, Ank holds Samuel in a sliver of moonlight that slides through the window. Listening to the rise and fall of the baby's breath. His mind with Ma. Her voice still silent, despite bringing Bridget into the flat, despite the birth of his own child, despite his love for Constance.

Ma, where are you Ma, speak to me.

Ank's mind floats back to the ship, to the scald of whiskey in his throat. *Was that it? Was that what scared her voice away?* So many years have been built around this belief, his life shaped by Ma's voice abandoning him because of the drink. But here, in the shadowed chill of the flat, Ank pulls the idea out from himself like half chewed toffee, stretched and sticky. He holds it by one end, eyes querying, mind like a scalpel, trimming.

The words of Bellicose wave at him from across the years. "*There you be. For the pain. Inside.*" Ank thinks about the pain inside, the fire under his skin. He gazes down into the corner of the room. Cockroaches are here, too, flickering in the darkness. And the pain inside has not died.

Ank up and settling Samuel in the basinet. Constance's face soft in a silky sleep. He flings his coat across his shoulders and treads to the door, not sure where he is going.

Outside, the full moon hangs in the sky, pulsating with muted light. He walks towards St. Olaves Church, near London Bridge. Ahead of him is the sound of men; not loud, but the quiet, clandestine talk of two men negotiating something in secret. One is tall with a fluid body that stretches up into the tip of his hat. The other; smaller, rounder, a rat man with a hunched back and bloated abdomen. They turn from the dim light of the inn to look at him, their faces now shaded from light. A cough, a cleared throat. Ank clipping toward them.

Neither of the men say a word as he passes them on his way to the water. From within the inn he hears other men's voices; words and sentences thrust out like arms and legs that tumble about in a cresting wave. He catches a phrase or two of men arguing about who paid for the last round, hears a lonely song hummed by an old man in the corner. The stench of alcohol and smoke waft out at him, threatening to encircle him, but he rushes on.

How long he has avoided that pub; perhaps the only man in the district who didn't sit on the wooden chairs nightly, gush his pent up emotions into a half filled glass. The other men laugh at him, he knows this, say he is the first Paddy they ever knew who didn't drink. *Imagine that, an Irish bloke who doesn't like the whiskey.*

Ank nears the church and hears the clambering of night dock workers on Toppings Wharf. As he approaches, he sees two figures on Tooley stairs that lead onto the bridge: a young couple, skirting each other in the darkness, playing a coquettish game of 'catch me if you can.' The man's voice is deep and lies low near the ground, the kind of voice that one must stoop to hear. Interlaced with his deep tones are the woman's mirthful shrieks. Ank imagines her dancing on a bed of friendly flames, the fire licking her legs with the adept tongue of a reptile.

In his head is Emma, bounding down the cliffs, lolling about in her hideout, huddled beneath the bush in the rain. Then disappearing. Never saying goodbye.

He hugs the stone of the church, hides in its shadows. From where he stands, he spots the enclosed walkway where the cloistered nuns are unleashed to enjoy a few moments of air. He thinks of them in there, hidden away in their clammy existence, their knees sagging and calloused with kneeling, their bodies untouched by human hands. Like the stone enclave providing respite at Christ Church Cathedral — when Bree and Mrs. Maynard finally met.

He hovers for a moment more, clings to the cold heart of the stone church and then bends down and removes his boots. He pitches them lightly into the corner of the church and they flop over to either side. Bree's shoes, just beneath the sofa, like tilting boats on the beach.

Then he walks to the wharf, descends the steep stairs that brings him closer to the river. Without boots, the path is cold; wet puddles with thick clots of mud wait to snatch up his feet and enclose them in its form. As he moves out of the close confines of the buildings, the shine of the moon pounces on him. He thinks about Constance, how she too loves the moon bloated in the sky.

The movement of water below; the mighty Thames. Home of battles, striking dock workers, vessel collisions, rowing races, all manner of import, relentless trading. Like the Atlantic. Like the Pacific.

He kneels down and dips his coat into the water. Then he whips it close to his face, allows the snap of the material to redden his cheek.

"Go on, do it," a voice inside him says. A deep voice. A male voice.

Ank banishes the half-formed thought that brushes against the inside of his skull. He rushes on. He has a curious sensation of being pulled, the tentacles of an unseen octopus seize him about the chest, wrap him wet, drag him along.

His feet begin to numb in the chilled night air and he stumbles awkwardly on the rough slope of the river. As he moves, he lets his mind spin to whatever thoughts rise up, gentle heat that prompts yeast to slowly swell in a formless blob of bread dough. Bree. Bree.

The water on his left side, the light from the inn and the nearby buildings not quite reaching him, as if there is a thin veil drawn from the heavens between him and the rest of the world. His steps, each one of them, heavy. His breath in the night air laboured. His determination to meet the silent challenge of the night.

He turns inland, climbs the small embankment, burrowing his feet into the mud. His toes fan like greedy fingers clawing the earth, webbed. At the top of the hill, his feet hit stone, then the uneven surface of the road. The gait of a soldier.

Eyes that do not blink. Dead eyes, watching me, dead.

The words float about his mind like tiny anemone in the ebb and flow of a tidal pool, thin, diaphanous creatures that roll, spin, dance in his mind.

A turn to the left would bring him back home, but he veers to the right. He is about to go down again, back down to the river. One more circle, then he will go home, kiss Samuel on the head, slip in beside Constance, and fall into sleep. This is what he knows he should do, but inside him once again is the egg of a giant bird, cracking open. Thoughts of a picnic long ago, memories wavering.

They're singing and clapping their hands and I want to join in, I need to join in. So I sing though I don't know the words. I just want to be loud. Rid myself of the quivering inside. The quivering that came when he mentioned the dead.

Ank breaks into a run. He makes for his boots, pausing only long enough to toss them on his feet. With unlaced boots, he saunters straight to the Inn, past the men who are still conspiring outside. Both heads watch him open the door. He steps inside. Smoke. The drink.

The barkeep tips his head in welcome.

"A pint of bitter," He says. Bree and the lazy smoke drift back to him. Opium, he knows now. Tired Bree and her opium dreams.

The man draws the beer. Ank reaches out and cradles it in his hand.

"Here's to you, Ma," he says, and drinks it down.

~

An outing to the parade, complete with baby. Samuel's first taste of patriotism, at almost seven months of age. Constance thought she would be a wreck, worrying about him catching cold. But she is calm. Almost haughty.

Ank leads them through the crowd of pawing children. They stick their heads all too close to the pram by Bridget's standards. Sickly beasts, the whole lot of them. She has little regard for the squalor outside the flat, her utter concern is Samuel. She has appointed herself his guardian, and like a gargoyle, her beady eyes strike any ill-intent in his path.

They make their way west on Snowsfields, continue as the road turns into Newcomen, leading them to the High Street. It has been a bumpy ride in the pram, but Samuel doesn't seem to mind. He gurgles away, wholly unaware of the havoc around him. On the High Street, Constance insists that she hold him, and wedges him snugly into the crook of her arm.

"Watch now you don't squeeze him." Ank and Bridget are on either side, coaching her. There is nothing done to Samuel that doesn't receive the debate of this triumvirate.

The High Street is a tangle of people and carriages and bowler-hatted men and women in their finery. A cart with long wooden poles narrowly misses them, the swaying goods undulating like a thick matted tail.

"Bloody hell, you fool!" Bridget calls out to the driver in her nastiest voice, but he continues on, deaf to her protests.

"It's bleeding crowded," murmurs Ank, "Maybe we'll have more luck down the way."

Constance is finally convinced to put Samuel back in the pram. They sidestep carts and hucksters selling their wares but are unable to avoid the stench. The closeness of unwashed bodies. The scent of roasted nuts. Constance barely contains the impulse to pitch her stomach.

They reach Long Lane and take refuge on the curb in front of Fogden's. The smell of fresh baked bread floats out of the front door where a baker stands wafting his long smeared apron to circulate the air. It is a hot day. The heat and comforting yeast smell engulf Samuel, lull him to sleep.

The decorations over the shops are disappointing. Bridget looks up and laughs at the rows of flags, draped in threes, in a triangle formation. There are bows too, strung along the buildings, all the way from the flats to the end of Fogden's where it rounds on to Staple street. She says it looks like Christmas gone awry. Constance doesn't much care for the decorations, either, but finds herself preoccupied with the flags. They look like giant paws that reach out from the brick, ready to seize someone.

"What about here?" Ank asks.

There is enough room for the three of them, though they are directly behind a man who has taken more than his share of sidewalk with the addition of a two wheeled cart. Constance wants to rip the burlap off the small square, see what goods the man deems so important as to gain an invitation to this Boer War carnival.

"It reminds me of the Diamond Jubilee, this crowd. Remember that?" A man with a thick yellow beard says this to no one in particular; a comment thrown like a buoy on an open sea.

"Queen was a grand dame that day, we got the fine show." Another man chimes in. They both nod, a silent partnership struck by the consent of opinion.

"Aye," a man with thick glasses begins, "was good of her to come out to see what the likes of us were up to. Being so precious and taken with her privacy, as she was." There is bitterness to his voice and a splattering of conversation begins.

"That's no way to talk about our Queen," protests a man with a scar on his chin.

"She died when Albert died," a woman adds.

"A truth, that. She was clear who she cared for."

"Right. It's bloody well not us."

"I'm standing with a pack of insurgents, I am. What's this all about?"

"Some people have no bloody respect." The conversation has come full circle, back to the man who began it with a toss of his opinion.

Ank and Bridget heed the debate with peaked interest. Any insult to the queen is entirely popular with them. They feel it is their Irish duty.

The bespectacled man, not yet saturated with controversy, begins again.

"Don't know what we're doing here anyway. They're putting them Negroes in concentration camps down there in Africa. Don't think that's right, meself."

"I'll ask you to kindly keep your opinions to yourself." The yellow-bearded man is crimson all over.

"I can speak my mind if I want to. It's a free country yet."

There is a silent standoff between the forces. Constance takes a step back, sensing the potential for a flare up.

"We're here to help families, mate. You understand that? Their men folk were fighting in the South African War, mind. What you doing here if you feel as you do?"

"I'm keeping my eye on the Imperialists."

"He's daft. Leave him be."

"Time we laid off, don't you think? Imperialism is dead, she is."

"Indeed," the woman adds, "We've not done right by the things we've done. Why Africa, and India — "

"What the hell do you know about India?" The bearded man blurts.

"What the hell do any of you know about India?" The words are fired out of Constance's mouth before she has a chance to stop them. The crowd is momentarily silenced by the severity of her tone.

She looks at Ank who rolls his eyes. Bridget giggles. Ank takes hold of Constance's wrist and pulls her away from the conversation. They nudge their way down the street a little, the crowd growing thicker as bodies move into closer proximity. Constance, who is already tired of standing, thinks about the previous conversation and realizes she would like to see the Queen, though she could not begin to explain why.

They stand for an hour more. The bodies on the streets form a clotted mob. Samuel sleeps easily in his pram, his pink hands open and tighten in silent reaction to his infant dreams. There is a sound that escapes his lips as he sleeps. Constance decides it sounds like "more".

Constance think about the word 'more', decides that the word is his message to her, his way of telling her that he has embraced his life, that he desires more. A full life wherein he will grow up to be an adorable boy, then an admirable man. A son and a friend to Constance. A boy who will go to school, and come home at the end of the term to inspire her with new ideas and salient thoughts. A man who will one day sit on the settee with a young bride who knows her own mind and befriends Constance with the energetic conversation of a lucid and intelligent daughter-in-law. A man who will always be her son.

Ank is shaking her arm. "Connie, they're coming."

Suddenly, Constance doesn't care to be here. Her interrupted fantasy begs her to return. Her mind serves up an enticing thought of her and Samuel travelling India. She fights with the external din in a bid to keep the image tucked inside her own head. But a sound draws her outward. Horses hoofs.

When Constance looks up, all she can see is horses. They parade by her, through the reams of waving and whistling people. She watches them closely. She knows that the horses sense her presence, the companionship of one who bears a splice of horse spirit in her own soul. Friends all, they are ready to have a conversation in unspoken words that will slide between their eyes, dip into their brains. Constance watches as they turn their heads in her direction, long to catch a glimpse of her.

She looks at them in pity, senses they feel trapped beneath all that awkward covering. After all, they don't know how fine the cloth is, how the glimmering bits of silk are coveted by everyone. All they know is that it is hot and they are swamped beneath tightly drawn leather and sweltering layers.

Then she hears one of them. "Take it off of me."

Constance glares up and down the street. There are dozens of horses, all clipping politely in order, each of them looking awkward and embarrassed at the spectacle they had no choice but to be a part of.

"Take all this off of me." The voice again. In her head, the front of her head this time, above her right eye.

Constance bolts. She sears through the crowd, jostles past elbows and turned heads and outraged expressions. She is in the centre of the street.

"Who said it?" Her voice comes out too loudly. There is a frenzied, desperate sound to it that even she herself doesn't recognize.

The movement of the parade does not stop, but people have turned to her, their expressions transformed into masks of fear and misunderstanding and pity. A guard jumps off a horse, makes his way to her, a bayonet warping by his side.

But he is too late. Constance has found the horse, wrenches the bit from his mouth. The man in uniform atop the steed reaches down and tries to grip her. Constance intervenes, yanks his foot out of the stirrup and thrusts him over the side.

She has the saddle off and the cloth beneath it peeled before they are on her, hands tight around her.

"But I'm a mother!" She cries. This is all she has time to say before they haul her away.

Left behind, Ank and Bridget watch in silenced shock. To Bridget, Constance is a woman misunderstood. To Ank, she is Emma, up and running half-sideways, half-forward away, face bruised. He makes after her but the shadow comes back, the shadow near his ribs. The feeling causes him to stagger and lose his balance. The cloud in his head gets altogether too thick while Constance gets away.

～

Back in the place of the outlines. The thought forms. They want me to take their thought forms and bring them somewhere . . . Where am I supposed to bring them? No one will answer me.

Oh, it's the yellow place. And now it is clear. I'm supposed to take the thought forms and crumple them, just crumple them into fine powder . . . and . . . scatter it.

And that's when the thought forms dissipate in the yellow and I go into the rainbow spiral and I'm cleansed.

～

The cell is dirty. Constance wonders why they don't clean these places. Are criminals, people like herself who are housed here against their will, are they not worth the effort of a clean floor and a wiped window?

Constance leans her head against the stone wall. She knows that Ank and Bridget cannot help her now. They are Irish, and their words have acted as testimonies against her, rather than in her favour. A woman living with Irish scum, is what she overheard the guard say. And a mother at that.

She wishes Father were here. He would waltz in with his clipped gait and speak to these fools in a way that would have them clearing their throats and exchanging nervous glances. He would take control. Remove his daughter from this cell.

And then what? Smack me?

Constance decides that a few good hits with the rod would be worth it. Even Father's silent, bludgeoning stare would be worth it.

But that is the hurt of a girl. Here, she is in pain of another kind. Her breasts scream with the ripeness of mother's milk. They are heavy, too heavy, clumps of brick and mortar, congealed sustenance. She is desperate to dispel some of the milk, banish the sagging reminder that she has been taken from her son.

Constance peers out to make sure she is not observed. She turns to face the wall, squats, slides her hand up beneath her blouse. To the left breast, its yearning a bedrock call.

But how to do this?

She has never had to wrangle the contents of her breast before. Always, there has been Samuel, his eager, pink mouth an expert in its draw. In his place, her fingers are blind, unable to feed themselves. She imitates Samuel's mouth drawing on her nipple, his easy suckling, but there is no release.

She tries a staccato pull but the engorged tissue merely buckles in reply. She twists her fingers, leading a waltz, a swing, a reel, but there is no reception, no flow.

Constance sinks to the stone floor. Rat faeces litters about her in small, compact black balls. The ache in her breasts a swelling rage. Never has she sunk so low. Here, with the smudge of cigarettes scarring the hard floor, she must offer her mother's milk into the filth where a thousand lice-infected criminals have lain.

She releases her hands in defiance, refuses to continue. But the agony in her breasts is too grave. She must expel.

She imagines Samuel, his slurping coos, his clean body smelling of her handmade oatmeal cakes, his almond-shaped blue eyes. A release begins. Constance opens her eyes and watches the flow of her milk's trail. Into the corner of the cell, onto the urine-scented wall. A surge of warm, white liquid tumbles onto the yellowed floor.

~

It is when her breasts have softened, lost their hard, mortar-like feel, that she notices the shadow on the wall. Grey stone muting into the shape of a baby. It is not Samuel. It's Elvin.

She shakes her head, remembers Elvin did not live, he rejected her. She reminds herself of this, once, twice, trying to shake his image out of her mind. But he is there. On the wall, in a white nightdress.

Constance never dressed him in anything of the sort, he having only lived for a few minutes. Who has slid him into this feminine looking robe, she wonders. The seam of the gown trails down in a flawless line. He is without nappies, she can tell. No bulking beneath the cotton flow of that unfamiliar garment.

He looks right at her. His eyes open now, open to the death he has chosen. But they are darker than Constance would have thought, devoid of a proper childish innocence. He has a look of an old man.

She longs to touch him. Touch the pale skin on his cheeks where the light patches of ruddy red lie. She wants to dip her fingertips into the red, lick it like strawberry cream. She wants to smell him, the air-bit freshness of his new skin. She wants to inhale him.

Her hands reach out, but she cannot hold him. Her fingers move right through his little body, the flapping nightgown a barrier no more. *Elvin. Elvin. It's Mummy.*

Constance wonders who is raising him, who cuddles and feeds him. Who sings to him, strokes his fluid white belly? Who uncurls his clenched fingers and toes with gentle kisses?

His arched lips move. He is talking to her. It seems strange, because his words are well formed. But Elvin can't talk. He lived only twelve minutes.

Still, Constance hears the words.

"Mummy, I'm lonely. I want Sammy here. I want Sammy to come."

~

It is Doctor Watts who advocates for her. He brings in a box of medical papers, designed to intimidate the police with jargon they couldn't possibly hope to understand. He stands before them, a lecturer in front of an invisible class of interns, explaining the nature of her accident. Constance has been allowed out of her cell and is seated on a gouged wooden chair. A specimen for them all to behold.

She listens to his explanation, the way he says 'crushed pelvis' as if he is suggesting a spice for a good dish of curry. The tone he uses when he says 'possible brain damage', as if he is sharing an opinion about Jack the Ripper. She's caught between tears and hilarious laughter.

Watts sees her home, leaves her at the front door of the flat with a promise to check in on her in a weeks time. His mouth smacks when he says this, making it clear to Constance that this whole business is distasteful to him. He, who knows the size and shape and twisted flesh of her pelvis with intimate knowledge, cannot bear to touch her hand when he leaves. She has been imprisoned, after all. Her hands are soiled.

Bridget calls out to welcome her home, but Constance charges to Samuel. He is asleep, his arms aloft and slowly falling, sails billowing down. She leans over him, the hair in her ears warming to the sound of his sighs.

Tears hit her cheeks like boots prints on sand. She engulfs his warm body, covers one eye with her mouth.

"You can't have him, Elvin," she says aloud. "I'll never let him go."

~

Two o'clock in the morning. Constance's head stings for lack of sleep. Samuel panting, his whole body caught up in the fight for breath. An attempt at air so vigorous, his legs and arms are towed in to his heart by the effort. Each inch of his body drawn in for support. Then, a pause, the limbs released, spring-like.

Constance cannot believe how loud it is. His gasps have turned the flat is a living lung; wrinkling in to a leathery bubble in the middle, unfurling out in haphazard seams. The sound, the volume of his attempts. Like a hole in the sand, a tunnel of ocean water that rushes, foams up only to be spirited away underground. It's all she can hear. It's the only sound in her world. Samuel seizing little bits of air. Trying to draw it in.

Constance thumps his back with her fingers, tries to break up the congested phlegm in his lungs. The pads of her fingers knock on two cavernous caves. A needle chipping away at a mountain. She needs to do this, but she knows it is futile.

Samuel's face is a rainbow. Yellow to green, blue to violet. His eyes roll back, sometimes so far back that they threaten to get lost back there, spin away forever. Moisture droplets on his eyelashes, thin blue veins that protest, pop out at the surface of his skin. A mine about to explode.

Constance rocks back and forth, her fingers plying into Samuel's back. Bridget has gone home for the night, Ank is at the hospital. An innocent cold blooming into pneumonia. Now, she is all alone with this boy that is caught between her and Elvin. The war for him now on.

Constance can feel Elvin wrench Samuel with celestial hands into a place she imagines is like a large billowy cloud. Elvin has power on his side though, help from others. Who is up there, helping Elvin tug?

This is a vicious game, a war. A deadly football match in which Samuel is the ball and they vie for him, try to belt each

MAGGI FEEHAN

other into the ground. But the size of the teams is not fair. Constance is all alone, no other players to help her. There are some people lined up behind Elvin, giving him tactical advice. Who are they?

Constance can see someone laugh, some man's face in the murky distance. Someone like Father, but older. Maybe Grandfather, whom she's never met. Maybe he is fighting on Elvin's team.

She pats his back and tries to pull his spirit with her thoughts. This is a mental game, a psychic skirmish.

Sammy, Mummy loves you. You wouldn't leave her all alone, would you?

Constance wraps Samuel in blankets and moves to the door. The hospital. Maybe they can help him.

But this has been so long, so tiring. What if they all had a rest and then continued later? Inside her body is a large black hole. It seems cold in there, distant, but she wants to crawl into it and sleep. Maybe she could rest inside and continue the fight later. It would be so good to recess. Then they could carry on.

But Samuel won't rest, his gasps are so loud that when Constance thinks of herself inside an inner cavity, she can hear his breath in there too. Breath like a heartbeat, a drum, beating down her cave door.

Go away Elvin. Go rest in peace. You can't have him, he's mine.

She leaves the flat and squeezes Samuel against the night's cold air. Elvin follows them into the street. He's crying, screeching like a baby, which he still is, despite the fact that he is dead. But being dead is his strong suit right now, Constance thinks, he can do things now that he never could before. He can think like an adult, plan strategies, take advice. He has power on his side. He isn't really a baby anymore. He is a baby spirit, and they have clout. But he still knows how to cry.

234

"Please Mummy, please. I'm so lonely."

He uses this little voice to get to her. Constance is aware of his manipulation, how he tries to win her pity. She doesn't feel sorry for him. She feels sorry for herself. She is exhausted and she doesn't want to tug anymore. Her legs carry her down the lane.

Just give him to me.

Maybe she should act more like a mother. How cheeky he is being. Maybe he will back down. He might be a good boy, say sorry.

No, no, you can't have him!

Her fingers on Samuel's back thudding. Her feet running. Her voice stern. A tired, angry mother's voice.

Now sit down and do what I tell you to. You can't have him. Do you understand?

⌒

Samuel is wrapped in layers of white cotton and everything to him is fuzzy warm. Except a cold streak down the front of him. Two, in fact. Two long icicles on his chest.

He's seen this all before. It is just like the pictures he saw when he was inside that warm place with Elvin. When they were curled up together inside of Mummy. He heard everything in there, before he came out of the warmth and Elvin left him. They heard it all. Nine months of it. They were listening.

But he forgets how this part goes. Who is he supposed to go to, Mummy or Elvin? He was told, the pictures showed him how it would be, but he forgets. It's bad to forget something so important, someone is going to be mad at him.

He has to try to remember. But it's hard to concentrate, because Elvin can talk right into his head. He doesn't even say anything. His thoughts are just there. In fact, Elvin is just there.

Curled up all warm inside of Samuel's head. A real friend. A real brother. Someone who won't leave you no matter what. Mummy, on the other hand, is much further away. She has to talk outside his head, in all that cold space. He doesn't have those words yet.

Samuel pictures all this lying in his momma's arms. Elvin inside him, Mummy outside. Elvin is warm, Mummy is cold. Elvin has friends with him, and they are all soft and warm too. Mummy is alone.

It doesn't take him long. He can't remember what the right choice is, but he knows which way he wants to go. The way that's easier. Warmer. The way that takes him away from the cold.

⁓

When Constance sees what Samuel has chosen, she walks back to the flat. She places his dead body in the crib and walks to the kitchen. There is a long, sharp knife lying on the counter, and she wonders for a second what it would feel like slicing through her wrist.

But she doesn't pick it up. Instead, she moves slowly to the bed and lies down. She thinks about how love takes and never gives back. That if you let someone inside your heart, they rip you apart. *It's not worth it. Children aren't worth it. They just leave you. People who love you just leave you.*

Then Constance makes a promise to herself. An irrevocable decision. She will never have another child. Not even if she dies and is born again in another life. Even in a different body in a different country. No babies. No love. No giving her heart away to anyone, ever again. Because they take your soul when they leave you.

⁓

Sammy and Elvin watch Mummy. She lies on the bed, fully clothed. Tears slice down her cheeks like sharpened finger nails.

Daddy isn't home. Sammy thinks about what he is going to find when he gets back to the flat. Mummy on the bed. The grate cold. A tea pot smashed on the floor. Silverfish in the pram. And his own body, all icy. Lungs frozen like the icicles outside the window in January.

But Elvin is so happy it makes Sammy happy. This is what is important. Elvin is all warm and open and soft. Sammy wears him like a blanket and they cuddle together, content. Too bad Mummy is so sad. But who is she sad for, they wonder. We're happy here. Everyone is inside of you. Together. Warm. Yellow or pink or blue.

~

Constance goes to bed and stays there. Nothing can get her out. Not walks to the river, not trips to the High Street, nothing. Constance doesn't even read. She doesn't laugh at Ank's jokes. She first forbids Bridget's stories, then she forbids Bridget's entry into the flat. She just stares.

Ank wonders what she thinks about but not even Constance knows. She cannot remember one thought. It is just black inside her head. Her face turned to the wall, she surveys the ants in all their military might. They march for food. Build. Feed their Queen. Their activity exhausts her.

Ank paces the flat, bringing Constance sips of tea, boiled eggs, slices of apple. He counts the days, then the weeks, clenching with the passing of one month, then two.

Finally, he demands she get up, go out for fresh air.

Constance blearily agrees. They hobble down Snowsfields, neither with anything to say. Constance stuck in a pause she cannot shake, Ank with his thoughts on water, the Atlantic, the Pacific, and the perfect shape of a once found oyster shell.

Neither of them see her coming until she is before them. Nurse Shoemaker.

"Ah, Ank and Constance."

Ank nods; Constance says nothing.

"I heard about your tragedy. I'm sorry. It's really a shame."

Constance moans, pivots her body into Ank, pressing him home.

"Thank you." Ank's voice, cautious.

"Are you alright, Constance?"

Constance shakes her head feebly, bears her weight on Ank.

"It's such a shame to see you like this, suffering needlessly."

Constance's body taut.

"Suffering needlessly?"

"Yes, after all, you were warned."

Ank's body screams with the intention to ignore, but Constance flames.

"What the devil are you talking about?"

"I only mean you well. That's all I ever meant you, Constance. When I heard that you were, well, foolish is the word, to have children - and then when you lost them, I knew — "

"You knew what?"

"I knew God in his wisdom had taken care of things."

Constance severs herself from Ank's grasp and reels to Shoemaker. She grabs for her hair, and wrenches Shoemaker's head with an ugly snap.

"Ignore her, Constance. Let's go!"

But Constance drags her outrage down to Shoemaker's chest, which she strikes once before Ank intercepts.

"Get away from me!" Constance screams.

Ank holds Constance as Shoemaker, with aching slowness, backs away. She recedes a few steps, then whispers.

"God took away those children away because you are a sinner." She is gone.

Ank expects Constance to slump over, to cry, to wail. Instead, she touches his cheek and motions for home.

When they return to the flat, Constance refuses to get back into bed. She makes a pot of tea, then asks Ank to undress. He knows what she wants to see.

First, he takes off his shirt, shows her the burn marks near his ribs. Then, he removes his trousers, where his thighs still show licks from the fire.

"Tell me." Constance's voice is clear.

"I started it. I knew what I was doing, love. I lay down in Emma's hideout and waited to burn. I wanted the big logs to fall on top of me, trap me. It almost worked, but didn't."

"What would your Ma say?"

Ank smiles.

"Ah, Ma. What would you say?"

I was trapped in the house, now too scared and hurt and angry to move. All locked up inside. And the baby blue. Don't tell me you don't know what a blue baby means. It means you never look in the glass again. You can't pat your own hair without thinking that this life is nothing but an endless curse.

And the baby lingers 'round the chute. Every time you open it, it's there. Hovering. Still blue. That wee baby that went from cherry red coughing and turning side to side to this strange sea blue — like where the channel mixes up with the light from the ocean and you get yourself a mess of it.

And I have to close the flue, try to chase that baby away. But she don't move. On and on the baby stayed. Lingering they say.

Ten

~

Ank
London, England
1891

STUNNED I AM. TRULY STAGGERED. I'M daft with not understanding how I let it happen.

First the trains across that blasted country, the rocks that cut and thrust into my thoughts for endless days and reckless, sleepless nights. There I was, sitting blind in a series of railcars. Rattled across more mountains than a lad could care to see in his lifetime, their whipped peaks thrusting to the sky. Menacing, the whole lot of them. Demanded my attention, they did, shocking me with their cheekiness, then luring me quiet into the dark caverns and secret curves of their bellies.

When I thought I could stand the chipped peaks no more, well, wasn't I lulled by the open prairie. Hour after hour a wavering sea of grass, nothing to stop the eye from wandering. Then rock everywhere, days of rock, until that Montreal come and saved me from the country that promised the sun only to deliver rain.

And the young woman, with her hat tilted just so, her thin mouth grinning. The one who chatted me up, saying she knew exactly what boat it was would get me home. Me walking beside her, all a' listen while she prattled along, not paying the mind like I needed to. Boarding with her.

The Atlantic crossing again, your voice still lost. But this time, Ma, I was sick. Too sick to talk to you. Too sick to realize that it wasn't home I was going to. Till we landed and I saw the sign. Southampton. Didn't clear remember a Southampton in Ireland. Turning about, asking folks, "Next stop Waterford, is it?" And they were laughing, they were. Till I told the lady, "I'm going to Ireland, M'am." But her mouth went up in a crooked leer and she said to me "Don't be ridiculous. No one goes there."

So on English soil stand I. Not on my own hearth of flesh and blood. Having spent the last of the money Mrs. Maynard gave me for all the helping I done. All the money I squirreled away from the livery. All the money that Bree kept wrapped in her wedding petticoat. Having no means to get home. Again.

So I'm going with her, Miss Grover her name is, and she's taking me along to London. She pays my fare on the train, says I can make it up in her brothers pub, cleaning and the like. Same as you did, Ma, when you met Da.

But Miss Grover is not like any other woman I've known. She's too thin and stiff and queer, sometimes talking my ear blue, then turning away when I begin to tell her the stories. I think now that she doesn't like the Irish in me, but she likes me cause I'm here, listening to her. Don't worry Ma, makes no sense to me either.

And aren't I in yet another country. One I never planned on seeing, never had any need to see. Could have lived my whole life missing the black soot and crumbling row houses and dank laneways we see on the train. But Miss Grover says I should mind my manners. Says my broad, crude tongue won't win me friends here. I should pay respect, be grateful for my opportunities.

So I go quiet and watch out the window, remember that Emma is from England, so it can't be all bad. Wondering whatever happened to Emma. Wondering what Bree did when she got my note, when she found her money gone. Wishing I done a proper goodbye.

⁓

Miss Grover bringing me here, and then feigning she doesn't know me from spit in the lane outside. She comes to the pub only when no one else is there, early morning, late night. Talks to her brother like I'm not alive and even if I was, I wouldn't understand the English language. And her going on pretending, as she does, that she doesn't drink. Except I smell it on her. Every day.

The workers and customers alike all laugh that a man is doing the cleaning up. Don't mind myself, 'tis a job that will get me back home. And even when they call me down, tell me 'tis woman's work, I pay no mind, owing the train ride as I do. Sometimes Ma, I wonder why 'tis so, though. I never wanted to be in this country, and now I'm paying for the privilege of it. But soon as I say this, I remember Da, the dignity he talked on about. So I keep my head high and do what needs doing. Go on smelling the hops on the men's jackets when they get work picking the fields. See the oil beneath the fingers of those who work the greasy barges on the river. Watch those lingering around the door of the pub, their mouths singing for an ale, but their palms without a penny.

Spend my time off walking the High Road, thinking about you all. Wondering how sore Bree is with me. Wondering if Emma is somewhere in this god-blasted country.

But we're not in London the way Miss Grover said. Ah, 'tis some long lost part of London, but not the town. We're cross the bridge, south a way. Here the lanes are full of mud and thin ribbed dogs and starving folks who aren't even Irish.

The whole lot reminds me of the wretched lands near the equator, like the squatting Indians in Canada, like the farm animals back home. God help me, Ma. 'Tis a sorry place.

~

I got my head down and I'm scouring the lavatory when in he comes. Drunk, Ma, smoking like a cat on fire. And isn't he big. Not the fat big, but a whole lot of angry muscle on a man. He talks to himself, scrambles words here and there. His whiskers burning near blue.

"Ah, if ya didn't pay for me round, I would have knocked your block off."

I keep my head down, stay out of sight with my slop pail and the filth from the drinking men who miss the toilets.

"I should have cobbed ya, cobbed ya good and hard." He swings at the air. He wants a fight, needs a fight. I hope he doesn't see me, but of course, with my Irish luck, he does.

"Eh, you little rat you, whattca want a penny for?"

He starts to laugh. So I nod my head, keep it all polite, but he wants the fight.

"I'm talkin' to you. Chin up."

"Don't mind, I'm working."

"Ah, a Paddy have we? Whattca doing here?"

"Cleaning."

"Why don't you get back to your filthy isle and do the mopping there?"

I turn to make haste away, but he grabs my neck. See, he's three sizes bigger than me, with a belly full of drink, and so many broken blood vessels on his nose I feel I'm reading a map and I don't see a thing before whack! He cracks me.

'Tis my blood on the floor now. Beside the spit and urine and feces making a pasty syrup from all the drunk men who can't or will not aim. Then another blow from him, this time cross my face. Now it's my map and isn't it all askewer and lost in the waves when I find myself down on the floor with him leaning over me, gawking like he knows the way home. But Mr. Grover, who owns the pub, he's come now.

"God for sake, Maguire, get your ass off that floor."

I'm scrambling up when the brute knees me in the privates. I'm hoping Grover is going to stop the man, help me up, but he holds his chin like he's got a flap of skin there riding the wind and the air's a bit crisp. He isn't no Bellicose helping me, this is clear.

"You get up in the count of five or you will never clean another loo in this whole bloody country."

I try to claw my way up, grasp at the urinal, but neither of them will help me. Doesn't Grover pat that man on the back, turn away from me.

"The Mick been bothering you, Wally? Next round's on me."

And they're gone Ma. I'm on my way back down to the floor, thinking how I got to get this place clean but good.

~

Everyone cleared from the pub. Grover comes over, sits beside me.

"Don't want you making trouble now."

"He's a beast and he hit me."

"He's me best drinker, Maguire."

"Think I might have a break."

"Nonsense."

"Do. You got something I can wrap it with?"

Grover moves behind the bar, his feet shuffle slow across the floor. He leans down and looks behind the bar, and he's down there so long, I think he must be giving it a good search. But when he comes up, he has nothing. Just his regular red nose and bloodshot eyes.

"Don't have a thing."

"I'm needing something. This cloth isn't gonna hold my arm much longer."

He holds his finger to his lip, thinking like.

"Tomorrow. Round noon. There'll be a bloke to help."

Then he shoos me off to my room. The bed in the back where the liquor bottles are stacked. Growling at me the way they do. I lie down and fumble my trousers off, rip them into strips and begin to tug the pieces around my arm. Till it's warm and tight inside.

～

I sleep late. 'Tis the aching. When I wake, I see the blood has dried, but my clothes and my bed are soaked through and through. And aren't I bruised some.

Into the pub and it's almost noon, but Grover is nowhere in sight. 'Tis June, the girl who pulls the pints during the day.

"You look roughed up. Too much drink last night Ank?"

"Don't drink myself."

"Then perhaps you should start, love!"

The men laugh. Of course this is nothing new because they laugh at anything June says. All of them but one. Off his chair he gets and comes round to me.

"Let me take a look at you."

"Got the fist twice."

"Yes, I can see that."

"Stopped the blood but good."

He lifts my shirt and looks at my ribs and asks to untie the cloth I got around my arm.

"You were bandaged well."

"Did it myself."

"You did a good job with one arm."

"Indeed. Had no choice."

"This needs to be cleaned."

"This I'm sure about. Have you ointment?"

"Come in an hour. I'll take care of you then."

"Where?"

"Guy's Hospital. I'm Doctor Watts. Call 'round for me."

And he leaves. His Sheppard's pie half eaten.

∽

'Tis a celestial place. Angels with flutes and harps carved into the stone and of course you're in my head, knowing the angels as you do. A mighty spiral staircase inside, too. Up I go as if on a ship and there's another country waiting for me at the other end.

He's waiting for me, Dr. Watts. Ushers me into a room and pulls out more bandages and gauze than I ever seen with Mr. Harrow. And he cleans me himself, wraps me up good. All the while, me telling him about the bandages and how deft I am with them.

Seems to listen, he does, with my Irishness and all. Then looks me in the eye, saying,

"How long do you plan on staying?"

"In England?"

"Yes."

"'Tis all I got right now."

"Where did you go to school?"

"Canada. A boy's school. With the English."

He doesn't move his face nor does he say anything, so I don't have a lick of an idea what's going through his head. He doesn't know that I didn't get a chance to go to the school. Left too soon, I did.

Then he hands me a bandage, says, "Wrap me."

Well, don't I wrap him but good. 'Tis simple with the right bandages, better than peeled bark or the Colonist or even Bree's stockings. He hands me gauze and scissors and I cut everything neat like, in the long, thin rectangles like I learned from the book. He looks me up and down.

"You know this is a teaching hospital?" He hums to himself, looks at the wrapping I did of his arm. "I could use you. In time, you might pick up a great deal."

"I'm quick as lightning."

"Yes. I need a good surgeon's dresser."

"I'm the man for you, I am!"

And Ma, oh Ma, I'm stone glad to leave the lavatory and the liquor bottles behind.

Eleven

~

Ank and Constance
London, England
1902

AND SO IT WAS, WHEN ROSA *died. Her not moving from the flue, wanted me to play with her some more, she did. So on I went, making light of it, while Mamaí sat in her chair and would barely have a drop of tea.*

Me searching for Rosa while up she popped here and down she hid there, teasing me all the while. Never leaving, see. Floating above us, hiding in the pantry, 'neath the tins, behind the grate, ready to jump out and give me a good friendly scare. Cause she knew I liked it. And so I did.

Her hovering all the time. Not being able to move on, cause Mamaí couldn't let the whole of her go. Me own Mamaí, not allowing the river to run, wanting to stop it up, control it, see? Like your own woman there. Trying to gather the water with her hands.

~

The door of the flat knocked and Constance knows that it is someone, someone who makes the tips of her fingers white, flattens her tongue.

Then she is there. Green-eyed gin lady, who smiles widely, offers her hand. Constance looks around for Father, gin lady shakes her head no.

Come in, come in, and still, after so long, her embarrassment over the flat. Green-eyed gin lady sits and looks about while Constance prepares tea. Neither of them talk, their heads full of India, standing in the rain, dresses flapping.

"Where is he?" Constance asks.

At this, the woman pales.

"Dead, Constance."

The boiling water stings Constance's hand.

"How long?"

The green-eyed gin lady ignores the question, reaches into her bag and pulls out a parcel, wrapped neatly in string and paper.

"I brought something for you."

Constance accepts the package, unwraps the crinkling paper to see folds of light blue silk. In her fingers, its fineness wavers with the thin yellow lines that undulate through it.

"Thank you. It's beautiful. How many memories it brings back."

Long rectangles of splashed colours, held up on either end by dancing arms. Billowing cotton.

"Have you been in India all this time?"

"Yes, until very recently."

Nancy, Constance remembers. Mrs. Frederick Newton.

"Constance, I've come to tell you — ." She pauses, her fingers licking at the folds of her dress. "You see, I did the unthinkable. I left my husband. For your father. I don't have to tell you what a scandal that created. We were instant untouchables."

And that's when I feel it. Her touching my skin, only it's my Father's skin and they are kissing, lips touching, heat on heat.

Constance takes a long sip of tea, her eyes not yet ready for the green eyes, her stomach not yet ready for the rolling, the rolling inside. She wishes Ank was at home, someone else to hear this, someone to pinch her and say, it is real, what you are hearing is real.

"And?" It is all Constance can think of to say.

"I didn't know about the accident, Constance. You must believe me. I would have sent word."

Constance merely nods her head.

"It was a while after he died that I learned. It's ridiculous, I know. I thought — "

"What did you think?"

"I wasn't thinking, Constance. Or, I was thinking only of myself."

Constance pauses. "Did you love him?"

"Very much so."

"And he allowed himself to be loved?"

"He was tender, Constance. I can imagine how much this might surprise you. He was gentle, even. You have every reason to doubt it, and yet it's true. He was very much a loving man."

Constance gets up and walks about the flat. Her left hip is throbbing, an ache she hasn't felt for many months. But there is something else that she feels, something surprising. It is a soft stroke, a loving finger brushing against her cheek. She raises her hand to feel the skin and she smells him: Father. Not the scent of his hot breath, or his moist armpits beneath the Indian sun, but something else. Tenderness. The smell of a freshly cut peach, shared between the two of them. Dabbed on her blistering cheek.

"He was a loving man?"

"Yes. He even loved you."

Constance looks into Nancy's eyes and sees a small wave of moisture folding out.

"Why didn't he tell you I was injured?"

Nancy will not answer. Instead, she sips her tea and looks around the flat.

Constance shuffles the cups on the sideboard. She straightens the tea towel. She brushes crumbs off the front of her dress.

"He left me too. He leaves people he loves before they leave him. Like your mother did." Nancy offers this with a kind smile.

Constance turns and looks at the woman. She wants to slap her, slap Nancy hard, scream: but you were a full grown woman, and what do you know about my mother! But she sees the folds about her eyes, the watery pain overtaking the edges.

"I was foolish. I was an outcast amongst my own people. I brought the misery on myself."

Constance picks up the sari material, unfolds it, drapes it over Nancy's shoulders. It forms an arc around her, and in the thin yellow lines, Constance remembers the golden wedding band Father wore in one of his ghostly visits to the hospital.

"Did you two marry?"

Nancy looks down, an ill attempt to hide her shame.

"We were in love. He wore a ring to prove it to me. But there wasn't time before — "

"Before what?"

"Before your father killed himself."

Constance plunges herself into a chair.

"My husband. The others. Pretty much the whole Indian Civil Service. You see, he'd lost all face, he lost his job."

Constance nods, trying to understand. Of course, this is why no one at the hospital would speak of Father. They knew. They all knew and no one would tell her.

The green-eyed gin gently removes the cloth from her shoulders, hands it to Constance, and quietly leaves the flat.

Constance goes to her wardrobe and lifts out the bangle Father sent, the blood red bangle with little white stones. Was this his last act before he died? His way of saying goodbye? She lifts it to her nose, and the outdoor market comes back to her. Ayah smelling flowers, the boy with yoghurt skin, the cool wrists of the woman as she slid it over Constance's hand. The bangle she could not wear lest Father rip it from her, spin its vanity into the garden.

～

Ank walks the long way home. Out to the high street, along the road. Not yet ready to go back to the flat. He longs to leave; another ship, another country.

Why didn't I ever go home? But he knows that there is no home for him in Ireland. He has always known this. Where would he go? Back to Galway, back to the bad luck, back to the lads who are now men who work the farms or who spend their evenings down at the pub, trading yarn. Back to Mrs. Cleary, to the red tongue licking coins she coveted? Back to the cliff and the cottage that is no more?

No, home is here. With Constance. A surgeon's dresser.

Then, a whistle from across the road, outside the pub. Ank crosses the street. It is a boy, a young boy, who holds out his cap, waiting for money. Ank stares hard at the boy, then reaches out to touch him. He disappears. That when Ma's voice finally comes back to him, fills his head.

Haunted, ye all are. Didn't I tell you that it's contagious. Like the fever? Ah love, needing to put it all away now. 'Tisn't so?

⁓

When Ank gets home, the green-eyed gin lady is gone and Constance is sitting in front of a cold cup of tea draped in a beautiful silk shawl.

"I need to tell you a story." Ank says.

"Alright."

"Listen carefully."

Ank stares at the shawl for a long moment, considers asking about it, but holds fast to his story, lest his courage disappear.

"I had a dream, love, that I was standing on top of a hill that slid its way down into a huge valley, where a river cut through far below. I stood there, just looking down into this exquisite valley, see, and my Ma came to see me. There she was, and she waved at me, and pointed down to the river. And when I looked to the river, she was standing inside it. Standing in it, saying, *come in, come in.*

"I walked down to the river, and it was moving, meandering its way along, over rocks, around sticks snapped off from the trees, underneath the wee moss bridges that were trying to grow from rock to rock. And Ma in the river, saying, *watch it love. This is how a river flows.*

"So I did. Watched it, sat for hours, just tending to how the water bubbled, gurgled, but kept on moving. And when I turned around, Ma was lying behind me, in the grass, looking up to the sky, her hand on her belly. But she told me, *isn't the belly boy, 'tis the womb. 'Tis the womb, grieving like.*

"And that's when I saw it, the things coming out of her womb. Shapes lifting out of her womb. They spiralled and vanished into the air above. A large key, first, and then a coin, a gold coin, spun into the air. Was colours too, black at first, then red, then grey and green. Splashing out of her. And that's when she called me over, told me put my hand in the air over her belly, move it in a circle. So I did, and I found I could draw things out, lift things up, all the hurt she packed inside there. Her wound. Her womb. A flock of crows cawing and flying forth, the blanket of her wee dead sister Rosa. 'Till all that was left was the dolphin, swimming about making sure there wasn't anything left lingering in the corners.

"Then Ma said to me, *the river's gotta run*. And I turned back to watch it, when in front of my eyes, doesn't it change course, undulate to her, slide inside, in her womb. Cleansing her.

"And I stepped into the river while Ma disappeared. As she went, she thanked me, said, 'I learned this from Rosa and now I pass it on to you'."

Constance has pulled the silk tighter over her shoulders.

"Constance, it's yours now."

～

Constance in bed, Ank's body warming her from behind, his sleeping sighs in her ears. That's when Father comes, accepts her biding. His presence enters the flat and slides across them.

Father doesn't look haughty tonight. He looks tired. Life has tired him, Constance thinks, the deception of a lifetime squeezing out any chance at joy.

As she knew he would, he has brought the snakes. He has heard her, answered her request. She can see them clearly now, the mottled skin, the beady, penetrating eyes. They extend from his shoulders, slink out of his arms, thin pink tongues flickering.

Constance sits up. *Mali, be with me now.* And a silent invocation to the snake wallahs. *Come. Come. All of you, come.*

Then she invites him. To put the snake around her neck. As she does, she remembers the first time. The other time.

She ran to the embrace of a Neem tree, while Father, cherry blushed by her retreat, marched over to grab her. Her spine hardened with his approach, the muscles in her body sucked in towards a shirking centre. His hands hot, his face cold. He clutched at her hair, shook it away from the back of her head, so she could feel the snake on her neck.

The wallahs were saying no, no, snakes only made to dance, but father shouted at them to be quiet as the cool muscle of serpent slid across the back of her neck.

Constance pleads for help with her eyes. The older wallah clasps his hands together in front of his chest in prayer position, bows his head, says, 'Snake no hurt you, Miss. No bite'.

That's when she heard the python's voice. It said, 'I know. You know I know'.

⁓

Father unfurls and undulates towards her. Constance breathes deeply; heavy, panting breaths. She forces herself to feel. To really feel the snake as he places it around her neck. There is a coldness, a softness, the crawling over and across, around and about. The snake cradles her, sways at the back of her neck, explores every inch of exposed skin.

She doesn't let her mind run away. Instead, she stays, senses how the hair on her neck first stands at attention, then retreats. Calming with the sensation of slithering, her mind ebbing from its terror.

"God in what scares you, also." The voice of the mali, across the miles, across the years.

"Thank you, Father."

Father bows his head.

"Thank you for coming."

Ank hears Constance's voice and wakes up with a start.
"It's alright, Ank. It's just Father. He left a gift."

~

Morning, Ank out back in the lavatory when the voice murmurs in Constance's brain.

Go to the window, go to the window.

She moves to the front window, sees him. Sitting on the kerb, staring at her. Samuel. He has grown. He looks two years old, the age he would be if he had lived. But he is dead.

Constance dashes back to the sink and pours water from the white ceramic jug into her hands. She rubs her eyes violently. Behind her, the door opens and Ank appears. She blurts out to him.

"Did you see out front? Across the road?"

Ank's breath stops.

"Did you see anyone who shouldn't have been there, Ank?"

Go to the window, love. Samuel, he's there.

Ank walks to the window and looks out.

"Who are you seeing?" she asks.

Constance follows behind him, presses her body into his back, her eyes shut against the thick cotton of his black coat. She doesn't need to look again. She knows exactly where he is.

"On the other side. Sitting up. You see him?"

There is a long moment when Ank doesn't breathe. Then he says calmly.

"Samuel. Yes. He's there."

They are out on the street in a beat like dogs snapping at moving air. Samuel is gone. The place on the road where he sat is now a large pile of horse dung. Steaming. Fresh. Constance holds Ank's hand. They dare not say anything to the children. It is a shared error. They are both complicit.

Then a black-eyed boy throws the ball at Ank. It is the boy with the ancient face, who strode alongside the wheelchair on Constance's first day out of the hospital. He has grown into a gawky, greasy young man, the anger of his boyhood marking his face now with a permanent sneer. The ball smacks Ank in the chest and plops to the ground. It does not roll. It spins in one spot.

"Who you after?" the boy asks.

Ank answers with a glitch in his throat. "A boy."

"The one who watches?"

Ank leans over to pick up the ball. Constance siphons breath up through her nose. A horse's snort.

"Perhaps. He was just here." Ank manages to sound calm.

"Ya, I know him, the little one? He's 'ere sometimes. Then 'e's off."

The boy wrenches the ball from Ank and tosses it with a fumbled arm into the crowd of children with their eager hands waving.

"Never stays long, that one."

The other kids disregard the conversation, blind and deaf to the emotion that wraps itself around Ank and Constance.

"You've seen him, then?" Ank says.

"Now and again."

"Does he say anything to you?"

"He doesn't talk yet."

The statement is simple. And honest. Samuel couldn't talk. He doesn't know how. No one has taught him.

Constance is overcome with the nearness of Samuel. She needs him, needs to smell him, run her lips across his pink cheeks. She marches over to the boy and grabs him by the arm.

"Tell me more."

"Don't know any more, ma'am."

"Do the others see him?"

The question is ludicrous to the boy and his face demonstrates this.

"Never asked them. They see you, though."

Constance looks down and sees that her fingers are squeezing the boys arm. Like Father squeezes her sometimes, when he wants to shut her up, when he wants to frighten her.

"How long has he been coming around?" Constance continues.

But the boy has had too much. He sneers in Constance's face and bolts.

"Wait!" Ank runs after him. "Don't mind her now, she's just anxious to meet up with him. They used to know each other, a while back."

The boy turns.

"Look, I haven't the foggiest where he lives. He comes, he sits, just watches. Then he's off. That's all I know. Now I got a match to continue 'ere."

"Of course." Ank backs away, smiling his crooked smile at the boy. "You got a good arm there, lad."

When they are inside, Constance wraps herself in the sari material.

In Ank's mind, Ma's voice.

He'll be coming again, see? You just mind it.

⁓

Constance dresses herself in a white dress with a black lace front piece. There are three waves of material that hang down from her waist to where the dress hits the top of her boots. For some reason, she thinks Samuel will like this. The flowing line.

Despite the warmth of the day, she swings a black shawl around her shoulders. Then she leaves the flat and walks towards London Bridge Station. Her dream was clear. The destination was exact.

Out on the street, she knows she is being watched by the women who live on Snowsfields. Mrs. Cartwright wears a black face today, covered with the relics of a cleaned coal stove. Her friend, who never seems to be out of gossiping distance, is Mrs. Longway, who has a perpetually rubbed down look. They watch as Constance walks past. They cannot understand her, a woman who lives on the same lost lane as they do, but lives a separate life.

She takes the train to Marble Arch and walks along Park Lane. She is moved by how clean things appear here compared to The Borough, how white and shiny all the buildings look. Constance feels as though she has been transported to another place, another century, where people live with a straight backbone and gloved hands.

When she enters the park, she is momentarily intoxicated with the green grass and trees. She comes to a dead stop and allows the gently vibrating leaves to fan her, send out wafts of clean air which she inhales. Then she sits on a bench and watches. She knows Samuel is near. She dreamed of this place last night. She will wait for him.

People in groups of five or six pass her, engrossed in conversation. They seem flushed and excited, milling about, waiting for something to happen. Constance longs to speak to the women, discuss politics, or leisure, or some remnant of her lost life with Father, but she will not allow herself to be distracted from her search.

Then she sees him. He is behind a woman who sits with three others, all of whom are talking intently. He doesn't stand, but floats behind the woman, behind her left shoulder. Constance gets up and walks closer to the group. Samuel sees her and smiles.

He is wearing a red hat that arches up at the front. There is a badge on it, a circle of gold. "Sammy?"

The group of women look up at her, compelled by her voice. Constance gives them a coy and confused smile, dissuading them from further inquiry. Then she hears the words in her head.

Don't talk Mother. People can hear you.

At this Constance wants to burst out in speech, let her tongue waggle forward and unleash the words she has prepared for him. Instead, she furrows her forehead and thinks loudly.

Samuel, where have you been? Speak to me, speak to me.

He answers her. The words in the front of her forehead. *I want to introduce you to someone.*

A man appears behind Samuel, dressed in a white suit, wearing the red hat. Samuel's head is now uncovered. The hat has passed from one head to another without Constance having seen it.

Who are you? Constance asks him.

Her husband. He answers solemnly, pointing at the woman in front of them.

The man's voice is deeper than Sammy's. It vibrates above her nose.

Constance looks into the woman's eyes. There is no misery planted there, no exposed roots of sorrow that might be evidenced on a widow. Constance cannot understand. Surely this man is dead. Otherwise, how would he and Samuel have met?

Sammy's voice cuts into her thoughts.

She doesn't know yet.

Constance lets a little cry escape her lips. The unknowing widow stands up and walks to her. All Constance can see is the woman's eyes, which she knows will change very soon. They will look like her own. Bloated with memory.

"Are you quite alright?" The woman holds out her hand to Constance, who shakes it away.

"Yes, thank you. Just a little faint I suppose."

"Well, I imagine it's the heat. Here, sit for a moment, won't you?"

The woman indicates the bench that has been cleared abruptly by the group of women.

"Are you here to listen to the speech today?"

Constance knows nothing of the speech. "Yes. But I don't think I can stay."

"Perhaps. Well then, do you need an escort to the trains?"

Constance dares to move her eyes away from the woman's eyes, look behind her. Samuel and the man have gone. There remains only a wash of grey air behind her. Their presence marked by a filmy coating that immediately begins to dissipate.

⌒

There is Mummy. Mummy so sad. Doesn't she know that she shouldn't be sad?

Bent over, tears. I try to tell her but it is too dense over there. Heavy. Murky. Like she is stuck in treacle. Not like here, where it's all light and clear and I can move anywhere, any way I want.

Mummy, Mummy. Don't be sad. Don't you see how silly sad is? I am happy, I am light. You don't need to be sad. How can I make you understand? You need to let me go.

Mummy, let go of me. Let go!

⌒

Constance has her hands in bread dough, braiding two pieces together, over and around. Her hands spiral over each other, the uncooked dough like interlocking serpents.

The feeling again, the hairs on her neck lifting to a wave, then the smell of liquorice. It is the mali before her, his words in her head. *Dance is how Shiva began the world.*

He spins around, laughing. Constance watches as he turns in a full circle, his arms up in the air, his tongue lying out the side of his mouth. He turns his back to her, black hair smudging her vision, and when he faces her once more, he has Samuel in his arms.

Her body wants to bolt, to wrench Samuel from the mali's arms, to put her lips to his forehead, inhale the smell of her baby. *Her* baby. But she resists, knows the mali will call her impatient and may even disappear. She wills herself to be still, forces a calm smile onto her face.

Shiva and Parvati never apart, like fire and heat, cannot be apart.

She remembers these words, from so long ago. The temple in India where she first saw the stone statues, learned of Patanjali.

She says it aloud. "Born from a snake in a woman's palm."

Constance looks down at her floured fingers circling in a lump of dough. A palm of white, lifted up, thrown. A toss, a laugh from Constance.

"Connie?" Ank's on the settee, his paper down.

"I'm playing. I'm playing with him!"

"Sammy?"

"Yes."

Sammy laughs. Constance takes another palm full of flour, dashes it into the air.

"There, got you!" She laughs.

Ank stands up, looks over to where the pile of flour is collecting on the floor.

"Do you see him?" Constance asks.

Ank pauses, unsure.

"Here, your turn."

Ank scoops some flour, turns to the air, flings the powder.

"There Sammy. From your Da!"

Ank has barely finished the words when Constance throws a dollop of dough on his neck. Thwack! Cold, kneaded dough. He plucks it off of himself, throws it to Constance. It lands on her blouse, tumbles off.

Then a halo of flour, thrown in all directions. Whitening the veil.

～

Constance awakes and puts her hand on Ank's warm back. In her head, the words from her dream. And a peace inside. She closes her eyes and in front of her is Father. He holds out his hand and Constance takes it.

In her mind, a rush of images: Ceylon stomping her, the snake temple, her and Ank throwing flour at Samuel.

She knows that it is time for Father to go. And he has come to her for help.

His warm hand in hers. Constance sees the colours, the thought forms on the other side. Some of them are waiting for Father. One of them is small, circular, playful. It is Samuel.

Then the words *In my head the light of a thousand suns rise.*

Constance enters the colour. She sees Samuel and blows him a kiss. Then, she leans into Father, touches his hand softly.

Father gives her a nod. A slight nod, then he is gone.

～

"No step is lost on this path, and no dangers are found. And even a little progress is freedom from fear."
—The Bhagavad Gita, 2:40

ACKNOWLEDGMENTS

MANY FINE WRITERS HELPED ME HONE this work. Thanks to all of you, especially my editor, Susan Musgrave, with whom I had rich conversations about burning peat. My love goes out to three writing friends who witnessed the evolution of this novel and gave me invaluable feedback on the first draft: Sherri Bird, Meg Walker & Peggy Herring. Also, thanks Florin Diacu, Margaret Gracie, Elizabeth von Aderkas, Kitty Hoffman and Paul Mohapel for reading reams of my prose over the years and helping me develop my craft. Thanks also to Daphne Marlatt and Audrey Thomas, in whose writing workshops some of these passages were birthed and shaped. Also, a very special thank you to the late Rona Murray, for lending me her Raj child's eye regarding the scenes in India.

I am inedited to others as well, including Valerie and Alison Oates who let me stay with them on Snowsfield Road all those years ago, and who introduced me to Guy's Hospital. Those were the days long before the area of London Bridge was gentrified, and the dark emptiness and ghostly streets are with me still. Also, to all my teachers of Yoga throughout the years, especially those at Yasodhara Ashram where I first learned of the *Bhagavad Gita*, to B.K.S. Iyengar and Geeta Iyengar for their incomparable yoga teaching, and to the ongoing tutelage at the Iyengar Yoga Centre of Victoria under the sage direction of Shirley Daventry French.

Also, my deepest appreciation to Martin and Dylan de Valk who lived with me during the years I wrote this novel and always believed in it.

This book is dedicated to my father, Joseph Bernard Feehan, 1929-2008, who dreamed, prophetically, that this novel would be published after his death.

~

I am grateful for the information and clarity I received from the following works: *Mr. Guy's Hospital* by H.C. Cameron, *Southwark, Bermondsey and Rotherhithe in Old Photographs*, by Stephen Humphrey, *The Story of Southwark* by S.O. Ambler, *Growing up Poor* by Anna Davin, *Southwark Story* by Florence Highman, *The Story of the Borough* by Mary Boast, *The History of London in Maps* by Felix Barker, *Shoulder to Shoulder* by Midge Mackenzie, *On the Street Where You Live: Pioneer Pathways of Early Victoria* by Danda Humphreys, *Victoria A History in Photographs* by Peter Grant, *Diary of Charles Hayward 1862* (City of Victoria Archives PR 118), *The Journals of Honoria Lawrence* edited by John Lawrence and Audrey Woodwiss, *Mediumship and Survival* by Alan Gauld, *The Other World* by Janet Oppenheim, *My Life in Two Worlds* by Gladys Osborne Leonard, *The History of Spiritualism* by Sir Arthur Conan Doyle, *Opium* by Barbara Hodgson, *Ireland, A History* by Robert Kee, *History of Ireland* by Desmond McGuire .

Also, invaluable experiential knowledge was gleaned through my visits to Guy's Hospital and the Old Operating Theatre Museum, St. Thomas' Hospital, the Spiritual

Association of Great Britain, College of Psychic Studies, Southwark Historical Society, John Harvard Local Studies Library, Southwark Cathedral, the Monument, the Imperial War Museum, the Museum of London, the BC Archives, the City of Victoria Archives, the Maritime Museum of British Columbia and the Royal British Columbia Museum. Travels throughout Ireland and India and my love for Victoria, BC, were a constant source of inspiration.

Excerpts from the *Bhagavad Gita* are from the Penguin edition, translated by Juan Mascaro. This edition of the *Gita* was published in 1962, sixty-seven years after Constance was introduced to it by the mali. However, I chose to use Mr. Mascaro's edition over translations that were available in 1895, because he captures the spirit and the poetry of the words so beautifully. I trust readers will forgive this minor adjustment.

The poem by Yeats is the first stanza of "The Stolen Child" and can be found in *Fairy and Folk Tales of Ireland*, edited by W.B. Yeats.

An excerpt of this novel, *This game, his affection*, won *Grain* Magazine's Dramatic Monologue contest in 2002. It appeared in the fall edition under the title, *Through the Bubbles*.

A freelance writer for many years, Maggi Feehan has published articles on visual art, literature, social justice, and travel for numerous periodicals. She has written scripts for four television documentaries seen on CHUM-TV and the Aboriginal People's Television Network, and in 2002, she won *Grain Magazine*'s Dramatic Monologue contest. *The Serpent's Veil* is her first novel. Originally from Edmonton, Feehan has made her home in Victoria, British Columbia for the past twenty years.